LUCY'S STORY

LUCY'S STORY

STUART COTTERILL

ISBN: 0692761845
ISBN 13: 9780692761847

Also by Stuart Cotterill

The Legacy of Ma Jun
Ma Jun's Lost Treasure

ACKNOWLEDGMENTS

I want to thank my wife, Pat, for encouraging me to put pen to paper after I told her about a dream one night. It involved a woman wheeling an aged father down a hospital hallway, unaware of what was crushing his will to live.

I also appreciate Rebecca Ramey and Susan Henning for reading an early chapter and urging me to continue to see where the images would lead.

As always, I'm indebted to editor Susan Snowden, whose guidance has been invaluable as I shape my stories.

Above all, I am deeply grateful for the inspiration China gives me when I sit down in a favorite spot in Beijing to lay out a first chapter. I often surprise even myself to see where those beginnings lead.

PROLOGUE

She wheeled her father down a long hallway, the squeak of the wheels telling her it might be time to get him a new one. Her nervousness had been increasing, and she continued to ask herself if this was the right thing to do. Whatever she felt over the years about her father, there was no turning back. She had involved too many people not to finish it. She pushed her father down the empty hall, knowing full well he had no idea of what she had set in motion for him. Would it achieve what she was trying to do for him? Or cause a further breakdown, as Dr. Weinstein warned, potentially killing him.

She stopped some fifty yards from the doorway at the end of the hall. He was still slumped forward, staring at the floor as he had done for three years since her mother died. At first she thought grief had simply overwhelmed him, but only later would she learn the truth. She hoped what she was about to do could bring him back into the current world, and enable him to communicate with her again. He'd shown no reactions that night she confronted him about a small part of his past, as ever silent he had simply stared at the floor. But, as much as he appeared to have no reaction, she knew him well enough to see something well up inside him that said to her, yes, something was there.

The doctors advised her to talk to him about her plans for that day, but she refused; her instincts told her they might provide the shock he needed to bring him back. It was one of her closest friends and one time lover, a psychiatrist himself, who supported her and gave her the courage to go ahead. He had dealt with serious traumas in patients before, some of which led to paralysis and an inability to continue functioning normally. She had met him when trying to save her own marriage. He supported her now in what she was doing, but warned her of the risks she was taking, that she should prepare herself for its failure.

As the distant hallway door drew closer, there was only one outcome she prayed for in the last moments before she reached the door. She closed her eyes one more time, saying softly, "If there's a god out there, make this right . . . bring him back."

———∽∾∽———

The noise of the wheels, echoing from the sterile walls of the hall, stopped as the doors swung open. The tiled floor changed to a quieter sound of carpeted floor in a large reception room. Comfortable lounge chairs, paintings on the wall, and the gentle sound of soft music eased a little of her anxiety. Across the room she stared at another doorway, still closed. A cleaner was just finishing her work and told her the room was ready for her. Dr. Weinstein was sitting in one of the easy chairs, catching up on patient notes, waiting for her to arrive. Fresh coffee and snacks she had paid for were sitting on the table, the smell drawing her over to shakily pour herself a cup, not bothering to waste any time asking if her father wanted one.

"You're here already, Doctor Weinstein?" she asked.

"Don't worry, I'm not staying, Lucy. I think I should, just in case, but I agreed not to. It's not my recommendation; you know that, don't you?"

"Yes, I understand completely. Thanks anyway."

" I'll be close by in my office, should you need me."

"I appreciate it, Doctor . . . I really do. I'll call right away if we need you."

"Good luck to you both," he said.

She watched the doctor open the far door, turning to look back at her father as he left. His expression told her, as so many times before, that he could see no good medical reason for her father to be in his condition. Glancing behind the departing doctor, Lucy could see another corridor with closed doors on either side; the emptiness and silence only heightened her fears. She came around to face her father again, knelt in front of him, and looked straight into his eyes. She spoke forcefully, wanting to be sure he was listening.

"Father, there's someone I want you to meet."

As she looked for any kind of reaction, the creak of a door opening startled her. A young nurse peered in. "Mrs. Summers?" she said.

"Yes, Nurse."

"Are you ready?"

"I am," Lucy said, not knowing what was going on in her father's head.

"Well, fine, I'll fetch them then. They're here."

"Thank you, Nurse."

She rose shakily from her knees, still watching her father for any kind of reaction, but there was none.

"Oh god!" she said. "What have I done?"

Chapter 1

Eighteen months earlier

Lucy Summers and her husband lived above a flower shop she owned and managed in downtown Blowing Rock. It was her husband, Phil, who insisted they sell their house so she could buy the apartment and storefront when it went on sale. She knew he did it to try to save their marriage, but it had not been enough. Their relationship, which soured after he left the military, was worsening. She often thought back to life before him, and a promising career that ended when her mother's illness became serious. It was during those many months of illness that Lucy met and married Phil Summers, but he was different then, and so was she.

Many had envied the two when they courted and married. Phil, for his popularity growing up and the promise he showed on the football field. Lucy, for her beauty, how well she had done at university, and in the business world far away from Blowing Rock. That Phil had joined the military out of a sense of patriotism further endeared him to the town, but his refusal to stay back and support Lucy and the problems with her mother introduced conflict, despite what many thought a perfect marriage. When Phil returned from Afghanistan, a hero in the eyes of locals, Lucy had to endure all the trauma of his capture, torture, and escape that he brought home with him.

Her mother's death was long and painful, and Lucy's life was dealt another blow when she was forced to put her father in a nursing home. He had voiced no objections to going, or to selling the home her mother left her. She hated to do it, but she needed the money to cover all the expenses; he needed round-the-clock care, more than she could provide. Her father stopped communicating in any way about a month following her mother's death, Lucy had found him alone in a chair one day, staring at a blank wall in one of the guest rooms.

When he finally stopped eating and wouldn't get out of bed, she panicked. Not long after, he was taken by ambulance to the local hospital. His doctor of many years tried everything to bring him out of it, but finally sent him to the regional hospital for advanced care and help. None of the doctors there were able to resolve anything either, nor offer Lucy any hope he would improve.

They struggled to understand what was going on with him, but told her something catastrophic must have happened that was locked up inside him. Their final prognosis was, in her opinion, a bunch of medical mumbo jumbo. Basically they said the trauma of losing his wife obviously triggered the issues. Although they managed to have one of the nurses get him to eat some things, he remained bound to a wheelchair. Lucy watched him slowly wasting away before her eyes.

Her old friend Sam Jones, Blowing Rock's one psychiatrist, tried to put the doctors' report into simple layman's terms for her. She still couldn't understand it, or believe it was a problem as simple as their report seemed to be saying. She knew her parents' relationship had been a difficult one, especially with his long trips overseas, but there was nothing in their relationship she saw to have triggered such a serious setback in hm.

She decided to put her father's things into storage ahead of the house sale, just in case some miracle occurred and he came out of this thing, whatever it was. There were a few items in the house and garage she knew might mean something to him, but most of their possessions were her mother's, things Lucy wanted to keep for herself. His office was a different matter. It was hallowed ground, out of bounds for most of her life. In there, her mother warned her, were "Daddy's things" and she was never to mess with the paperwork, or computers. As with all children, being told it was restricted made Lucy more determined to get inside. When she did sneak in one time he caught her sitting in front of his desk. She was surprised at the time by his calm reaction to her being there, not at all what she'd expected, based on her mother's warnings. Her father had sat across from her at his oversize black desk, trying to explain everything to her in the room.

She was too young to understand exactly what he was saying to her about this computer, that contraption, or what "files" were, or even what his work really involved. She would laugh to herself years later, thinking about that special day when he talked to her alone in there, the financial terms he used going over her head completely. Finally he had warned her to stay out in future, that this was his special place and no one, not even her mother, was allowed in. She promised him never, ever, to go into that room again. "Cross my heart and hope to die", and she had kept that promise all these years.

At school the next day she told her closest friend, Sally Sweetland, about her adventure into the "special room" and that she could never, ever, go in there again. Asked what was inside, she told Sally, "I'm not sure really . . . I think he said sacks of gold."

The next day the door to her father's room was locked, and she had never found a key to it since.

⸎

She stood before the door of the room, thinking back again to that day as a child; she felt strangely guilty doing it, but there was no other way. It was not easy to open, but a rummage around the garage turned up a good-sized sledge-hammer she hoped would do the trick– if she could lift it. She was going to ask her husband, Phil, to do it for her, suspecting he would have taken it down in minutes, but this room was special, and to her alone. The door finally gave in to her efforts after ten minutes of pounding on it, sweat pouring down her face. She stood there looking through the splintered mess of a door with some trepidation about going in. There was obviously something in there her father needed to hide, but what was it?

She wrenched the broken door aside to where she could walk into the room without cutting herself, pausing to take a deep breath before going in, just like she had as a little girl. Apart from the mess she created, the room looked almost as she remembered. It was a little dusty, but had clearly been used up to the time her father became ill. She walked around the room, touching every cabinet and item she could see and decided she would store its entire contents.

She could see her father had the best of everything in there, though some of the things were different from what she remembered; two computers near his desk looked quite new. She had worked with hardware at university and in her early career enough to know they weren't purchased at any store she'd ever been in. How had he afforded them? Provided by the company he worked with? The printer alone was more elaborate than any office home would need. Then again, she thought, maybe his work called for it before he retired, but even that didn't make sense to her. It was way too powerful for that.

She moved over and sat in the same spot from all those years ago, staring at the empty leather seat in front of her. She could see him there, talking to her so gently, the deep brown leather chair more worn than she remembered, but still with the same smell. The ashtray filled with cigarette butts was there too but empty now. Looking up, she saw a large exhaust fan in the wall that was new; so much for his claims to have stopped smoking all those years ago.

⟨⟩

After a while she moved onto the leather chair and started to open the side drawers, hoping to discover what her father had been doing in there every night. Most of it provided no surprises, but the back of the top drawer held several old notebooks filled with numbers and dates. Was it her father's business financial information, or personal records? On closer examination she decided it was not, nor that he would ever tell her what it might be. She moved the top drawer in and out, noting a rattling sound at the back of the drawer. Lucy pulled it all the way, but the drawer would not come out. She found nothing to make the noise she heard, shook the drawer back and forth rapidly again; there was definitely something there. As she looked closer she suspected that the rear hid a locked compartment. She could have given up, but a strong desire to see what it might be told her not to; after all, her father and this room had been off limits for some mysterious reason, even to her mother.

———— ✣ ————

Another trip to her father's garage yielded a smaller hammer, a chisel, and a thin pry bar. Taking these, she returned to the desk and tried to figure out how to get behind the drawer. First she emptied the drawer's visible contents; then, with the pry bar, managed to remove the entire unit, figuring she would be able to see the back of it. The last three inches, however, were enclosed, a kind of compartment, along with a small keyhole that could open it. She searched the office for another key, but found nothing. Should she just ask her father about it? Deciding there was no point, she knew it was better to break it open in any way she could.

The compartment proved more difficult than the office door. After trying everything, the large sledgehammer became the only answer. When the drawer was battered open to reveal its contents she saw two hard drives there, and nothing ordinary about those either. They were encased in metal and sturdy enough to survive anything; they had already come through the battering of a fourteen-pound sledgehammer with only minor markings on them. She wondered what they held that needed to be hidden this way. She decided to check them out, expecting them to be protected against any third party accessing them.

She turned on what she thought was her father's main computer, expecting to wait for it to load a welcome screen, and request the password. She was shocked when the screen came alive in an instant, and said welcome back to some name she had never seen before.

Checking the menu screen she soon found her father's files, but there was nothing suspicious in them at all. His business and personal files were clearly laid out; even the last correspondence he had started to write before sinking into silence was there. It was sitting open with a request to save or delete it, but there was nothing typed in it. Why was the computer not shut down fully? Why had it opened up to her without asking for a password? It made no sense to her after all the efforts he'd taken to secure the room.

She went to the inbox to see if she could find anything that might have triggered leaving it open. The last message he received had come in from a third party, addressed to him, but originating from an email address she didn't recognize at first. The message had only two words in it. They seemed to practically scream out to her from the screen . . . simple, but direct.

"FUCK YOU."

———∞∞∞———

Lucy turned on the machine behind her, hit print on the computer, and sat back to see if the printer would work. The machine whirred into life quickly and spat out the two copies she had requested. Looking at it more closely she highlighted the original sender's e-mail address, folded the page, and put it into her pocket. She was not done; there were still the two hard drives to contend with, but in the meantime she typed in the original sender's e-mail address and proceeded to send a reply. She apologized for contacting the person, but asked if the party could contact her directly; she typed in her own e-mail address and phone number. She ended the e-mail by noting that her father was John Wainwright, that she was interested in what was behind the e-mail, and that something terrible had befallen him.

She was surprised to receive a response right away, but disappointed to see it simply say that all such correspondence to the party was blocked for security purposes.

Lucy then tried one of the hard drives to see if there was any hope of accessing them. As she expected, it called for a password and rejected everything she entered. She sat back in the old leather chair and looked around for a password book, or some scrap of paper indicating what it could be. She doubted her father was as loose with them as she was. Small yellow notes were stuck on the side of her desk at home, with most of her passwords for all to see. She could, of course, consult her father about them, but doubted she would get anything out of him. In the back of her mind was that old warning to stay out of that room and his things. She could not bring herself even now to tell him she had broken into his office, especially the desk.

It was getting late in the day and she needed to get home to her husband. She knew she could not talk to him about what she had done, or found. Phil could barely switch a computer on, let alone have a serious discussion about hard drives and password security. A hard drive for him was pulling his Harley bike out of the garage and heading for a long road trip with his three town buddies. The thought about why she was still married to him flashed through her mind, changed as he was after returning from overseas. She couldn't desert him in the state he was in, even though his mental abuse of her was worsening. She knew it was post-traumatic stress disorder, but felt trapped by it all and not sure where to turn. Wars were terrible things; she knew that from the day she married him, but never imagined things would become so difficult.

On a sudden whim she decided to call Sam Jones again. She knew she was playing with fire, but needed to talk to him about Phil. She would also ask him if he knew anything about computer security and passwords, or could at least give her some ideas on how to proceed.

She called his private number and left a message. Within minutes he was on the line, arranging to see her the following afternoon, disappointed when she preferred to meet in his office. The last thing she needed, with Phil in his current state, was his finding out about his own psychiatrist's involvement with her. It wouldn't be easy, but she had to put a stop to the affair, for now at least. Her friend, Sally Sweetland, had warned her that there were whispers about them in town, and she needed to be careful.

—⊗⊗⊗—

Lucy arrived at Sam's office shortly before the appointed time, his assistant Jane welcoming her with a warm hug, and saying how she hoped Phil was doing better. Then Jane began telling her the latest gossip in town, how awful it was the way so and so was cheating on his wife. Lucy started to take a seat but the assistant continued. "You can go in right away, Lucy. He told me to send you in as soon as you got here. He's not so busy today. We're happy to see you here. By the way, you look very pretty today, as always."

"Thanks, Jane, I don't feel it today."

This really is small town America, Lucy thought, as she knocked on the door and walked in, to find Sam Jones jump out of his seat to greet her. He quickly closed the door behind her and pulled her into his arms. She returned the passion of his kiss but soon pushed him away. "Not here, not today. We need to talk."

"We can talk later," Sam said yanking her back into his arms. She told him she couldn't, that they really needed to talk. She told him she wanted his help and had something serious to tell him.

He relaxed his hold, then led her gently to the seat by his desk. He had always been this way with her, a sharp contrast to Phil's occasional rough handling. "Okay, you win. Where do you want to start? Phil? Us?"

"Phil will do."

"How is he at home now, Lucy? He seems more distant in our sessions. I suggested he head over to the big veterans hospital in Greensboro, see if they could help better than I can. He won't go, says he prefers talking to me. Does he know anything about us?"

"I doubt it, Sam. You wouldn't be sitting there if he did. No, I'm sure he doesn't. I'm worried about him though, he's been more difficult than usual of late, and I'm not sure why. Something's happened."

"You don't know?" Sam asked.

"Know what?"

"I don't believe it. You mean the hags of Hampton have kept it from you?"

"What the hell are you talking about?"

"Phil defending your honor at that old bar on Sixth Street."

"How do you mean?"

"They say he put three guys from the bar in hospital . . . for saying you'd make the best lay in town. They're right, of course, in that regard. Anyway, his buddies pulled him off them."

"That can't be; he's never come home looking as if he's been in a fight."

"He wouldn't, as far as I heard. None of them got to touch him apparently. Whatever else he came back with from Kabul, he certainly knows how to take care of himself."

"That's why we can't go on like this anymore. If he finds out about us he might hurt you. I can't bear thinking about what he could do to you."

"You can't do this to me, Lucy, just like that. We need to talk about it a whole lot more. You need me, and I certainly need you."

"No, Sam, we won't talk more, and certainly not with me lying on that couch having you convince me otherwise. The time isn't right. Did you know the hags are starting to talk? If we don't stop now it's only a matter of time before he finds out."

"But we both know we're right for each other, Lucy. Why not just divorce him and get it over with? I love you."

"I love you too, but I can't right now, not in the state he's in. Make him well again, Sam, and I will. If you really want me you'll have to wait."

"Oh, I'll wait. But let's see each other still," He begged.

"No, Sam, only like this; no other way until he's acting better. I'm worried for you in the future."

She watched him sink back in his chair. The dejected look on his face told her he knew she would not relent. She walked behind his chair and slowly massaged his shoulders.

"Just wait for me, Sam, wait for me."

"Always. You'd better go now before this adult cries like a baby."

"Not yet. I do have something different to talk to you about . . . my dad."

"Why? Isn't he doing okay with those doctors over in the nursing home? I've heard the facility is great for people in your father's situation. Expensive though. Can you afford it?"

"He's there and alive; that's about all I can tell you. No, I wanted to get your advice about something I've found in Mother's house."

"I've heard you're selling it, right? How does he feel about that?" Sam asked.

"He doesn't feel. Anyway the house was left to me, so I'll use the money to take care of him. Where all his investments are nobody knows, and he certainly isn't speaking, about that or anything."

"There's always hope, Lucy."

"I keep telling myself that. I really do. But it's getting harder all the time."

She began to relate what happened at the house, and the things she had found. Inadvertently it turned into Sam analyzing the whole situation and how the event as a child made its mark on her, why she was feeling so guilty about what she had done to his things. They talked about everything, including the two hard drives she needed to access. It was not his area of expertise he told her, but tried to assist her by talking about the psychology of different types of individuals, and how they handled passwords. She told him she found nothing in his desk to hint of a likely password, except for a book full of numbers.

Sam told her she should try to find a specialist company, not that they might be able to break into it either. She didn't think that was a good idea. What if it was something that could get her father into trouble? She still preferred to try herself. He offered to go back to the house with her to help, but she told him he needed to stay away. There were nosy hags close by who would assume more than there was with the pair of them alone in the house. No, she would continue to look for an answer.

"Look, Lucy, unless it's on some scrap of paper, a notebook, a password program on the computer, or hidden in some other part of the desk or room, then I don't know what you can do. Let me write out a list of the kinds of passwords people use based on their character. You can try it, but I don't hold out much hope. Maybe the book of number strings holds the answer, somehow."

She got up to leave. He reluctantly followed her to the door, until she turned and they kissed again.

"That's it then? Just like that?"

"No, but there's no other way right now. It's on hold, but please don't think it's over, unless you want it to be."

"Never, and I'll be here to help you with anything you need. Anytime, night or day." She reluctantly opened the door; he yelled out to Jane to cancel everything for the rest of the day, he wasn't feeling well.

"Is he okay, Lucy?" Jane asked, as she walked by her desk.

"He's fine, I think. Maybe he's starting to catch what's been going around."

"You may be right; my mother's been sick all week."

Lucy kept her composure until she made it to the car and turned the ignition on. She burst into tears, sobbing for a long time before slipping the car into drive.

She was heading home to Phil, praying that things would get no worse than they had become. It was not his fault, she understood that, but how much more could she stand without seeing Sam again? How long could she last before running back to Sam?

Chapter 2

Lucy Summers sat in the corner office of her flower business. Her assistant, Sarah, was taking care of the customers who stopped by while she caught up on the wholesale orders they needed to place. Afterwards, she pulled out the copy of her father's last e-mail, and decided to try a reply from her own computer. Looking at it again she wondered who the sender really was, then sent off another e-mail asking the sender to reply. The response this time was more concerning; the account was closed, "no longer in service."

She knew enough from her intern days and work after she graduated from Duke University in North Carolina, that the e-mail originated in China. Looking at the name she assumed the sender was a Li Buyun, the surname first, following the Chinese custom. She considered herself lucky to have gone over there with her manager at the time for meetings. Global Oil in Dallas, who she had interned with initially, had not wanted her to leave the international area of their business, but after two years her mother had developed cancer and begged her to move back to Blowing Rock. Taking her to Beijing was Robert Jenkins' way of thanking her for her hard work, and she appreciated it. She wondered if anyone in the office there might remember her and be able to help track this person down.

Lucy rummaged through some old phone books and placed a call to Global Oil. It took time to get through a series of recorded prompts before she ended up speaking to a human being,

"Good morning. Global Oil, Dallas. How may I direct your call?" the voice asked.

"My name is Lucy Summers. I'd like to speak to Mr. Jenkins in international operations please. "

"I'm sorry, Miss, there's no one by that name on my list."

"Are you sure?"

"I've been here for a year now, and there's no one in the employee directory by that name, not even close."

"Well, could you put me through to someone in that department then? I worked in the area for two years for him and I'd like to speak to someone about him. It was a long time ago, I'm afraid, right after I graduated."

"I can put you through to our Dick Humphrey if you like. He's been here for a while and might be able to help. I'm sure human resources won't give anything out to you, company policy and all."

"That would be great; he may even be able to answer my question." Lucy said.

The phone flipped over to a recorded message while the call transferred. It highlighted the achievements of Global Oil and its diverse business activities around the world. Lucy was surprised at the extent of the businesses they were now involved in since her time there. She hung on for what seemed an eternity before the recording stopped. The receptionist came on to apologize, saying it had taken time to run Humphrey down. Lucy thanked her as another deep voice came on the line.

"Dick Humphrey, Global Oil, can I help you?"

"I hope so. My name's Lucy Summers, but at the time I worked for Global my maiden name was Wainright. I worked for Robert Jenkins in international and have a question for him, if I can ever find him."

"You worked for old Bob? Great guy. My boss too; retired now though. Finally hung it up three years ago and headed off to Florida. I can try to find his contact details if you like?"

"That would be great, but maybe you can give me the information I'm after?"

"Shoot."

"Is Mr. Wang Jun still chief representative in the Beijing office these days? He wasn't much older than me at the time."

"Boy, you have been away a long time," Humphrey said.

"Oh . . . he's gone too? I was over there working with Bob and him for three months. I had the impression Bob thought he had a great future as chief rep for Global."

"No, I wasn't implying he was gone, not at all. You see, the rep office doesn't exist anymore. We joint ventured with a Chinese company after the time you were around, then closed it."

"Really? We were all working on a JV then. Do you know where he went? I'm actually looking for some help from him on a personal matter."

"I can give you the number of the JV for you to contact if you like . . . Lucy Summers you said, right"

"Yes, but they would remember me as Lucy Wainright."

"Well, I'm happy to tell you how far off base you are asking if Wang left. He's the president of the JV now, the whole damned thing. Doing a great job too."

"That's good to hear," Lucy said.

"That's when I came in here, Lucy. It was a difficult time for Bob though; he was the one who pushed the deal through the board. Frankly, between us, it was a disaster for the first couple of years. Almost cost him his job. It was Wang who helped pull it out of the fire. It's the most profitable division in the group now. Shouldn't be telling you that though, so keep it to yourself."

"Of course. I'm glad it worked out."

"Look, I'm not allowed to give information like this out to just anybody, so why don't I e-mail him direct and give him your contact details. I can't give you Wang's direct line information – policy, you know, for someone at that level. If you call the main number there yourself they'll never let you through to him. Do you want me to try that for you first? I 've got to e-mail him anyway today; his quarterly numbers are due."

"I'd really appreciate that. I think he'll be happy to hear from me again. Could you tell him it's urgent, and personal?"

"Sure can. If I can help anymore, let me know. What info do you want me to send him?"

Lucy gave her phone and e-mail address and thanked Humphrey profusely for his help. The call over, she began thinking about a visit to China, pleased to hear about Wang Jun's rise in the company. They had talked about their futures a lot while they were together in Beijing. She doubted that if Bob Jenkins had known the two were sleeping together, things would have turned out so well for him. She hoped Wang Jun would not misinterpret the urgency of the call after all these years, although they parted with good feelings on both sides. When she left the company he sent a warm thank-you letter on behalf of the rep office in Beijing, along with a beautiful cashmere shawl she still treasured. She had even received an invitation to his wedding later on, not that her attendance was expected, simply a gesture of his fondness for her. All she could do now was wait for him to call while she tried to uncover what her father might have been hiding.

***

Dick Humphrey put the phone down after Lucy's call; he thought it better to check the caller out before sending anything on to Wang Jun. He knew how busy the man was, and did not want to push a crank caller on to him. He called human resources, gave the manager's secretary the name of Lucy Wainright, the year she claimed to have worked for Jenkins, and asked her to check if the caller was for real.

He was close to sending off his e-mail to Beijing when he received confirmation; Miss Wainright had worked there as he was told. Her exit interview file still contained recommendations to employ her again; two of them were from Bob Jenkins and Wang Jun in the China rep office. He was pleasantly surprised at what he heard about her, but intrigued as to why she was trying to contact Wang Jun after all this time. He added a note about Lucy to the end of his memo to Wang, passed along her details, but kept his comments business-like. He had typed in one last sentence, smiled, but then deleted it as soon as he had finished. It read, "Hey, buddy Jun, you didn't screw this one too, did you?"

***

Lucy was surprised to get the international call so quickly. Phil was still watching his Miami Heat basketball game on their big screen TV, and paid no attention to the call she was taking, or that she left the room.

"This Miss Lucy?" a female voice said on the line, with a Chinese accent.

"It is, *ni hao*," Lucy replied.

"Oh . . . you speak Chinese?"

"No, not at all, but I was in Beijing many years ago."

"That's good. My name is Mei Rui, assistant to President Wang. He will talk to you now, but asked me to explain he's very busy and won't be able to talk for long. I am to give you my number for future reference. Is that okay?" Lucy grabbed a pen and quickly wrote down her e-mail address and phone number. Clearly Wang Jun didn't want her calling him direct at this point, no doubt wondering what the call was about.

"Okay, hold on please. Mr. Wang is on the line now."

"Lucy! It's so good to hear from you after all these years. We can talk more later, but what's your urgent call for? I was worried hearing from you like this, after all the years too."

"I'm sorry, John, if I can still call you that. It's nothing life threatening at all. I can explain another time if you're busy. To tell you the truth, I need help to track someone down in Beijing who knew my father when he worked there."

"No problem. What's their name?"

"Li Buyun, I think. I don't know if it's a man or a woman, but it's very important to me."

"Okay. We'll see what we can do. It's really nice to here you calling me John again after all these years, Lucy. I'll tell Mei, my assistant, to work with you. She's excellent in that regard, and I'll make sure she gets what you need, if she can. Of course, we have to speak again when I have more time. I'm sorry, but I have a flight to catch to Moscow later today and need to get going. I mean it, we must talk as soon as I get back."

"Don't let me hold you up for your flight, especially with what I read about the traffic in Beijing these days, and all that pollution. Sounds awful. I appreciate you taking the time to call me, honestly. I hope we can talk when you get back."

"We will, but I'll be busy for a month over there; big deal to work on. You would have liked it. So how come you never called me after you left? You broke my heart, you know."

"That's nice of you to say. I just figured at the time it was one of those special flings that couldn't go anywhere. I still have the shawl you sent me, and your wedding invitation, as fancy as it was."

"Well, we'll never know now what could have been, will we, Lucy?"

"That's true."

"I'll ask Mei to call you tomorrow when I'm out of her hair. It really is good to hear from you, Lucy. You must come to Beijing and meet my family. Bring your husband; I can arrange everything."

"Not so good in that department. If I was able to come it would be alone."

"Mm . . . that sounds even better!"

Lucy smiled to herself at the change in his voice. It had the same lilt she remembered from all those years ago–in bed, after they'd made love.

"You haven't changed, have you? Go and make more money for the company. And congratulations, by the way. Bob always told me he thought you had it in you."

"Yes, dear old Bob. He was my mentor, boss, and friend. I miss talking to him these days. Take care. I have to rush. All my love to you; we'll talk when I get back. Mei will call you tomorrow, guaranteed! Or she's fired. *Tsai tien*, my lovely Lucy."

The phone clicked dead. The excitement of hearing his voice wilted as she walked back into the den, saw Phil sitting there, beer in hand, watching his game, and barely giving her a glance.

"Who was that, honey?" he asked.

"Just Sally. She wants me to go over there Friday night and see her; she's taking the night off."

"No sweat. I'll be out with the boys anyway."

Lucy went back to her bedroom and slumped onto the bed. She thought of Phil in the other room and what he was like before Afghanistan, the career her mother's illness ruined, Wang and their nights together, of Sam and his love for her too. How had it all come to this? She burst into tears.

Minutes later she was startled by Phil at the door. "Are you okay?"

"I'm fine, just thinking about Dad's situation."

"Don't worry; he'll come out of it one of these days. I've seen stuff like that with my buddies. It always gets better."

"What about with you, Phil?"

He ignored the comment, asked only if she minded him slipping out for a quick one with the guys to celebrate his team's win. She told him to go and enjoy himself. As soon as she heard the door click shut, she picked up the lamp by the bed, screamed in frustration, and threw it against the far wall. She cried some more before finally getting up and going downstairs to the flower shop. It was late, but she needed to work on a flower arrangement for the next morning to take her mind off things. Her thoughts soon returned to her father and the e-mail she found on his computer. She wondered if looking for one person in Beijing, with a population of twenty million, was realistic, and whether in the end it would help at all.

⟨⟩

In the morning she left Sarah to manage the shop and headed for her mother's home. She planned to search for passwords and go through all her father's files, to see what she could find to help Mei Rui in her search. Whatever guilt she felt earlier about rummaging through his things was slipping away; she realized her father may have had things to hide, even from her mother.

She decided to check every filing cabinet carefully, still not knowing what it was she was looking for, but with the hope that something would stand out. She spent the first hour that morning with one of the hard drives, inputting every string of numbers in the little black book she found. Finally she gave up on it as a password source, and set it to one side. After another hour of going through the first cabinet something odd struck her; she confirmed it with a quick overview of every other cabinet. There was not a shred of paperwork referring to her father working for Goldman Sachs all those years, or about the company in any of the files.

She remembered him telling her he reported directly to their New York headquarters. He had spent considerable time in China on projects, which was probably the reason she felt a connection with the place when she was there with Global

Industries. Why not just call them up and ask about her father? Not sure of the best way to handle it, she decided to go through their human resources department, pose as her mother, and make up some story about her father's pension. She would ask them to confirm the details of her father's care benefits. After all, Goldman was a great company; its employees must have had good pensions. Her mother had always commented on how nice it was for them to retire so comfortably.

<hr />

It was not difficult to get through to New York, and on the phone line to the human resource group. It did take her a while, however, to get someone dealing with pensions to speak to. When she was finally able, Lucy told the administrator she was a Mrs. John Wainright, and that her husband was seriously ill. She told the lady about her husband being mainly involved in China when he retired, how he was facing more medical expense, and could she please confirm that his long-term retirement care was still in effect?

Lucy gave the woman all of her father's details, spelled his name out twice to be sure she had it correctly, gave his birth date, and the approximate date of his retirement. She could hear the tapping of computer keys as the information was being entered. Asked politely to wait for a few moments, Lucy was put on hold. While she listened to some kind of market commentary in the background, she suspected something was wrong; it took more than fifteen minutes for the woman to come back on the line.

"I'm really sorry, Mrs. Wainright, but we have no record of an employee at all by that name."

"That can't be!"

" It is . . . I've checked the files thoroughly . . . the pension records . . . even made a quick call to one of our old China hands. The answer was the same from everyone; a John Wainright never worked for Goldman Sachs. I'm so sorry to tell you that, but I'm a hundred percent sure of it."

Lucy thanked her then dropped the phone to the desk. "What the hell is going on here? What have you been doing, you son of a bitch? Were you lying to us all these years?" she asked aloud, flinging her pen down in disgust.

Chapter 3

The call from Mei Rui came in early the next morning. She jumped out of bed, grabbed her cell phone to avoid waking Phil, and headed down to her office.

"So sorry to call this early, Lucy Summers. I thought I better call you before I left for the day."

"Call me Lucy, please," she said breathing heavily. "Should I call you Mei or Rui?"

"Everyone just calls me Mei."

"Did John leave already? Excuse me . . . I mean Wang Jun, of course."

Mei laughed. "So that was the English name he used? You don't hear it around here at all. That must have been a long time ago. He never uses anything but Wang Jun here, usually *laoban* with me, of course."

"*Laoban*? Oh yes . . . boss in Chinese . . . right?"

"Good memory, Lucy. Around here I have lots of *Laoban*, but he's number one for me and I like working with him."

"I enjoyed him too . . . back then. I had a great time over there."

"You must come back; you wouldn't recognize it. Anyway, let's hope one day you visit and we can have a good talk about my country."

"Your English is really excellent, Mei."

"Thank you for saying so. I think my language skills made the difference when I applied for the opening. Look, Lucy, I've done a little work today, researching your Li Buyun character. It's not a common name, but I assumed that would help. Buyun is more of a lady's name, you know. Some men have it, but it's rare. It means "steps to the clouds". Quite an auspicious name I might add. If you believe some of our traditions this would imply the person is ambitious, and strong. Of course until we find your Li Buyun we'll never know if she is or not."

"What were you able to find?" Lucy asked, well aware that what she was asking was difficult.

"Well, there are seven Li Buyun names in the phone system here in Beijing, not many at all. If you give me something to ask in regard to your quest we can see if we get a match."

"That sounds like a lot of work for you, Mei. I hate to put you to so much trouble."

"Oh, no trouble, might be fun, depending on why you're looking for her. *Laoban* is gone for a month, and things will be quiet until he gets back. I'm not sure what went on between you two, but I assure you he insists I spare no effort helping you."

"That's nice to hear. We were just good friends. I was in Beijing for three months with my boss, working on a JV partner project. It was intense, as I recall, lots of meetings, late nights on documents. I'm sure things haven't changed in that regard."

"They certainly haven't."

"We were both young. It was just a close working arrangement in a small office; he had fewer than five employees back then."

"Wow . . . he's got sixteen thousand at least under him now!" Mei said.

She told Lucy more of the company's recent history, how under Global Oil's joint venture the number of businesses had grown to over twenty diverse companies; the original oil part now accounted for only 10 percent of the revenues in China. Wang Jun and his boss in the U.S. had been responsible for its success. She added that along the way Wang made a personal fortune, enough to quit any time he wanted. Lucy was not surprised the business had done so well, but felt a pang of disappointment in leaving the company when she did.

"Well, okay then, Mei, I really, really appreciate you doing this for me."

"No problem. What kind of a story can I use when calling them all?"

Lucy suggested she ask if they had ever known or worked with a John Wainright of Goldman Sachs, that his daughter in the U.S. had news of him she would like to discuss. She smiled as she said Goldman Sachs, remembering that day in her father's office and the next day at school when she told her best friend about the "sacks of gold" hidden there.

Mei told Lucy she would get to work on it the next day. She didn't expect to be too busy, but warned that she might not be able get back to her right away. She urged Lucy to see if she could find something, anything, to indicate where the person might be or worked. The call ended pleasantly and Lucy headed back upstairs, hoping Phil was not up and wondering what was for breakfast.

The call, given her current circumstances, did nothing to improve how she felt about her life. She was, however, feeling better to at least be doing something out of her normal routine. She couldn't help but think about what might have been if her mother had never begged her to come home to Blowing Rock. She soon felt ashamed for the brief feeling of bitterness toward her own mother for stalling her career; she should never even think that way.

Searching through her father's office continued, becoming almost an obsession until she struck gold, or so she thought. It was in the form of an unopened package addressed to John Wainright with a New York address, but no sender's details. She felt the package in her hands, shook what felt to her like a book, and then unwrapped it carefully. It was an eye-opener for her, a copy of a new book by Henry Paulson, someone she knew ran Goldman Sachs before becoming the U.S. Treasury Secretary. She opened the book, encouraged to see that it focused on his views of China, and gave the history of the company's efforts there.

She flipped through the book, looking for any marks to indicate who sent it, or why. There were no markings at all. She sat down in her father's chair and began to read. After glancing at some of the text she flipped through the many photos in the book showing Paulsen's visits, and his meetings with Chinese dignitaries. As she worked her way through the photos her eyes fell upon one in the early chapters. There it was, the proof she was looking for, a picture of four Goldman Sachs personnel from their China office, each one named except for the man in the background who looked like her father. The date under the photo was 1994. He wore heavy-rimmed glasses and his hair was combed differently, but it was him, of that she was certain.

She wrote down the names in the photo and noted the page number, studying each face to guess their ages and if any of them were likely to still be working. Two were senior executives; she was sure they would be retired or dead. The youngest looked at least ten or fifteen years behind her father, but it was somewhere to start. She went over to the scanner and printed a copy. She circled her father and the young man beside him, wrote "Attention: Mei Rui" at the top, added a comment to the bottom, scanned it again, and attached it to an e-mail. She advised Mei this was not her own computer she was using.

The message read, "Mei, can you call me please? Know anyone with Goldman Sachs who can identify the man standing next to this Peter Rawlings? Call me for more details." She mentioned nothing about it being her father, wrote that she would be working late, then hit send. Lucy studied the photo again, called Phil to tell him she would be busy that evening, and home late. She put her feet up on her father's desk and began reading the book to see if she could find any other clues.

In Beijing, Mei Rui received the e-mail and printed a copy for herself. She smiled broadly. This was something she could get her teeth into for Lucy, not to mention showing Wang Jun how competent she was. She scrolled through her contact list and called Goldman's headquarters, asking for Madame Zhang, their office manager. She had met her, and others from the Beijing office, on several occasions, when they visited Wang Jun to secure acquisition and investment business. So far they had fallen short every time, but Wang Jun let them compete for their business, throwing them minor projects just to get free investment advice when he needed it. She told Madame Zhang an e-mail was coming her way, and that she needed to talk to her about it as soon as she read it.

———— ∞∞∞ ————

Within two hours of Lucy sending the e-mail to Beijing, Mei was on the phone.

"Lucy? It's me, Mei."

Lucy sensed an air of triumph in her voice.

"That was the easy one," She said.

"I'm happy to hear it. What did you find out?"

"Lucky for you Laoban Wang has dealt with their office for years. They've been falling over themselves to get some of our business. All I needed to do was talk to my good friend there, old Madame Zhang, and it was done. Piece of cake, as you Americans say."

"And?"

The Peter Rawlings works in New York now. He left China a few years back, but he's about to retire, so she says. They also have copies of this book of yours in the office. I guess the staff have been told to read it. I must get one for myself."

"What did she say about the other man in the photo, the one who's not identified?"

"She had no idea."

Lucy's heart sank, "No idea? None at all?"

"Patience, Lucy, Mei Rui doesn't give up so easy. I told her someone in the office must know who the man was, even if she didn't, that it was important to Wang Jun. That was enough for her to tell me she'd call back later."

"And did she?"

"Oh yes. Anything for Laoban Wang! She told me she'd tracked down old man Chu; he started as a driver and office helper when Goldman opened up in Beijing, and he knows everything. The man retired four years ago, but stops by the office every week to say hello. He brings sweets for all the girls there, apparently he's still loved by everyone there."

"So he said it was a John Wainright, yes?"

"Who is that, Lucy?"

"I should have told you before; that's my father."

"No, Lucy, then it's not your father after all. That man standing next to Peter Rawlings is a Richard Towers, guaranteed."

"That can't be . . . it's my father. I'm certain of it. I have other photos to prove it. Oh my god, Mei, what's going on here?" She asked Mei to hold on while she calmed herself, then got back on the line. "I'm sorry for the outburst, I just don't understand it."

"What's happening? Does this have something to do with asking us to find this Li Buyun?"

"I've no idea. I don't understand anything yet. I should have told you more about what was going on, but I didn't want to influence how you might look at it."

"And how should I be looking, Lucy? I thought all along this was something to do with Wang Jun. Please tell me. You can trust me. If you don't want me to tell *laoban* then I won't."

Lucy told Mei she had no problem with her telling Wang anything but she planned to tell him herself later. She asked her to keep it confidential for a while until she knew more. At that point she relayed everything about her father's situation, and what she'd found. She told her nothing of the issues with her husband, or her problems.

For whatever reason, she found talking to Mei Rui a relief. She was someone other than Sam she could talk to, well away from the gossipmongers of her small hometown. She found a sympathetic ear in her new friend, someone as intrigued by her situation as she was. By the end of her story Lucy was weeping, mostly with relief at getting her worries out in the open. Was this Li a woman her father had slept with? Who was Richard Towers? Who was the man she called father?

"Lucy," Mei interrupted, "stop crying. I'll help you as much as I can. Before you say no, I'm going to talk to Wang Jun about getting you a ticket to come over here. I'll help you get to the bottom of this."

"Oh no, absolutely not. My husband would never let me. I can't afford it anyway."

"Nonsense. I know you can't afford it on your own. A flower business in your small city must be a struggle. Don't worry, Wang Jun drops more on a lunch meeting than covering your expense to come here. I told you before, he's a rich man outside of Global. Anyway, for whatever reason he wants you to come."

"My god, you've talked about me already? How do you know about my business?"

"Wang Jun told you I was a good investigator, right? Well I also protect my boss. I'm ashamed to tell you I used some resources to check you out. If you knew how much I can find out about companies around the world, and their people's personal lives, you'd understand how easy it was for me to find out about you. Need to know more?"

"I don't think so. I may not like what I hear. Tell Wang Jun I really appreciate his offer, but there's no way my husband, Phil, would let me come over, even if I wanted to."

"That's something we can't do much about for you, Lucy. But I should warn you, a birthday card will arrive from Wang Jun. In it will be an open round-trip ticket from New York to Beijing. You'll stay with me, of course, while you are here, and Wang will give me time off to accompany you. It's plain to me, Lucy, what went on between you two back then, so please don't try to tell me otherwise. Please come. I'm anxious to meet you. Meanwhile, see what more you can find out on our mysterious female to help me locate her, and this Mr. Towers."

"If I could come I would; nothing would please me more. Tell Wang Jun I can't say enough about what you're doing for me."

Lucy put the phone down, happy that Mei Rui called her shop direct; the lengthy overseas call would not be on her home phone bill for Phil to see. She began to think more about the call, especially the Richard Towers business and how to make sense of it. The man in the photo was her father, no matter what anyone said. If only she could go back to Beijing, that would be special, and maybe she would find some answers. She needed to watch the mail in the coming days, to make sure Phil did not see the note from Wang Jun first. How would she explain it? Voices in her head said to tell him the truth, but her heart told her otherwise.

Chapter 4

Phil Summers arrived on time for his session, stopping briefly to chat with the receptionist until Sam waived him in. He headed to the couch in Sam Jones's consulting room without being directed to it, the usual routine.

"So, Phil . . . how did the last couple of week go?" Sam asked, listening intently while Phil gave him a rundown on some of the issues he had tried to deal with.

"And that's it? I've asked you time and again to lay everything on the line, to leave nothing out."

"I've told you everything, Doc. There's nothing more to tell."

"This is Blowing Rock, Phil. You think putting three guys on the floor is nothing to tell me, something I won't hear about? We've talked about anger management before, haven't we? You're slipping again."

"It was nothing, Sam."

"I'm not sure I can continue with you. I think you need to get over to the VA and see Dr. Robertson. Maybe they can help you more than I can."

"No, Sam. Not there. I could never talk to them like I can to you. Hell, we've known each other since we were kids. I trust you. I need you, Sam. You're helping me . . . really."

"And what about Lucy? How are things there these days?"

"Okay, not so good. I do the stupidest things, and keep saying the wrong things to her. Don't know what gets into me. Will you talk to her for me? As a friend?"

"I can't. It doesn't work that way, Phil. You need to do that. Why don't you?"

"The words won't come out. She seems so unhappy with me these days. I thought buying the flower business from old Alice would help. It did, or I guess it has for her, but I can see in her eyes she's still unhappy with me."

"She seemed okay the last time I chatted with her. I'm not her doctor but I'd say she needs a break from Blowing Rock, something like that. Why don't you go on a trip together? Take her somewhere nice. That assistant of hers is good; she could run the shop blindfolded."

"Buying the place took a chunk of our cash, Sam. We get by all right, don't get me wrong, but there's not enough to pay for a nice trip anywhere."

"I thought you said you boys were planning to head to Sturgis again for the big Harley meet, stay in some rental place for the whole week. What about skipping it this year and using the cash on Lucy?"

Phil's demeanor changed quickly. "That's the only damned week I can get away from this shit, and you want me to give that up too? No fucking way, Sam. We've planned that for months. Anyway, I think Lucy will be glad I'm gone."

Sam backed away from the subject and shifted the conversation back to the nightmares Phil was still having, wondering if he had gone too far. He nearly choked when Phil suddenly sat up from the couch and said, "Do you think Lucy is fooling around, Doc?"

"Course not, Phil. I can't imagine anything like that with her. No . . . not Lucy. No way."

"I hope not. I don't know what I'd do if she was. I think I'd really lose it.."

Sam recovered his composure and shifted back to talking to Phil about pain and anger management, explaining yet again to him where all this was coming from. Phil calmed down, assured Sam he was ready to face the world for the next couple of weeks. Sam brought the session to an end.

Before he left the room Phil hugged Sam again, as one would a brother. He said how much he appreciated the help and left, the session having run well over its allotted time. Sam still could not find a way to get Phil to open up on what really happened in Afghanistan. He knew it was the key to Phil's recovery. He tried to convince him to spend some time in the veterans' program, but Phil would have none of it. He agreed, however, to go back on the prescription pills that had helped calm him in the past.

Sam watched his troubled patient depart, wondering if Phil's question about his wife having a lover was only a concern because of their problems, or whether it was a subtle warning directed at him. He shuddered at the thought of what Phil might do to him if he found out what was going on behind his back. He'd never been in any kind of fight in his life, and had no idea how he could defend himself against someone like Phil. Maybe she was right to cool things off; before they got out of hand. He knew Phil was not what she needed in her life; he would wait.

Chapter 5

Tracking down Peter Rawlings by phone was easier than Lucy imagined. She was put through to him in his New York office right away, as soon as she told the main reception to say her name was Lucy Towers, daughter of Richard.

"Good morning. Peter Rawlings, Goldman Sachs. How can I help you? How's your father? I haven't heard from him for years. Lucy, did you say your name was?"

"Yes, it's Lucy. You knew my father?"

"Of course. Had the corner office when he was in Beijing. We didn't work much together, but we did lunch or dine occasionally when he was in town. How old are you now, Lucy? I clearly remember him not being married at the time. You must be quite young."

"Not that young anymore."

"How's he doing these days? I'm out of here myself in a few weeks. Maybe I should look him up, or at least talk to him."

"Mr. Rawlings, I'm afraid I may not have been quite truthful. Please forgive me, but I'd appreciate you hearing me out."

"Go on, I'm listening. If I don't like what you have to say I'll just ring off."

"It's nothing like that. My name is now Lucy Summers, but my maiden name was Wainright, my father's first name John. He said he worked for Goldman

Sachs all the time I was growing up; he traveled to China a lot. To be honest, we hardly knew him until he left your company."

"Never heard the name, but what's that got to do with our Richard Towers?"

"Mr. Rawlings, the man standing by you in Hank Paulsen's book I just read is my father; I'm sure of it."

"Absolutely sure? The photos in that book aren't the greatest, you know."

"I can e-mail you more photos of him to look at if you like?"

"Why don't you? I'll look at them for you, but I'm afraid you'll be disappointed."

"My father is sitting in a wheelchair these days staring at the wall. He doesn't talk to anyone and is getting worse by the day. I'm trying to find out what put him in that state. Something is going on here, and I need to get to the bottom of it to help him. By the way, does the name Li Buyun mean anything at all to you from your Beijing days?"

"Absolutely nothing, I'm afraid."

"What can you tell me about Richard Towers? She asked.

"As I said, not too much. He traveled a lot between Beijing and New York, stayed in China for long stretches, but seemed to disappear quite a bit; except of course when dignitaries from the main office or our government were in town. He always seemed to be in the background though, sometimes just listening; never said much either way. He was one of our folks who never learned the local language that I knew of. Even old Chu, the driver, tried to help, but finally gave up on him."

"Chu was his driver? Madame Zhang never said anything about that."

"Oh! You've talked to her already? Well, I'm surprised she didn't tell you. That woman knows everything about the place, or rather Chu does. Come to think of it, maybe she came in after Richard left."

"Is there anything about him you can tell me that might be out of the ordinary?"

"I'm thinking. Give me a minute or two, you've got my attention."

Lucy could hear Rawlings tapping his pencil on the desk, the beat never changing. It was obviously a habit while thinking something through.

"Steve Hardy. That's the man you really need to be talking to. He was our VP at the time. Richard reported directly to him, but I know Steve didn't like him. Come to think of it, I might have been the only one in the office who did. I'd talk to him if I were you."

"Do you have a number for him? I'd really appreciate it."

"Not right here. I heard he moved again a while back. Give me a day or two and I'll call you back. If it works out it's best you tell him I told you to call; he never liked talking to anyone about Richard as I recall. Let me know what you find out in the end, but I'm afraid you're going to find this man is not your father. Send me those photos anyway, I'll look them over for you."

Lucy noted Rawlings e-mail address and gave him her own just in case. She picked out some good photos of her father from around the time he would have worked out of Beijing and sent them off. She also sent a set to Mei Rui, along with notes about the conversation and the comment about Chu being Richard Towers' driver. The man was her father; she had no doubt about it. What he had been playing at all those years was the question she wanted an answer to.

Mei Rui received the photos and update from Lucy with interest. She had to admit the man in the book looked like the same person in Lucy's photos. She wondered why Chu hadn't told Madame Zhang about driving for Towers. Did he feel that part of his work there was somehow demeaning? She determined to speak to the old man herself, alone. He supposedly showed up at the office every Wednesday around ten in the morning, according to reception, walked around, gave out some homemade sweets, then left within the hour.

She checked the time and figured the driver could have her over there by 10:15, if they left right away. Once in Wang's company car she told his driver,

Mr. Han, that she needed to be in the Goldman Sachs lobby before ten-fifteen. They were there by ten.

———

She waited in the lobby area, hoping Madame Zhang wouldn't see her and invite her up. She asked one of the receptionists to point Chu out when he was leaving. At 10:30 the young girl waved, indicating Chu was heading out the door. Mei quickly tapped him on the shoulder, told him he must be the famous Mr. Chu, and, since she was new to Goldman, could she pick his brains on the history of the business there. He hesitated at first, but when she offered to buy lunch for both of them he readily agreed, especially being told she now worked for Madame Zhang. Mei had made a point of finding a copy of the infamous book Lucy referred to. A copy was sitting in Wang Jun's office all along. Goldman must have sent it to him. He'd never opened it.

She let Chu ramble on about the early days for quite some time at lunch before she thought the moment was right and pulled out the book. She flipped open one of the pages, pointing to a photo with Chu in the distant background.

"And that's you, Chu . . . am I right?"

"Oh yes, that's me," he said. "I used to drive all the bigwigs around, you know. But I did much more than just a driver; invaluable I was."

"That's what everyone says. You are a legend in there."

Mei turned a few more pages in the book until she came to the one she really wanted him to look at. "And those guys?" she asked.

Chu identified everyone, but he did not point out Richard Towers.

"So who is that one?"

"That's Spook."

"Who?"

"I mean, Mr. Towers."

"Why'd you call him Spook?"

"No reason really."

Mei knew right away there was more to be said. She ordered a small bottle of baijiu, hoping to loosen his tongue a bit. She changed the subject, let him wax on about his life there until she had him where she wanted.

"So tell me about Spook, Chu. Didn't he work for Steve Hardy? You knew everybody there back then, didn't you? Why Spook?"

"Mr. Hardy gave him that name behind his back; didn't like him. Said he was a bullshit man from New York. I heard him telling Mr. Rawlings once that he was a spook, in no way a financial man."

"A spook? You mean like a spy?"

"I guess not a spy like in the movies, no, not that, but everyone did think he was sent by head office to keep an eye on us. You know, check what was being expensed, make sure no one was breaking any laws . . . that kind of thing."

"So he was, let's say, like a compliance guy?"

"What's that mean?" Chu asked.

"He made sure the company followed the corporate rules and practices, that everything was above board."

"Nah, couldn't have been that; he was hardly there. The only driving I did for him was to and from the airport, none around the city. He had no friends in the office to speak of, except Rawlings, of course. He was the only one; they appeared too friendly at lunch for my liking. Why are you asking about Spook anyway?"

"No reason. Just seemed funny to a friend that he was the only person in the photo unnamed. Anyway, how did you like the book? You do read English, don't you?"

"I read some, better than most in my work, but not everything. My daughter does; she's been to university. They all have a copy at the office these days, but I don't. Madame Zhang says she'll get me one, but I haven't got it yet."

"Here you go then; have my copy, but don't tell my boss we talked or she'll ask for it back."

"But it's brand new. You must keep it."

"I can get another one, Chu. You take it home and show the family. Not a word though about our chat, okay?"

"No problem. Anytime you want to know more, you just call me. Catch me in the lobby every Wednesday, rain or shine."

Mei found her driver and headed back to the office. She wrote a long e-mail to Lucy and fired it off. She was becoming more certain that Lucy was right about her father. The question was, what was he really doing in Beijing, and who was this Li Buyun. Was she his mistress perhaps? She began to imagine all kinds of possibilities, especially after what Chu had told her. Also, why had he relayed none of that to Madame Zhang? She smiled to herself. This was becoming much more interesting. She knew she had to find Li Buyun somehow, maybe Lucy could find out more about Steve Hardy from her side. He might have something to say about this so-called "Spook" character.

———— ∞ ————

Phil Summers arrived at Jake's Bar in a good frame of mind, ordered a drink, and headed over to where his three friends were waiting. Bill asked him how his session went with the doctor, and if he was feeling any better these days. Phil told them he was back on his meds, and asked them to watch that he didn't overdo it again. He looked at his friends joking with each other, and felt better to be there with them. Phil sometimes felt guilty leaving Lucy at home. Even Sam had told him not to overdo it, that he was likely using the company to soften his guilt over the loss of others on his team in Afghanistan. He had been the only one to survive the raid, and it still bothered him, aside from the terrible nightmares over what the enemy had done to him. None of his friends knew what really happened, only that he was seriously injured in the groin by a roadside bomb. If only it had been just that, he thought.

As the evening wore on Phil finally pulled something out of his pocket and asked for some quiet.

"What you got there, Phil? Another citation for bravery?"

The three friends chuckled, not in humor but with respect for the medals he won over there. While they remained in Blowing Rock, their biggest risk in life had been the number of cigarettes they continued to smoke.

"I need you guys' advice on something, but it's personal. Tell anyone and I'll cut your balls off; then you can all join me in the eunuch's club."

All three laughed at his half-joke, assuring Phil they were his men, they were brothers. If he said don't tell, then that's how it would be.

"Okay, I think I may have screwed up a bit."

"How's that?" Joe asked.

"Opening Lucy's mail without telling her."

"That's a dumb thing to do with any woman, Phil," Bill said. "Unless it's a love letter or something."

"Nothing like that. Get serious guys and listen to this." Everyone moved closer in, although the likelihood of anyone else hearing was unlikely; the bar was almost empty.

"First there's this cover note from a Global Oil outfit in Dallas. I know she worked there before she moved back to Blowing Rock."

"And the rest is romantic history, right?" Joe said.

"No, just listen to me, asshole. It's actually a nice letter. It says, 'Dear Mrs. Summers, we have been contacted by Global Industries, China Region, to invite you to a special event. We hope you will accept this invitation in the spirit it has been sent to you. We know our records show you only worked two years for us, but it is clear from your exit file and comments of others that you made an impact. The reason for your resignation mentions your mother's health; we sincerely hope that everything worked out in that regard. We would really appreciate you attending the ceremony, especially for the reasons outlined in the invitation by Mr. Wang Jun, President of Global Industries Asia'.

"Wow, Phil, that's cool shit. Where's Asia?" one of them asked.

"The invite's from China, you dickhead, now listen up, here's the second thing. 'Dear Lucy, it has been a good many years since you and Robert Jenkins participated in our first joint venture negotiations in China. The seeds from those first efforts have grown to something special. The agreement, signed after you left us, generated twenty million dollars in the first year of operation. Next month we will celebrate a special anniversary within Global Industries China for that first JV's investment in rail and transport technologies. We will commemorate reaching five hundred million dollars of sales for the prior year, and the birthday of the chairman of our joint venture, Mr. Xin, whom you may remember from the negotiations.

'You will recall how warmly he treated you in particular, and how much he respected your tenacity in the negotiations for someone of such a young age at the time, as he put it. As a result of this, and our desire to have you participate in this farewell ceremony, we are enclosing a round trip ticket to China for you to attend the banquet, and to see the changes that have occurred here in the recent past. I do hope, Lucy, that you will accept this gesture of respect and friendship by agreeing to join us. We will ensure that your visit is a memorable one'."

"Who's the letter from?" Joe asked.

"Some guy called Wang Jun, says he's president of this Global Asia."

"That's really nice, Phil. You should be proud of Lucy," Bill said.

"Especially with all the shit she's been through with you lately," Joe added.

"You mean, you guys think I should let her go off there on her own?"

"Of course you should, if not go with her."

"We can't afford it. Anyway not me, not after the last flight I took back from Afghanistan with those friends of mind in boxes. Swore I'd never get on a plane again. I haven't and I won't."

"Well then, don't be a son of a bitch, let the lady do something she'll never have the chance to do again, and get her a trip out of this dump of a town."

As soon as Bill finished, Joe jumped in. "We'll have a ball while she's gone. We can polish the bikes up, and have our own road trip. It'll be great."

Phil wondered aloud how he was going to tell Lucy he'd taken her mail and opened it without telling her. He was sure she would be angry. He proposed throwing the letter away and saying nothing to her. All three of them told him to get his act together for once with Lucy; he had the prefect opportunity to treat her right. They told him to tell her he opened the letter by mistake as soon as he could, to say how proud he was for her, that the "boys" all voted for her to go, and would be taking him on a road trip while she was gone. Phil knew they were right, then ordered drinks all round before telling them he was going home.

"Go for it!" they yelled as he left the bar, earlier than usual.

⸻◈⸻

Lucy was surprised when Phil came home before ten, then angry when Phil explained how he opened a letter for her without having the time to tell her about it.

He surprised her with a bear hug. "Read this, Lucy. The boys and I are really proud of you; you have to go."

"What are you talking about?" she said.

He gave the note and letter to her, and stood back while she read them.

Lucy acted as shocked as she could. "I don't believe it . . . after all these years! They want me to come? No, I can't do it, I can't leave you here. Could you come with me?"

"Lucy, you know how I am with flying. Look, things haven't been right lately, I know that. It's the opportunity of a lifetime. Remember when we first met how much you said you liked the place? It'll be fun for you to see how much it's changed. No, you go, the boys will take care of me. We're already planning a road trip, as soon as you can tell us when you would go."

He completely surprised her; she never dreamed he would agree to her going. She pointed out needing to go soon, according to the event's date of only two weeks away. He pulled her to him, told her again to get it all planned.

"I'm proud of you, Lucy, I do love you. I wish I could be my old self, but I just can't get the hurt out of me. I mean, why me? Why not them? And with what those bastards over there did to me . . . I'm so sorry."

She kissed him on the cheek, held him tighter than she had in months. "I know, Phil. I know. None of this is your fault. Yes, you've hurt me, but I understand why. It'll get better, I hope. I still love you."

The last three words came out naturally, but inside they held a hollow ring. She knew any love for him was dying after Afghanistan. She would protect him as long as she could, but she wasn't going to throw the rest of her life away on him. She was unhappy to hear that he showed the letter to his friends, but could tell they pushed him to agree to her going. For that she would at least be grateful to all of them.

"Okay," She finally said. "I'll go ahead and see what I can arrange, but those boys better take care of you while I'm gone."

"Oh, they will Lucy, they will."

———⚮———

Lucy went into her office leaving Phil to pour himself a beer. She opened her computer and typed an e-mail right away to Mei Rui.

"Thank you so much for the letter, and don't tell me it was from Wang Jun because I remember very well how he writes. The best part is my husband surprised me tonight by agreeing. I can't wait to meet you, and please thank Wang Jun. Meantime I'm still looking into Steve Hardy, searching for anything here on Li, and trying to open the two hard drives I found. Thanks again, Lucy."

About ten minutes later a reply came in.

"Great news, Lucy. Laoban will be so happy. I have lots of room in my apartment for you; we will have a good time together while we do our detective work. Why don't you bring the hard drives over with you? We have some experts here that I'm sure could help. Send us your flight info as soon as you have it."

Lucy replied right away. She would have to think about the hard drives. What if there was something bad on them that no one should see? She started work on her flight booking.

Chapter 6

Two weeks later Lucy walked up to the United Airlines counter in Kennedy Airport to check in, still in disbelief that she was flying to Beijing. She had sent her passport, a copy of her flight reservations, and the visa application to the New York company referred by Mei. Along with the application form, she included a copy of another invitation letter received by e-mail from Global in Beijing, in Chinese, with instructions to request a ten-year multiple entry visa. She paid added fees for a rush turnaround.

She was amazed to receive her passport back, visa inside, in only four days. She remembered that the last visa for China had taken six weeks to come through. At first she was impressed with how efficient things had become, until she saw a slip of paper accompanying the passport asking her to thank Wang Jun for his continued business. They hoped she would pass along her appreciation to him for the visa company's prompt action, especially during such a busy time of the month.

The suitcase she wheeled behind her was the same one she used all those years ago. Travel had never been much of an option with her husband's condition, or on account of the expenses getting the flower business up and running. Phil told her to buy new luggage, but she declined, opting to use the money towards new clothes she needed for the trip.

She researched the best way to communicate with Phil while she was gone. Using her cell phone overseas would be prohibitive from all she read, so she signed up to use Skype on her laptop. She would be able to stay in touch with Sam Jones easily enough, but showing Phil how to work the office computer, and use the service turned out to be frustrating. In the end, her assistant, Sarah, promised to help him with it. Phil warned her, however, that since he would be on the road most of the time, he wouldn't be near a computer. They determined that Lucy would call Sarah, and she could pass messages back and forth by phone.

Sam had offered to close his practice and travel with her, but she told him no, not to even think about it.

She presented her passport at the check-in counter; the agent greeted her with a warm smile. "Welcome, Mrs. Summers."

As the ticket printed out Lucy watched the agent immediately tear it up.

"You're a lucky lady, Mrs. Summers, your ticket was changed yesterday; you're upgraded to first class. We do hope you enjoy flying with us today. Is this your first flight to Beijing?"

Lucy told the agent she had traveled there once before when she was younger, that she appreciated the upgrade, and would make the most of it.

"Here you are . . . your tickets, baggage claim check . . . and the invitation to the first class lounge. You're a bit early I'm afraid, but you can relax there."

Lucy took her carry-on, thanked the agent, and with some bemusement headed toward security, excited to be traveling in the front section of the plane. She remembered the last time she boarded the Beijing flight with Bob Jenkins, how he turned left to the front section, she to her right and the rear of the plane. Bob had been apologetic at the time, but told her it was company policy, and not up to him. She had understood, just his taking her along on the trip was enough; she remembered telling him she would have traveled baggage class for the opportunity to go. The memories flooded back. He'd warned that the trip would be tough, with difficult meetings; she would get to see the Great Wall and Forbidden City, but she needed to be prepared for long nights. She laughed at that thought. If Bob had only known about Wang Jun and her; those were indeed very long nights!

———∞∞∞———

She settled in her seat, amazed at the luxury in first class, the vast array of seat controls that could turn it into a bed, the flat screen TV in front of her and other amenities. She received a first class gift bag and rummaged through it, determined to save it intact to show Sally when she got back.

A young man soon sat next to her, leaned over and welcomed her. "Hi, Lucy? Call me Chen. I'm here to make sure you have everything on the flight."

"Excuse me?"

"Wang Jun wants you to have a wonderful visit. I'm to accompany you through customs and security before his driver meets you on arrival. Mei Rui will be there to greet you."

She was almost speechless. This was too much; she wondered how far this was heading with Wang Jun, nervous about what might happen, but excited about what could.

"I won't bother you if you prefer to sleep. If not, Mr. Wang has instructed me to give you an update on China and Beijing, so you have some idea of the changes, what you might want to see there, that kind of thing."

"I doubt I'll be able to sleep with all this going on. By the way, do you know anything about the celebration next Tuesday? It's at a hotel."

"Of course . . . big event. We'll all be there. I heard, aside from Mr. Wang wanting you to come, that Chairman Xin insisted you be invited. You must have made quite an impression on him."

"I didn't think I made any kind of impression. I liked him though, even when he was tough in the negotiations." She laughed. "A real pain in the ass, my boss called him, but he was the nicest guy to me. I think I called him "uncle" at someone's request."

Chen reaffirmed how important those kinds of relationships were in China, both in business and personal life. He told her to rest, enjoy the meal, and urged her not to feel she needed to talk to him. During the meal, and for about an hour afterwards, they talked about Beijing and its recent history. Chen even pulled out a power point presentation to highlight places she might want to consider visiting. She finally tired and decided to try to sleep. He helped her with the controls and wished her goodnight. She felt somewhat relieved when Chen explained none of this was any inconvenience, that he was already in New York on Global China business, and happened to be traveling on the same day back to Beijing.

She closed her eyes but couldn't sleep. Too many things ran through her mind: updating Mei Rui on Steve Hardy, who Li Buyun was, and if she should let anyone look at the two hard drives in her bag. She also wondered if she would feel the same about Wang Jun after all these years, and about her regret over having to leave Global Industries. Concerns over her marriage to Phil and the affair with Sam Jones were also mounting by the hour. Could she return from this trip and accept the rut of a life she'd fallen into? A voice told her to make the most of the trip, and embrace everything that came with it, whatever that might be.

<hr />

A gentle shaking from Chen woke her from a sleep she never thought possible, complimenting her on being able to sleep for so long, but advising it was time for breakfast. The plane would be landing in only ninety minutes. Lucy wondered how Phil was doing on his road trip, but only for a moment. Once she arrived and could get on line, she would call Sarah. She would not say anything about her ticket being changed; if the invite had come with a first class ticket that could make Phil suspicious. She would only tell Sally, and perhaps Sam.

Upon landing Chen led her through passport control to a special area, then on to baggage claim. Their bags were picked up for them and delivered to another separate room, where a man and woman were waiting.

"Here she is, Mei Rui," Chen said, as Mei rushed over to greet them.

"Lucy, so glad you are here."

"Me too, Mei," Lucy said, hugging her as if they already knew each other.

"You look just like I imagined," Lucy said. "Very pretty."

Mei looked at her longer, cocked her head to one side. "You too, Lucy, very special. Not quite what I imagined. Even better."

Lucy blushed.

"This is Wang Jun's personal driver, Han. The car is outside and waiting for you. Come . . . come along. My home is ready, no hotel for you. This is going to be fun. I know it even more now I meet you in person."

Lucy turned to Chen before leaving; he had his own car there, but hoped to see her again in the office. He gave her his card, and told her to call if she needed anyone to show her around. She gave him a hug and surprised him with a kiss on the cheek. "You guys really are too much!" Lucy said, before they headed to the cars and out into the city she had enjoyed so many years before.

———

Riding in the back of a Bentley was a first; she had never been in such an expensive vehicle. She knew Mei was looking at her, amused by how awestruck Lucy was with everything. The Beijing she knew was transformed. Incredible new buildings were everywhere; construction cranes pierced the sky like the redwood forests in California. She was impressed how modern Beijing now looked, the number of fashionable women walking the streets, and the masses rushing in every direction using cell phones. The traffic was something else. New York was awful, but now, as they crawled along one of the inner of five ring roads, she understood Beijing's own traffic problems. She couldn't help noticing the number of luxury cars of every make and type running alongside the Bentley. Phil and his friends would have been in awe of the Lamborghinis and Ferraris that passed by, not to mention the Porsches and Mercedes SUVs, often with young and pretty drivers inside.

As they drove towards Mei's apartment, her host pointed out key buildings and businesses on the way. Tomorrow they would tour the city with Wang's driver, visit some of the key tourist spots, and on another day see the Great Wall at Badaling. Mei told her that in China, a man was not considered a man until he walked on the wall. Lucy had been before, but wanted to visit it again. Mei warned her the Chinese were wealthier now; the wall would be swarming with more locals than ever, so she needed to avoid the weekend at all costs.

Sheepishly Lucy asked about Wang Jun. Mei smiled knowingly and told her they would meet soon enough; he was due back that weekend from Moscow, in time for the celebration. Lucy tried not to blush, but felt her face redden.

"We'll talk more about Wang Jun when we get to the apartment," Mei said, "and be careful what you say. Our driver understands everything . . . don't you, Han?"

"Of course. That's why I'm his driver, Miss Lucy. Five languages I have, not bad for a driver, is it? And he pays me well for it."

"You'd be surprised," Mei said, "what we learn about our foreign partners when Han picks them up at the airport. Especially when they discuss their strategies while he drives them around."

"Very smart of you," Lucy said.

Han and Mei chuckled. "Oh, you don't know the half of what we do to get the edge, and we're good at it, very, very good."

Lucy joined in the laughter, telling them she was absolutely sure they were.

———◦◦◦———

The car finally pulled into a development called Palm Springs, right across from Chaoyang Park, Beijing's modern equivalent of Central Park. Mei and the driver escorted Lucy up to Mei's apartment in one of the side towers facing directly toward the park. A spectacular view lay before her, on a remarkably clear day that Mei warned would not last long before the pollution rolled in again.

As Lucy glanced around at the luxury, Mei Rui turned to her. "Before you ask, no, it's not mine. I do live here . . . but it's one of Wang's earlier apartments. It comes along with what I am able to do for him, my capabilities, and the position I hold. Of course, if I leave or am fired, I lose it. But I don't intend to let that happen. Anyway I've worked for him for five years and I'll soon buy my own."

Lucy gave her a quizzical, but knowing look.

"Wrong, Lucy. Let's get one thing clear, so we understand each other. I'm not one of his mistresses. Yes, early on I slept with him, four times to be exact, and I still love him, as others do, but I work for him and his well-being. You have nothing to worry about with me. I would die for him though; he's taken special care of me. In return I do very, very good work for him."

"You said 'mistresses'. Plural?"

"This is China, Lucy. Wang is a powerful and popular man, still good-looking, as you will see. Read our history. Concubines and mistresses have been a part of life here for generations, though not so common these days except maybe at his level. I can tell you his marriage is not a happy one, but he's an honorable man and will not leave her. Frankly she's a bitch, as you Americans would say. I say nothing more on the subject, but if anything happens between you two I don't want him hurt again."

"Again? We had a romantic fling when I was here, nothing more."

"Maybe for you, but ever since I've known him he has referred to you as his American flower, the one that got away."

The subject was changed, and Mei proceeded to show Lucy where everything was, including the huge guest room she would stay in. As Lucy unpacked her few belongings, Mei put her hand on the suitcase and stopped her, walked her over to another cupboard, and opened the doors. There were several dresses and other things hanging inside, including a gorgeous chipao dress that Mei told her was special.

Embarrassed, Lucy stepped back from the cupboard. "I can't have these, Mei, I'm sure they won't fit anyway."

"They will, and they're all yours, a gift."

"No, Mei, I can't. This is way too much. I just can't."

"You can, Lucy, and you will. For once in your life enjoy the attention. If you are afraid to take them back with you, then leave them here. We'll give them to charity since they won't fit me. Bit too heavy I'm afraid."

"You have a figure to die for. How do you know they'll fit me?"

"I told you I know more about you than you could imagine, didn't I?" Mei said.

"Yes, but that information is a bit much, even for you."

"Not really. Anyway, the photos of you were pretty useful to determine the right size to get you. You've kept a remarkable figure, you know, even Wang Jun commented on that."

Lucy was flabbergasted with how much they knew about her. She wasn't sure whether to scream at Mei's intrusion of her privacy, or ride along with it until the trip was over. In the end she decided to accept everything with grace and show appreciation for it all. What she really wanted, however, was answers to who her father really was, and how this Li Buyun fit into the puzzle. She was no fool; she understood Wang Jun's intentions. If he was anything like the person she remembered she would not be able to deny him anything; feeling a tingle of guilt, and desire, as she thought about it.

Mei left her to shower, telling her they needed to change the subject and discuss the celebration evening, and importantly what each of them had learned in their investigations. Once Mei left, Lucy took her travel clothes off, ran the water for the large whirlpool tub, and stepped in, grateful to have the chance to relax and be alone for a while. It was early morning in Blowing Rock with the twelve-hour time difference, but she planned to call Sarah as soon as the shop opened. Mei had already told her to forget using Skype, and gave her a Samsung smart phone to use. Lucy had sarcastically said to Mei that she assumed, of course, the phone numbers for home were entered in it already. Mei had her speechless as she showed her the pre-entered numbers in the contact list. Lucy laughed about it later, thinking about Mei's parting words. "Told you I was good . . . didn't I?"

Out of the shower Lucy tried on some of the dresses; they all fit. She stood before a mirror with the special evening dress on. The chipao looked gorgeous, its long side splits showing off her legs to advantage. She looked at herself with some pride, thinking that not having a child was the reason for her perfect body shape. She admitted to looking good in the dress; the men in Blowing Rock would go crazy over her in it, especially Sam. She understood, however, she was being dressed for Wang Jun. Was the dress his idea, or Mei's?

The excitement of the trip had exhausted her, even with the unusual amount of sleep on the plane. She longed to try out the large king size bed, but knew Mei wouldn't let her. She was under strict orders to stay awake until eleven that evening, follow a rigid program of time difference management, and get adjusted as quickly as possible. The last thing she needed was to eat, but dinner was next on Mei's activity program. She changed the chipao for one of her own casual dresses and tried to place calls to both Sarah and Sally. She shook her head in disbelief as she scrolled down the contact list in the phone; there, right above the name Wang Jun, was Samuel Jones, psychiatrist! She decided she wasn't going to ask Mei how that came about. Was there anything about her these people didn't know? It felt worse than identity theft. The calls went through quickly. Lucy kept them short and sweet, said nothing to Sarah about the details of her journey; she kept those for Sally.

Mei took her for a stroll along the busy road outside the Palm Springs complex and its million dollar plus apartments. They were not going to the park itself, but to a small noodle restaurant within walking distance, apparently one of Mei's favorites. Lucy was pleased to see it was a small neighborhood restaurant, nothing at all fancy. The two of them were the best-dressed women in the place, but no one paid much attention, despite her being the only foreigner in there. One lady smiled, waved her chopsticks over the noodles, and spoke to her in Chinese. She remembered the words right away and smiled back. "Delicious food here," she said.

They sat down at the only available table, the sound of noodle slurping everywhere, a sign the food there was popular. She listened as Mei yelled an order to the waitress, who screamed right back, confirming her choices and then shouting the order on to the cooks in the kitchen. It was obvious everyone there knew Mei.

"What did you order, Mei?" Lucy asked.

"Your favorite noodles, and two large beers for us. Good for sleeping." She laughed as Lucy shook her head yet again.

"Mei, I'm not even going to ask about the dresses, or the damn phone, but my favorite noodles? How the hell did you find that out?"

"Easy. You don't remember?"

"Remember what?"

"Wang Jun. He's always kept lists on everyone he's met or dealt with. Some of that stuff is handwritten from his early years, but most of it is on our computers now. It's invaluable to our work, nothing special though. Usual profile data; family, hobbies, likes, dislikes, all that sort of thing . . . and, of course, favorite foods. I just asked to look at yours."

"Can I see mine?" Lucy asked, as the piping hot noodles arrived, along with a large bottle of local Yanjing beer. Mei told her it was up to Wang Jun, not her; meanwhile, it was time to eat.

Despite being full when they walked in Lucy was soon feeling hungry. The delicious aromas around her, and her own dish, reminded her how much she loved the wide, spicy noodles. She slurped along with the best of them, remembering the first time she ate them, eating as quietly as she could, only to be asked why she was not enjoying her food. These were definitely some of the best noodles; she wolfed them down, out-slurping the next table, washing the noodles down with the entire bottle of beer, much to Mei's delight.

By the time they got back to Mei's apartment she was exhausted, but happier than she felt in years. Before closing the door to her room, Mei told her again they were going to be great friends, and that next day they would discuss what each had uncovered regarding her quest. Lucy sheepishly asked when exactly Wang Jun would be back. Mei said he was still scheduled in on the weekend and couldn't wait to see her. Lucy wondered if she would be able to get to sleep thinking about him.

Chapter 7

Lucy woke late the next morning, surprisingly fresh thanks to Mei's insistence on her staying up the night before. By the time she was showered and dressed Mei was already at the kitchen table, typing on her laptop. Mei quickly closed the computer, told Lucy she was just answering some e-mails and that coffee was made. Mei had eaten earlier and offered to take her out to breakfast, but Lucy wasn't hungry. She reluctantly accepted a pastry as being more than enough, then told Mei she was raring to go, anxious to see Beijing. Mei decided they would take a general tour first with driver Han, and then rest at the canal district of Houhai for coffee. There they could talk about the progress of the investigation, in a small place that roasted coffee on the premises, in her opinion the best in Beijing.

Lucy liked the way Mei embraced everything around her, the contrast of the absolute luxuries on the one hand, compared to her caring for less fortunate people living in places tourists would look down their noses at. Han drove them first down Chang'an Avenue to the Forbidden City, then around Tiananmen Square, past spectacular new buildings that had only been construction sites when she was last there.

Like other tourists, Lucy insisted on jumping out the car for a photo of herself in front of Mao's portrait hanging high over the entry to the walled city, hundreds of tourists jockeying to get in. Mei told her it was too busy to go in that day, but promised to arrange something special for her on another day. Later, as they drove over to the canal district, for coffee and lunch, a phone call from Wang Jun came in; she passed it over to Lucy. She said hello to "John," thanking him profusely for everything Mei was doing for her and adding that it was all too much. Lucy blushed as Mei gave her a knowing grin; she too understood what was going to happen in the days ahead.

She passed the phone back to Mei at his request, and the two talked in Chinese for about five minutes. By Mei's tone, Lucy understood it concerned whatever business deal they were working on. Mei switched to English on purpose, making it obvious she intended for Lucy to hear some of it.

"Oh yes, just as you said, but I think more beautiful than you told me. Of course I'm taking good care of her. What do you expect? I'm number one in that area." She paused for a moment then added, "No, we haven't talked about that yet, but we will after lunch." Another moment of listening was followed by laughter. "Of course I'm taking her to the best place, and she'll love it . . . yes, of course she enjoyed the noodles last night . . . she can't wait to see you." With that the phone went dead, Mei poked a red-faced Lucy in the ribs, and smiled.

<hr />

It was a beautiful day around the lake and canal district of Houhai, where empresses and emperors had been rowed in royal barges during the hot summers away from the Forbidden City, en route to the Old Summer Palace. The sight would have been magnificent back then, Mei told her, with their entourage of eunuchs and servants in other boats plowing through the waters. They would stop for lavish meals at he same place that is a popular restaurant today looking out over Beihei Lake. The pair sat out alongside the lake and spent the next fifteen minutes discussing the menu, its different dishes and Lucy's tastes. Mei finally ordered far more food than they could ever eat, but told her she would be giving the leftovers to driver Han for his mother.

They drank no alcohol; Mei ordered fresh pear juice for both of them and more coffee, which Lucy was desperate for. Lucy ate well, despite being asked to leave something for Han. Mei reminded her of the old traditions that looked down upon guests cleaning their plates; she apologized, but did it anyway. The food was better than Lucy remembered. When lunch was done with, Mei told her it was time to discuss where they were with their quest. Lucy was pleased to be finally talking about the main reason for her visit, or was it becoming as much about seeing Wang Jun again?

"I'm afraid it's not looking good, Lucy," Mei told her. "I know I said Li Buyun was an unusual name, which would help. Well from that standpoint it is; only seven people here have that name. Two are male, but still no match, I'm afraid . . . with any of them."

"But doesn't one of them know something?" Lucy asked in a disappointed tone.

"No. We've used all our resources, which I assure you are good to dig around in these people's lives, but I found nothing to link one of them with your father. I've tried both of his names, the Goldman Sachs thing, but so far there's nothing."

"You mean it's a dead end then, after I've come all this way?"

"I didn't say that at all. I don't give up so easy. Not Mei Rui. Oh no, not at all."

"But what can we do? Where do we go next?"

"My money is on someone outside of Beijing. Who knows where though? For that I think we have no choice but to break into those hard drives you told us about."

"I'm not sure, Mei. What if we can't get into them?"

"Well, then nothing is lost, right? But if we're able to, maybe there's a clue where this Li Buyun fits in, and where he or she could be."

"I brought them, just in case, but everything seems more sinister than when I started out. I don't want to get my father into more trouble."

"Why don't we do this. You let our guys have a crack at opening them, look through what is there, and if you feel you can't show it to me we leave it at that."

"Mei, I'm no idiot. Some whizz will make a copy while they're trying to open them up."

That was the first time Lucy saw Mei visibly offended, and understood right away she had insulted her. She apologized profusely, and promptly agreed to her suggestion. Mei said the work to try to access the drives would not be done at Global. They would go to another company owned directly by Wang Jun, one Lucy could not talk about to anyone, certainly not Global Industries. Mei explained knowledge was everything in their business, but that bribery and corrupt practices were avoided at all costs. Intelligence, on the other hand, was more powerful than any illegal activity. Lucy didn't want to know more. Whatever they were really doing couldn't be completely legal, she thought, but it might help her cause.

Mei asked what, if anything, she had to report from her efforts. Lucy began to explain how Peter Rawlings had seen the photos she sent, and agreed there was a remarkable resemblance in the photos. Unfortunately, he told her Steve Hardy said the last person he would talk to anyone about was Richard Towers. Rawlings himself was sympathetic to her dilemma, but declined to reveal Steve Hardy's address. What he did give her were enough general clues to help find him on her own; that way, he said, he could deny betraying Steve's confidence. Lucy said nothing to him about old man Chu's reference to Towers as the "spook." She felt that was something to confront Hardy with directly.

"So did you find him?"

"You're not the only detective around here, you know. It took a while but I did find him."

Lucy told her it turned out the man was living in the next state, only a four-hour drive away. She had left Blowing Rock at six that morning, telling Phil she was off early to buy fresh stock for the shop. In the town that Hardy supposedly lived in, she was directed by locals to a large home set back from the main road. The entryway was not gated and she was able to drive all the way up to the house, where a pleasant- looking woman was working in the garden.

"Mrs. Hardy was very nice. As soon as I complimented her on how beautiful her garden looked, and named every flower growing there, I was a friend for life. I told her I was hoping to speak to her husband, so she invited me through the house to the rear. He was sitting there, just reading the papers."

"What did he say about you being there?"

"Well, he wasn't happy, especially when I said I wanted to talk to him about Richard Towers. If not for his wife I'm sure he would have thrown me out."

"What did he say?"

"He told me the "son of a bitch" Towers was the last person he wanted to talk about. Thank goodness his wife was there. She told him not to use that language around me, and to be polite."

Lucy told Mei how Mrs. Hardy insisted they all calm down, while she brought some fresh lemonade out, and for him to listen to whatever the young lady had come to visit him about.

"And did he talk?"

"It was frosty for a while, but his wife was so sweet about it, really a nice woman. I showed him the pictures, same ones I sent to Rawlings, and told him I thought this man Towers was actually my father, John Wainright. He admitted the likeness was remarkable, I knew right away from his expression there was some kind of light going on in his head, especially when I threw out that I heard he used to call him the spook."

"Did he open up then?"

"Sort of. He admitted he didn't like the man, wouldn't call him my father, just referred to him as Towers, that he'd never wanted him in Beijing in the first place; he was forced on him from high up, as he put it. He told me it was clear from day one that Towers knew little about high finance and investments, but admitted he picked it up quickly."

"So why did he think he was there?"

"He initially thought this Towers was sent over by headquarters to make sure there was no funny business going on, that New York was terrified at the possibility of any blemish on its reputation in China and other Asian countries."

"Makes sense."

"Then he noticed how Towers only seemed interested in specific projects, that whenever he didn't want him involved there was usually a directive soon after to include him. When he did participate, Hardy said, he would show up at meetings only to disappear, and then reappear when the meetings were almost done, always refusing to say what he was doing. That's why he nicknamed him the spook."

"What else did he say?"

"Not much. He did say Rawlings was a big buddy of Towers, and that old man Chu was the only driver he used to go anywhere. Told me if I needed to know what my so-called father was up to I should talk to this Chu. He was surprised when I said I would, that I was going to China to do just that. Look at this. He wrote a personal note for me to give to Chu. It's a nice note, tells him to tell me anything and everything he knows."

"Good. We'll use that while you're here. Anything else?"

"No, but he did make a crack about the man being with the CIA or FBI. He suggested they were using his office to try to figure out what the Chinese were up to, especially with the new leadership in control then."

"He may be onto something there. Did you mention Li Buyun?"

"I did. He had never heard of her. He suggested I ask Chu about her as well."

"Did he mention Madame Zhang?"

"No, but *I* did toward the end. He said she came in shortly before he left; called her a real pain in the ass. Mrs. Hardy jumped all over him again for his language. It was quite funny really. I did tell him a lot more about my father's situation, but he wasn't too sympathetic."

"What else did he say?"

"Not much. He muttered something about not being surprised if Towers was some kind of special agent, that maybe he was my father after all. If I ever find any more out to change his views he wants to hear from me."

"Did his wife say anything more?"

"Not really, just said she hoped my father recovers and wished me luck. She said her husband was a wonderful husband, even if he didn't show it, and to come again any time to talk about her garden."

"That does it then," Mei said. "Back to where we were. The mist is clearing a little, but we have to get into those hard drives. We have to, Lucy . . . and quick. We don't have much time before you leave. We should start first thing in the morning."

Lucy agreed there was little more they could do, maybe talk to old driver Chu again, but the drives might hold the key. Lucy's jet lag was kicking in, so she asked if they couldn't go back and take a nap. Mei agreed, warning her she would only allow her a half hour, that sleeping any longer was the worst thing to get over the time difference.

Mei phoned Han, who was waiting at the entrance to Houhai to be ready for them to drive home. Once back at the Palm Springs apartment Lucy went to her room, lay on the bed, and was fast asleep within minutes.

⎯⎯∞∞∞⎯⎯

Mei looked in on Lucy, then went back to the lounge, called their facility, and organized the meeting for nine o'clock in the morning. The specialists were to be ready to hack into the two hard drives. She instructed them to make separate copies for her if they could, but in such a way that her visitor would not realize it was being done. The copies were for Mei and Wang Jun's eyes only.

As soon as Wang's name was mentioned, any protests about how busy they were on other projects ended abruptly. She couldn't wait to see what the drives contained. She was convinced there were things on them Lucy was not going to be happy about, but they might hold answers to many questions. She sent a text message off to Wang Jun updating him on the day's events, advising they would be over at the "black building" in the morning. If anything useful came out of it she would let him know right away what they found.

Chapter 8

The two women left the apartment early the next morning. Lucy slept only until four o'clock, waking with a headache and sore throat. Mei thought it was related to the change in time, or perhaps the effect of pollution creeping into the city again. Lucy was amazed at the changes in the landscape since her last visit, impressed with the expansion in highways as they traveled along the third of six ring roads around Beijing. She was stunned by the modern architecture filling the skyline, interrupted at times by old-style apartments of the sixties, reminiscent of what she had seen before. The sterile blocks of apartment buildings had been everywhere on her last visit. Some were still now in use, but many were renovated to a more modern appearance. Others were sidelined for demolition.

Lucy lamented the disappearance of the old hutong neighborhoods, and some of the large courtyard homes, which she heard were now being sold for ridiculous amounts of money. Mei agreed it might be a shame on the one hand, but told her on the other, many areas were in very poor condition, some with no real services and a lack of running water. The loss of the sense of tradition and neighborly community saddened Mei most.

After an eternity, in some of the worst traffic, the car arrived at an abandoned warehouse in the south of the city. It was surrounded by what seemed to be many families of garbage sorters, hard at work; the smell was sickening. Mei apologized for the poor location as the steel gates in front of them drew open. Han drove straight in, passing through two more plain steel doors that closed behind them.

Lucy was impressed with the transformation on the inside of the complex. Mei came around to her side as Han held the door open.

"Welcome to the black building of Wang Jun, Lucy. Remember, this has nothing to do with Global at all. It's entirely owned and dedicated to Wang's side of the business. Please respect that."

They signed in at a lavish reception area. The receptionist welcomed Lucy by name, presented her with a special visitor's badge, and advised it only allowed entry to certain areas of the facility. She wished Lucy a productive visit and asked if she wanted coffee or tea. Lucy was surprised to be provided an elaborate menu of drinks and foods in such a poor area of the city and ordered a large coffee. Mei walked her along a corridor lined with modern art, on to another area where a technician was waiting for them. Lucy was not allowed in until her card was swiped over a lock along with Mei's card, and only after the young technician greeting them entered his own code.

Once inside Lucy noted the large number of technicians working at different screens. She knew Mei was amused by her look of astonishment. Mei introduced her to everyone there.

"Too young for us," Mei whispered to her as they shook hands.

"Who says?" Lucy said with a grin.

"Guess where they come from?"

"No clue. Some computing university of yours . . . maybe?"

"Prison."

"You're kidding . . . really?"

"Sort of. All top university trained, as you suspected, but not there, from prison. Best hackers in China, every one of them. And getting better, eh, Mr. Li?"

"Damn right, Mei," Li said in perfect English, to Lucy's surprise.

"So what do you have for fun today?" he asked.

Mei turned to Lucy, who removed two metal hard drives from her bag, nervous about handing them over.

"Don't worry, Lucy," Mei said. "As soon as they can get into them you'll sit with Li to look them over. If you want to have him delete them, or give them back at that point you can. Obviously I hope we find something to tell us what is really going on here, or at least help us track down Li Buyun."

"Can I stay?'

"You can either sit here, if you don't trust us, or come with me to the waiting area and have your coffee while Li goes to work."

Lucy felt embarrassed and told Mei she was okay with everything; it would be nice to relax over a coffee. The room they went to was lavishly decorated. There Mei answered as many questions as she could about the operation, continuing to assert they did nothing illegal here, but admitting they strayed close to the limits of the laws in China. She laughed when asked about international laws, especially those of the U.S., a whole different question Mei never did answer to Lucy's satisfaction.

It was some time before Li came into the room and asked the pair to come through to the lab. He gave them a lengthy review of what they had been doing for the last hour, most of which neither Lucy nor Mei understood.

Eventually Mei stopped him in his tracks. "Okay, Li, that's enough. Cut to the chase, as the Americans say, what have you found?"

"Okay, just for you, Mei, and your lovely visitor."

"She's too old for you, Li."

"Who said? I always did go for the older ones, especially with a little Asian in them." Lucy blushed, flattered by the young man's compliment.

"So you noticed?" Mei asked.

"Oh yes, very much so."

"Never mind that now. Li, What the hell have you got for us?"

The discussion returned to a more serious side as Li announced the first drive's contents, and hit enter on his computer. The screen filled with an official U.S. Government login screen, accompanied by a gasp from Lucy.

"So you see, here's the user name, John Wainright, and here . . . the log in password box required to open the files."

"We can read, you know," Mei remarked.

"Well, we've never seen anything like this before. We struggled to get this far. We were able to open one other screen, but had to shut it down right away."

"Shut it down . . . why?" asked Lucy.

"Well, any further and it claims the whole disc will destruct somehow. If we enter the wrong login . . . over here . . . more than three times, same thing will happen. We thought you wouldn't want us to do that just yet. Unless you want us to try now."

"Final prognosis?" Mei asked.

"This is military, top secret or something, definitely not commercial—"

"Not Goldman Sachs?" Lucy asked.

"No way. It's beyond any commercial company. Most sophisticated drive any of us have seen. Has to be U.S. government. We'd like to keep it if we can, Mei . . . play with it some more. Could destroy it though."

"That's up to Lucy."

She thanked them for trying, but preferred to have it back. Li hesitated with it still in his hand, until Mei ordered him to give it up. Lucy slipped it into her bag while Mei asked about the other drive. This time Li smiled from ear to ear.

"Tough. Difficult yes, but not like the other. Well within our capabilities, thanks to our Mr. Zhang over there." As Zhang rose and bowed to Lucy, he too began to give a dissertation on how he had done it, until he recognized Mei and Lucy's eyes glazing over again.

He transferred his computer screen to the large central unit. "There you are. All personal files, two main governing files, a "Richard Towers" on one, and a "John Wainright" for the other. Different password trails require opening the drive with separate password protection installed for each main file group. Wainright's was difficult, skillfully done we would say; Tower's was brilliant, but no match for us."

"Have you read the files yet?" Mei asked.

"We can. There's a lot of correspondence for sure, but we thought to hold off until you told us what Wang Jun, I mean, Miss Lucy here, wants us to do with them. We can source things if she wants, you know, like names, figures, files . . . special words . . . whatever. Or she can use the guest room to go through them alone, with you, or me. Your choice." Mei looked over at Lucy for her decision.

"Just Mei and me, please. Can you sort anything by the name of Li Buyun first? That'll help."

"No problem. Zhang will load it to an independent computer in the other room. He'll program the sort, then leave you to it. Okay?"

"Thank you for your efforts, Mr. Li."

"No sweat. I hope Mei can change your mind about letting us have your other drive. It's really interesting, and Wang Jun isn't going to be happy we didn't succeed."

"Well, he didn't give it to you, so you're okay there. I'll think about it though. If I change my mind you'll be the first ones to have it," Lucy said.

"We hope you bring it back to us."

With that Lucy was led to another room. Zhang came in, loaded the drive, then handed her a typewritten process for accessing data on the disc. He spent a few minutes tapping on a keyboard before standing up to leave.

"There you are, Miss, a separate file heading for you. Every reference, no matter how small, is in it for Li Buyun, all in chronological order. There are two files under that master file. I created one series from Towers, and one under Wainright covering that name. Hope it helps."

"That's great, thanks," Lucy said, and finally began to smile, knowing at last they had something on Li to work on. As she sat down Zhang headed to the door, followed by Mei to make sure it was closed. As he left she whispered in Chinese, "Did you get a copy?"

He grinned as he walked away, then mouthed to her, "Of course, both of them. Piece of cake."

—⌘—

The two sat for three hours, looking at the files on the one drive that Lucy could access. It was everything she'd hoped for and more. She took copious notes from the Li Buyun files, Mei suggesting it might be better to print the files out.

Lucy agreed, but was eager to write down some of the highlights, especially the confirmation that Li Buyun was female as she suspected..

She scanned the material by content first, and then by date, looking for what led to the final rebuke of her father by Li. Meanwhile Mei left her to organize lunch. Lucy appreciated being alone for a while to look at correspondence that was changing every notion she had about her father, and who she thought he was. In a way she was glad her mother was not around to know any of it. While her parents' relationship had not seemed the most loving, her mother cared about him deeply. Lucy was loved more by her mother, however, and would have gladly died for her. She never had the same feelings for her father; he was never there.

⁂

Mei told the front desk to order sandwiches and salads for the visitor room, along with natural juices and coffee, then hurried off to Li's office. He told her copies of the hard drives were already in a package, along with four binders of printouts in the trunk of Han's car, but warned she wouldn't be able to carry the weight of material on her own.

"Okay, so what's on the other disc . . . in general? I need to get back in there before she gets suspicious."

"In a nutshell, you were right," Li said. "He was definitely a plant, not CIA directly as Wainright; he was State Department. A lot of material in there is high level, China-restricted material in its day. If released then it would probably have been as bad for China as Snowden was now for the U.S. "

"And Towers?"

"No question, CIA."

"And what about Li Buyun?"

"You'll see when you read the files Lucy hasn't seen."

"And?"

"Read them. Li got screwed, literally and royally."

"Okay, good. I can't wait to get Lucy away somewhere so I can read them."

"That's going to take a long time, Mei."

She gave him a brief hug, told him how great he was, complimented the team as always, and rushed off to the room where a waitress was bringing in their lunches.

"Let's break for a while, Lucy. You need to eat something and I'm famished."

Lucy briefed Mei on where she thought things were, not knowing for a moment Mei would soon know a lot more than she ever would. Mei casually suggested she hand the other drive back to the team, but Lucy would have none of it. Mei pushed only so far, hoping it would confirm their story that the team had not been able to break into it. Lucy admitted she plugged in the drive while Mei was out, but never penetrated as far as she saw Li's team get to. All she saw on the screen was the same warning, that any attempt to access the drive was a criminal act.

While they ate, Mei cautioned that time was running short. Wang Jun would be back within a day or two before the celebration for Xin, the other purpose of her visit. There was evidence from the files confirming Towers and Wainright were indeed one and the same, also that Tower's work for Goldman was his cover as an intelligence specialist. Some of the businesses he worked with, as Towers, seemed to connect with Li Buyun somehow, whoever she was. There were earlier references under Wainright indicating the relationship had been passionate, a deep affair going on between them for some years. There was no mention of any family back in the U.S., or of Li's.

Mei thought she might glean enough references to locate Li Buyun; it could take a few days but likely go faster if she worked alone. She recommended Lucy meet with Wang Jun and leave everything to her since he was expecting to be with her alone over the weekend.

Lucy couldn't see anything in the files to pinpoint where Li was living, or if she was still working. Any references to a company involved were carefully worded in such a way to keep it hidden from others. The question was why. She wanted to keep working on it alongside Mei, but understood that once Wang Jun returned he would insist on being with her. She had been dreaming every night about Wang Jun, longing for him to get back and seduce her again, fantasizing what it would be like. She could leave this work for a couple of days. From everything Mei had said, or hinted, it was going to happen with Wang Jun.

Mei finally told her they had done as much as they could, that they should take everything back to her apartment and work there. She would head to the office later and get to work on chasing this Li down. Lucy could stay in the apartment while she went off to handle things, but if she wanted to move into a luxury hotel it could be arranged. Lucy, as subtly as she could, asked what Wang Jun was likely to want her to do. Mei smiled, told her he would find the apartment more relaxing after the last couple of weeks stuck in a hotel in Moscow, and not to worry about her; she had other places to go.

Chapter 9

Mei arrived at the Capital Airport to meet Wang Jun. Mei watched him exit the arrivals area. Several officials welcomed him, bowing and scraping as he thanked them for their assistance. He rolled his eyes at Mei as they brought him into the executive arrival waiting area, looking tired but excited to be back. He began peppering her with questions about Lucy.

"So what doesn't she know right now, Mei?" he asked as Han loaded his bag into the trunk.

Mei held the door open for him in the back of his Bentley. "Well, one thing she doesn't know is we have everything, including access to the secure drive."

"Does it solve the mystery and help her?"

"Oh much more than that, boss; it helps us." Mei said, grinning from ear to ear.

"Global or *us*?"

"Mm." She thought for a moment. "Global maybe, maybe not. But for our side? Oh yes, very much so. You're going to like this a lot. I mean more than a lot."

"What do I need to know as far as Lucy's concerned? Fill me in on that, tell me what the plans are, and then where we go from here."

Mei gave Wang Jun a brief summary, told him what she planned to do for the next three days prior to the celebration night, and where Lucy would be over the weekend. He told her again she was a very clever lady, that if he was a few years younger he might have whisked her away. She laughed, told him they already tried it briefly, and he seemed to prefer the current arrangement more. She changed the subject and asked him about his Moscow trip.

"It went very well. Trouble is it might be a conflict with our Global friends. I want the deal, but I can't appear to be personally involved. I'm going to have to back door the thing, someone I trust has to run—"

"Me?"

"I'm sorry, Mei, you're too valuable where you are. I know you could do it with your eyes closed. It'll come soon enough, so don't worry your pretty little head about that. Anyway the part of Russia it's in sucks. I wouldn't put you through the mess where it's located."

"You said that the last time. Maybe I need to leave you hanging, go out on my own. I did a lot of work with the Black Building boys on this deal for you. Don't forget that."

"Check your bank account Monday morning, and then tell me if you are leaving; have your five hackers check theirs too."

She brightened immediately, leaned over and kissed him on the cheek. "What's she got that I haven't anyway?"

"Now that would be telling. Let's just say she was very special. Maybe she's changed though after all this time. We all do."

"Oh no, I doubt that. She's ready for it, you evil man. Just don't break her heart again. She's a treasure."

"Wrong way round, Mei; she broke mine. Or I guess I should say her mother did, indirectly. But don't tell anyone I said that."

<hr />

The conversation turned serious as they drove off, Mei filling him in on the information gleaned from her efforts, plus the new possibilities it could open up for their business. He congratulated her on the work, and told her he had no idea it would be going the way it was, but was pleased with how it was developing. It had started out as an effort to have some fun and help a woman he was in love with a long time ago to find whatever she was looking for. He also wanted to repay something that Lucy didn't even know she helped start for him— his relationship with Chairman Xin.

Since her first contact he had wondered what it might be like to relive those days together. More self-assured now, he had been with many women since Lucy, married too. Would it be better this time, or a huge disappointment? He closed his eyes for a moment as if about to doze off after the long flight. Whatever Mei thought he might be thinking, he was remembering the nights he and Lucy spent together, somehow managing to work through the daily negotiations and nightly banquets until they could be alone.

She was insatiable . . . he remembered that. Whatever Lucy was so hungry for, he never put his finger on. She always denied it was anything, other than desire for him, but he was sure it was something deeper, a desire to belong in some way to someone. There had been nights her passion and hunger frightened him, to the point he felt used for her pleasure alone. Those nights he lost himself, during her hunger for every part of his body, were nonetheless incredible. Nothing had come close since, and not for want of trying, something that drove him into his many affairs. The short tryst with Mei ended quickly enough; she was looking for love, not the lust he was seeking to satisfy.

When Wang Jun awoke to ask where they were, Mei told him they were close to his home. He rolled his eyes, as if to say he was not looking forward to seeing his wife again.

"Can you be on your way early so I can have Lucy picked up at seven thirty?" he asked.

"Of course, I've already booked tickets to Nanjing."

"Will you be back for the celebration?"

"I'll try. I'm taking young Zhang from the lab with me so we can take care of things on the spot."

"I really can't believe our luck, Mei. Lucy really is a lucky talisman."

"Let's hope so."

"This whole thing might not go off how I'd like it to though."

"If you mean, the you and Lucy in bed in my apartment part, then I'd say you have nothing to worry about."

"It's more than that, Mei. Much more. Too late now . . . I expect. She's married and everything, but it sounds like something isn't right with her. Not just the father and all, I mean the no family bit. I always thought she'd make a great mother."

"I want to know all about it when she leaves, boss. She really got to you before, didn't she? I certainly couldn't."

Wang told Mei she was still special, in different ways, and that he wouldn't trade her for anyone. He promised to tell her as much as he could when it was over; for now, she needed to follow the agreed upon plan.

Wang was dropped off at the door of his huge home, refusing Han's offer to carry his bag in. As Mei was leaving she looked back at the lone figure standing in the courtyard, his bag on the floor, staring at the house as if it was the last place he wanted to be. Whoever was in the house must have heard the car on the driveway, the loud horn blast, as well as the opening and slamming of the trunk and doors. Yet no one appeared at the door or a window to welcome him. Mei spotted a curtain pull back on a top floor window, and a figure glance out; the person showed no sign of interest or acknowledgment of the man searching for his keys below. She could only hope Lucy would turn out to be everything Wang was longing for, regretting that it couldn't be her.

When Mei got back to her apartment Lucy was sitting in the lounge, dressed and trying to appear casual in waiting to hear about Wang Jun's arrival. She told Lucy he arrived safely, and arrangements were made for Han to come back and pick her up at seven thirty for dinner. She had a quick business trip to make for Wang Jun, but hoped to be back for the celebration. If Lucy needed anything she was to phone her, day or night; otherwise, driver Han was assigned full time to her. Lucy was welcome to study the files from her father's hard drive in the apartment, or Han could take her over to use Mei's office. Lucy said she would stick around the apartment until Mei came back.

Mei looked at Lucy and asked her to stand up, which Lucy did, straightening the dress she had on. Mei looked at her again, tilted her head to one side. "No, definitely not. Not for tonight. Follow me."

Lucy followed her into the bedroom, back to the closet filled with the dresses and clothes bought for her. Mei ran her fingers along the hangers until she found what she was looking for.

"This is the one, Lucy. You'll kill him in this!"

"I already tried it on. The side slits seem a bit high. Don't you think so too?"

"You never wore one of those mini skirt things, Lucy? You have perfect legs; you need to show them off."

"You're sure he'll like it?"

"Lucy, he loves, and I mean loves, a chipao dress. He'll go nuts over it. Anyway he picked it out especially for you."

"He did?"

"Of course, insisted on being with me when I shopped for you. You should take it back with you. You don't need to tell your husband how expensive it was though." Lucy gulped as she ran her fingers over the embroidered design and small pearls.

"You mean these things could be real?"

"Oh yes, and don't ask how much it cost either. I promised I wouldn't tell you."

"I won't keep it, Mei. I can't accept something like this."

Mei told her not to be so stubborn; if Lucy felt like it she could cut the pearls off, throw the rest of the dress away, and pay off her business loan from the pearls alone. She tried to make Lucy laugh, telling her it wouldn't matter anyway having the dress on that night; it was unlikely to stay on very long. An embarrassed Lucy told Mei to be on her way while she changed into it. When Mei came to say she was leaving she stood still for a moment, looking Lucy up and down.

"By the gods! You do look incredible. I only hope I look that good when I'm your age. Enjoy yourself tonight, but be good to him. I love him too."

"I know you do, Mei. I'm nervous though. So many years have gone by. I feel like a teenager on a date again. Do you think it's going to be okay?"

"It will be. Just don't think too much about it and enjoy the moment. He really is special, and I've told him you are too . . . unfortunately for me. Anyway, I have to rush for a plane. See you Tuesday evening, I hope."

⸙

Alone again in the apartment, Lucy began watching the hands of the clock move closer towards seven thirty. She poured a glass of wine to steady her nerves, but couldn't get Wang Jun out of her mind. She remembered the nights she had practically devoured him in the hotel, wondering if it could ever be the same now they were older. No one had satisfied her like him, ever. She had begun to lose herself like that once with Sam, but he had been frightened by her passion and she backed off, knowing she was only imagining herself with Wang Jun again. She never experienced that level of passion with Phil; now it was impossible, even if she wanted to.

She felt calmer after finishing the large glass of wine, deciding another one might be too much. She took the remaining time to go around the apartment, rearranging things and adjusting the lighting. She paid special attention to the bedroom, leaving the door ajar for later, a lamp glowing inside as if to draw anyone sitting in the darkened living room in there. She made sure she had photos, which Phil had never seen, of the two of them in Beijing all those years ago to show him. Anyone who saw them, and only Sally Sweetland had so far, would have recognized that the couple in them was in the middle of a passionate love affair. Sally had wished her well the night before she left Blowing Rock, and extracted an agreement from Lucy to tell her everything if she slept with him again.

She grew nervous, wondering if she was doing the right thing. It had all happened so fast. She was beginning to feel like a concubine being readied for a night with the emperor. Once it was over would the emperor visit her again? Or avail himself of many others in the palace? Even grace the bedroom of the empress? She told herself she was being silly. This was the dream trip of a lifetime. Her life wasn't easy, nor would it be when she went home. All of this would be over soon. She had to make the most of it.

The shrill ring from the doorbell startled her, breaking the silence in the room. She looked at the clock. It was 7:20. He was early. Then she remembered driver Han was picking her up. She went to the door, half hoping Wang Jun was there, but Han was alone as planned. She tried not to let Han see her disappointment, and told him she would be ready in a few minutes. He stepped into the apartment, waited at the door, telling her she was going somewhere special.

Han was handsome in his own right, and clearly in love with Mei Rui. Lucy could never understand why Mei didn't see it. She was flattered by Han's comments on her beauty, and the dress she was wearing. It gave her confidence, and added excitement for the night ahead.

Han held the door open for her and motioned her to follow. "Come with me, princess. Your carriage is outside."

They both laughed at his comment as they rode the elevator down and walked through the lobby area. Other residents' heads turned as she walked by. One old lady stepped in front of her to speak but Lucy indicated she only understood a little Chinese.

"You very beautiful, wear dress like this, years gone. You lovely. Have nice evening." The old lady was proud of her effort to speak English; Lucy thanked her as best she could and the woman bowed affectionately. Han gripped Lucy's arm gently and drew her away, not wanting to be late.

Chapter 10

The flight landed at Nanjing Airport on time. A local manager, not from one of Global's group companies, met Mei Rui and Zhang at the exit.

"Mei Rui, welcome to Nanjing. You too, Mr. Zhang . . . good flight?"

"Not really, we had a late booking so they couldn't get us in business class. Anyway, we're here. Did you arrange everything for the morning?"

"Yes and no. But don't worry, I'll get you in, I'm sure," he said with obvious uncertainty.

"What's wrong?" Mei asked.

"I have the Bentley limo as you requested," the manager said. " Wang Jun's old friend was pleased to loan it to us for a few days. I also managed to get the chauffeur outfit for Zhang, and an official-looking Party flag for the car too."

"But?"

"They don't want to meet with you."

"How can Sunrise Chemicals not want to meet with us after all those meetings with Wang two years ago?"

"Well, Mei, I couldn't tell them what the meeting was for because you still haven't told me. They must have assumed we were coming after them all over again. Is that what we're doing?"

"All in good time. Give me the names of the persons that turned down a visit from Wang. We'll make sure they get their comeuppance in the future."

"What is this about, Mei? Why the theatrics?"

"I figured this would happen. Leave everything to me. In the morning we'll leave the hotel at nine and Zhang can drive me there. I'll explain everything to you later. Do you have the copies, Zhang?" Mei asked.

"Absolutely, and the labs are all set up too."

"How long will it take them?" she asked

"Hours at most. We're paying extra for special services, plus I know the guy from my old hacker circles. Good man. He's straight now . . . just like me." They both laughed while the manager looked on, wondering what was going on.

———— ✺ ————

By the time Han worked his way through the traffic along Chang'an Boulevard, Lucy was more anxious over how she would react to meeting Wang Jun after so long. She was impressed, on arriving at the China World Hotel area, by the eighty-floor tower that now soared above the complex. Han drove up to the Shangri La entrance where a hostess was waiting. She welcomed Lucy to the building as a special guest, commenting on the beauty of her dress as they walked to the elevators. There was already a line of visitors heading to the observation deck and upper bar, but Lucy was led to a direct elevator up to the Grill 79 restaurant, one floor below the Atmosphere lounge on the eightieth.

The ride up the seventy-nine floors to the dining area was extremely fast. She felt her stomach squirm as the car decelerated quickly and came to a halt. The door opened and another hostess led her towards the "Beijing," one of four private dining rooms. She gave Lucy a history of the building, while pausing to point out the sights. The views were spectacular, the night clear thanks to strong winds. It seemed to Lucy the lights stretched on forever beyond the building. The hostess told her to be sure to come during daylight when all the sights could be seen, and gave Lucy her card to call anytime to arrange everything. They arrived at the door to the private room. The girl said the host was already waiting and tapped gently on the door. Lucy thanked her for her help but insisted on opening it herself and entering alone.

Lucy stood looking at the door, waiting until the girl had left. She straightened the chipao dress one more time, felt her hair to make sure nothing was out of place, and finally took a deep breath to calm herself. She opened the door and walked in. Over by the window, with his back towards her, was a figure gazing out of the window, hidden by a beautiful array of flowers. She coughed slightly to let him know she was in the room. He turned toward her and she was speechless for a moment.

"Xiao Lucy, Little Lucy, welcome to Beijing! It is wonderful to see you after all these years." The older man strode over to her and the two embraced warmly. It was Chairman Xin.

After a moment or two she gathered herself following the letdown of Wang Jun not being there, and told "Uncle Xin," as she called him all those years ago, how she had missed him. Xin laughed warmly, telling her he was sure it was Wang Jun, not him she was missing, but that he was very happy to see her. He told her Wang Jun had been delayed due to a late business deal and discussions with Mei Rui. He would come later.

"I'm so glad you could come to my party, Xiao Lucy," Xin said. "I want the best of time for you here. I was so happy when Wang asked if I could come to see you tonight until he arrives. It gives us some time together. The celebration will be very big, you know. I may not be able to speak with you too much. Afterwards you must visit my home and we can talk there."

"I'm happy to see you too, Uncle, but I don't think we'll have much chance to talk after the celebration; my plane leaves right away."

Xin told her he hoped she could stay longer. She was already thinking about it, but knew it would be difficult getting Phil to agree. Xin looked at her closely, stepped back, held both of her hands, then looked her up and down. "You are stunning, my dear. You have grown lovelier than I remember. Mei was right about your beauty. I must say Wang Jun knows how to pick a chipao. My wife would marvel at it. We're so happy you came. I want to say one thing to you, and then I will never mention it again. Is that okay for you?"

Lucy was puzzled, but readily agreed to hear what he had to say.

"Wang Jun has been like a son to me, Xiao Lucy. Working with him, as we have after you left, has brought us very close. We never had our own son, you know."

"Wang always spoke highly of you. I remember that. He respected you greatly, Uncle. We all did."

"Thank you. Anyway, the truth is I know everything about you both, and I mean *everything*. My greatest wish would have been that you stayed in China and not left us, but I understand why you had to. I was sorry to hear about your mother, but your caring for her was very Chinese."

"You mean Vietnamese."

"Whatever. You still mean a great deal to Wang Jun, and I know you are not here for long, so make him happy for the short time you have together." Xin leaned over and kissed her gently on the cheek, as if asking her to do it for him.

Lucy was embarrassed for a few moments, but as they talked and Xin poured more wine, the conversation moved on to all that had happened over the years. She relaxed even more as another glass of wine disappeared in toasts to their past dealings, and to the negotiations she and her boss, along with Wang Jun, held years before. Finally Xin excused himself to take a call. He moved to the corner of the room, not that she would have understood what he was talking about, was soon back, but did not sit down.

"I'm sorry to leave you, Lucy, but I'm sure you will be happy to know Wang Jun is in the lobby and arriving soon. I really enjoyed seeing you this evening, and I do hope you stay beyond Tuesday. I want you to meet my wife, so please ask your husband. Do try . . . for me please."

Lucy told him she would, but knew it was unlikely Phil would agree. She gave Xin a warm embrace before he left the room; then she stepped into the private restroom to check her appearance. The conversation and drinks with Xin had calmed her, but the delay in seeing Wang Jun had increased her level of anticipation. She took up her own position at the window where Xin had stood, purposely hiding behind the floral display. She made a note of it for when she got back to Blowing Rock, not that anyone there could appreciate, or afford, such a stunning arrangement. She began to take deep breaths, holding them in the way her one-time yoga instructor had taught during relaxation classes. It wasn't working this time.

Zhang drove the borrowed Bentley up to the security gates of Sunrise Chemicals, Nanjing Limited, the sign over the gateway in Chinese and English characters. Off to the side, under the large SCNL logo, the sign read, "Improving the World's Food Supplies." Zhang drove to the gates, honking the horn to be let in. As Mei had gambled, the sight of such a luxurious car with a party flag and darkened windows brought the guards to attention. Saluting the car as it passed through the briefly opened gates, the Bentley whispered its way along a driveway toward the corporate headquarters building. The trick now was to get into the leader's office; any meeting or phone conversation had been refused point blank over the last two days.

Mei had discussed the entire approach with Wang Jun prior to coming; he had made a few minor adjustments to it, but went along with most of the plan she laid out. He also approved the proposal she was to make to them, then wished her luck before leaving for his evening with Lucy.

Zhang parked in front of the main door, walked around the car and straight up to the reception desk, knowing the receptionists could plainly see the Bentley outside, the Beijing Party flag on it, and the lone female figure in back. Both girls stood to attention as Zhang approached. An armed security guard straightened up, stepped back, and saluted. Zhang passed over an envelope, telling the girl it was urgent their leader saw it immediately. He would wait outside in the car until his visitor was called in for a meeting.

"Who shall we say is here?" the girl asked.

"I'm not at liberty to reveal, I'm afraid; your leader will see who it is in the envelope. Please deliver it right away. We have to fly our visitor back to Beijing shortly. Her plane awaits her." Since it sounded like someone important was there from the central government, the girl rushed to a private elevator accompanied by a guard, to speak to the company leader.

Zhang and Mei sat in the car waiting for the response. After twenty minutes Zhang wondered aloud why it was taking so long, Mei told him the leader was obviously reading the documents. She told him not to worry; if they were going to be turned away it would have happened already. As far as she was concerned they were in. Wang would be pleased.

Finally the girl came out and knocked on Zhang's window, it lowered and she asked the visitor to enter alone. The girl appeared flustered and worried. Zhang came to the rear and opened the door and Mei climbed out, suspecting the girl had received a tongue-lashing for letting her in through security. Zhang was told to move the Bentley to a different parking area, out of sight and away from the main building.

Mei was surprised to see the amount of security closer to the leader's office and living area. She knew right away she was dealing with a recluse, someone who ruled the company and those around her with an iron fist. She was not sure what to expect, but prepared herself for the worst. She was led into a huge office area where windows allowed the occupant visibility over the entire operation. The room was darkened, except for low lighting around a long desk where the visibly displeased leader was waiting. There were no pleasantries exchanged.

"How the hell did you get these?" the leader demanded in English.

"So you don't want to speak in Chinese?" Mei asked.

"Until I wipe the tapes, no. That's not a problem for you, I see."

"Not at all; that's why Mr. Wang Jun hired me."

"So he's behind this after all?"

"Not really. Let's just say this is a bonus for him."

"If you think it changes anything, it won't. I really don't give a shit anymore. I may not be here much longer anyway."

"Oh, you will be. I already accessed your doctor's files. You're in excellent health; another twenty years it says."

A smirk crossed the leader's face. "Is there nothing sacred in this goddamn world of ours?"

Mei laughed. "Not really, and by the way your American slang is very good."

"Good teacher. Now get to the point. What do you want . . . really?"

Mei said she was thirsty. Her host begrudgingly pointed over to tea and water for both of them. They moved from the austere surroundings of the desk to comfortable easy chairs. Mei remarked there was no need to describe the business activities in the buildings outside. She had analyzed SCNL on a number of occasions, except for the new leader, whose personal life was a mystery. As they sat down Mei pulled more documents from her briefcase and spread them across the large coffee table.

"We have a stack of these if you'd like to see them," Mei said, watching the expression on her host's face stiffen and its color drain further.

Mei could see she had hit a mark. It was time to talk more seriously. "Okay, now let's talk about what we have here, and what we want."

The leader drank some water, claimed she had to leave for a few moments, and then stepped out of the office. Mei could see the leader was shaken, the brashness gone. She was likely headed to the bathroom to calm down. Now alone, Mei completed another of her tasks, then waited for the meeting to continue, confident she was now in control of the discussions. When the leader returned, Mei summarized the documents she had laid out, saying there were more, and she could bring them next morning for a follow-up meeting.

"What makes you think there will be a meeting tomorrow?"

"Read these through tonight. You've only glanced at them. The other documents are far more incriminating. If you don't want to see me, I'm sure your major shareholders will enjoy looking at them. I'll be here around ten." With that Mei stood up, added a couple more documents she thought would get the reader's attention, then left.

Chapter 11

Lucy purposely continued to look out the window at the lights over Beijing. She could feel the man's presence, his crossing the room toward her, and she watched his reflection in the window. Her heart beat faster; she sensed him standing right behind her, his warm breath touching her neck, before he whispered. "Lucy, its me."

She turned around to find herself in his arms and his lips on hers. They embraced for a long time before separating.

"Yes, it's definitely you." She looked down and could see he was already aroused.

"What do you expect, Lucy? You look great . . . and the dress . . . it's perfect on you."

They hugged again and John, as only she called him, led her to the table. "We should eat. I'm starving, and I want to hear everything about you. I've really missed you."

"So much that you never tried to contact me again?" Lucy said.

He told her he tried, but once he found out she was in a relationship and then married, decided not to continue. The conversation started to seem awkward, so Lucy moved it back to talking about the time she spent with him in Beijing, pulled out the old photos of them together, and said how grateful she was for him bringing her over again.

Wang Jun said the visit was not only his idea, but involved Chairman Xin Zhiming too. He explained that the work she did with him not only benefited Global Industries, but also Xin's company. As the economy opened up in China over the last decade their initial joint venture had blossomed for all parties, far more than anyone had thought possible.

"You know, Lucy, you made a huge impression on Xin. He always told me you were a big factor in his agreeing to go ahead with us, even though he never agreed to Global taking fifty-one percent of it. I don't know if you remember that was what we wanted. Bob Jenkins got the board to gamble on a forty per-cent position."

"I heard it was a struggle for a couple of years."

"That's an understatement, Lucy. It was a disaster. I thought Bob and I were finished over it, but Xin came through . . . it worked out great."

"I'm glad for you. Looks like it certainly did."

Wang Jun halted the conversation while he ordered more food and wine. As he did, Lucy couldn't take her eyes off him. He had aged handsomely; she was sure he took good care of himself physically and mentally. He was better look-ing than ever. She couldn't help but notice also the way the waitresses looked him up and down.

He didn't ask what she wanted to eat; he remembered everything she liked from before. He had the waitress pour more wine, then waved her away. "Xin and I got on well after everything settled down. He was really sorry when he heard you had to leave the company to take care of your mother. It was after that, when he seemed to take me under his wing more. He asked me to quit and join him on all his other ventures, but I wanted to stay and see things through with Global."

"You always were an honorable rogue, John," Lucy said, smiling.

"Anyway, in the end he began mentoring me, I guess more like a son than a colleague. It was his idea— if I wouldn't leave Global— to get them to agree to my being involved in other businesses with him."

"That's unusual. I'd have thought you could run foul of the legal and corpo-rate folks . . . conflict of interest and all that."

"Me too. We started out with an agreement for me to transition out of Global and into Xin's area, but it worked out so well for everyone that they figured out a way for me to continue."

"You never gave up on Global? Why not?"

"Well, for one thing, I knew that if Global put anyone else in there they would screw everything up. There were too many good people by then in the company and the JV to let that happen. We'd worked too hard to succeed."

"But you could have taken them across with you to Xin's businesses, couldn't you?"

"Yes, but that was pretty tightly controlled in the agreements we had."

Wang continued to explain how well he had done on the Xin side of things, not that Global wasn't really happy with theirs either. He changed the subject. "So how are you and Mei getting along anyway? Any progress with your research?"

"She's a treasure, John, and she worships the ground you walk on."

"I know. She's an incredible assistant . . . her investigative talents are quite special."

"Also a very good-looking young woman."

"True, but I didn't want to get things mixed up. Knowing her, she probably told you already."

"That she did. You don't change much."

"For you I'd change. Anyway, aside from that fill me in on everything. Mei gave me a thumbnail sketch of your problems, but with the negotiations in Moscow I couldn't pay too much attention to her."

———— ✷ ————

The food arrived to satisfy their desire to eat; Wang Jun hungry from a day without eating, Lucy out of sheer pleasure the evening was going so well with him. She began to talk about her father, totally comfortable in his presence, and trusting him as implicitly as in years past. He asked right away about the two hard drives, and if his people were a help.

"You've one hell of an operation there, John," She said. "Are you sure it's all legal? It would never fly in the U.S. you know. I bet Global's legal guys would go into high gear if they knew about it."

"Let's just say that here in China my research capabilities are exceptional. We're okay providing I steer clear of politics, the military, or any corrupt behavior. I keep it completely separate from Global, and never use its resources in connection with that side . . . so, did they help you and Mei yet?"

"Yes they did, with one of my father's drives; the other stumped them all. They wanted to continue to work on it, but I was a worried what might be on it, so told them no. Was that okay?"

"Of course, Lucy, none of us want to get into something we shouldn't, right? If you change your mind just tell Mei, but don't worry about it, it's a big computer game to Li and Zhang."

Lucy told Wang how she came to meet her husband, Phil, how he was captured in Afghanistan, and the terrible consequences from it, even her recent affair with his psychiatrist. She talked about her mother dying, her father's illness, how she broke into his office, and what she was trying to do. Lucy left nothing out.

"Look, if we can help you we will. I hope you know that. Mei is at your disposal. The only thing is it could take a bit longer than you've planned; you ought to think about delaying your return. I know I'd like that."

Lucy smiled back. She knew exactly why he wanted her to stay. She was happy to, but knew Phil would have none of it, replying only that she would see about it. The how was another question.

When dinner was over, Lucy was asked if she was too tired to take a late night stroll around the Houhai canal district. She readily agreed, recalling all the times they wandered around there until two or three in the morning, while Bob Jenkins slept, doing their best to appear fresh for the negotiations that went on day after day. She told him she was worried about walking around Houhai late that night in such a beautiful, and valuable, chipao dress, especially since Xin had asked her to wear it at the celebration. Wang just laughed, shouted something in Chinese to the waitress, who soon walked in with a small but expensive-looking lady's bag.

"You can change into these, Lucy. Mei put them in the car for you earlier. Go with her; she'll show you where."

Lucy took the bag from the waitress. who accompanied her to the ladies room, turning back momentarily. "Is there anything you haven't thought about for tonight? she asked suggestively.

"Oh, I've thought of everything, I hope. Get changed and we'll get out of here."

Han was waiting at the exit with the car. Lucy imagined the bill being horrendous for the evening— the private room and the flowers— but Wang Jun made nothing of it. The manager thanked Lucy for coming and reminded her to come again during the day sometime. By the time they got to Houhai, Wang Jun had shed his business jacket and they looked like any other couple taking a walk there. The crowds were heavier than she remembered, with more locals than tourists out late. She felt his arm around her waist and responded with hers. She did nothing when his hand slid lower as if to confirm the firmness of her figure.

They stopped alongside the canal where Wang Jun held her to him and kissed her forehead. "After all these years, Lucy, it feels like you never left. Can I stay the night?"

She looked up at him and said nothing, watching him wait for her answer. She held back as long as she could. "Of course. Did you think for a moment I'd let you leave? Tonight of all nights?"

They laughed, and he asked if she wanted to walk further or go back to the apartment. He was disappointed when she wanted to walk further; then she dug him in the ribs and said she was joking.

Once in the back of the car Wang Jun couldn't keep his hands off her. She was embarrassed at first, but noticed Han smiling with approval in his rear view mirror, trying to appear focused on his driving but glancing back at her frequently. A darkened screen rose between Han and the rear seats after Wang Jun pressed a button. At that point it would have been difficult to decide which of them was the aggressor; they were both hungry for each other. When Han dropped them off, Wang Jun told him to wait for Lucy's call before picking her up in the morning and bid him goodnight .

Han smiled as he left the couple behind. Once he was clear of the Palm Springs apartments he parked the car, then ran the recording of the couple in the back of his car. He knew his boss would kill him if he knew, so after watching it several times he deleted it. He liked his job too much to be caught with it. He drove straight to a club he used and asked for one of the girls he visited regularly. The video had aroused him.

The cell phone next to Wang Jun rang early. It was Mei Rui. He turned to look at Lucy, made sure she was sleeping, and slipped out of bed. He crept into the living area and stood naked by the window, looking out at the dawn rising over Chaoyang Park. He could tell it was going to be a polluted day by the early haze. He was tired but happy; his night with Lucy had been all he had hoped it would be, and more.

"Yes, Mei. What do you need?" he whispered, "It's early for a weekend."

"I know, but you can't stay in bed with her all day either."

"So you talked to Han already?"

"Of course. I had to know," She said.

"Well, call him back, and tell him if I find any tapes of us in the back of the car last night I will not only fire him on the spot but have his balls cut off too."

Mei laughed. "Don't worry, he won't even tell me about it, but he did say he was surprised to see she was more athletic than you. You must be slipping, Boss, or are you just tired?"

"No more of that, Mei. Let's just say that, for all the years that passed between us, nothing has changed."

"I'm sorry. Neither Han nor I mean any disrespect. We can tell how much you feel for each other. I'm just jealous. We both want you to be happy . . . and away from that bitch of a wife you have."

"Enough of that too. Remember your place. What do you want that's so important this early?"

Mei told him about the meeting in Nanjing, what had been said, and how she had one more meeting later that morning.

"Did Zhang get what he needed?"

"Yes, we should have the results by nine. How do you want us to handle it?"

"We better talk before you go in. Let's check if the results are what I think they'll be. That will determine how we proceed. In any event we still make the offer."

"Do you think it's too low?"

"No, I've talked to Xin too and he agrees with the numbers. We went over your figures yesterday. He went to the restaurant to wait with Lucy while I talked things through with the banks. It's a good offer all round."

"Seems overly generous to me."

"Even they thought we were being a bit generous, based on our proposal two years ago. At any rate Xin wants this to go through as amicably as it can, but he agrees we need to use our leverage, force their hand this time if we need to."

"Okay, I'll call as soon as Zhang hears. Make sure to keep your phone on."

Lucy wandered into the lounge naked under a silk robe she had found in her bathroom.

"Who was that, John?"

"Mei. She's working on a new deal for us down in Nanjing. She'll hopefully be back for the celebration and in time to work some more with you. Meantime I want us to be together as much as we can."

"Sounds good to me."

" You'll have to excuse me taking her calls; you know how that goes."

"Is it a big one? Shouldn't you be there?"

"Not with you here. Anyway, she's good, very good. She can handle it."

There was a knock at the apartment door and Wang Jun excused himself to grab a towel. Two women stood there with packages waiting to be allowed entry; as soon as Wang Jun welcomed them in he waved them over to the dining room.

"What's this?" Lucy asked.

"Your favorite. Fresh fried dough pancakes, the best tea eggs in Beijing, bowsers, and of course your eight treasure soup. You just have to make the coffee yourself if you want any."

"What, no bean milk?"

"Shit, I forgot that."

Wang laughed as he thanked the two women, gave them a big tip, and ushered them out. He told Lucy the two ran a cart down by the side of Chaoyang Park. It was the genuine street food she loved, not from some restaurant. She stood at the table absorbing the aromas and smiling, "You've thought of everything, haven't you?"

He told her he had tried to, that he wished he'd not let her go so easily all those years ago. She came to him and he held her close. He thought about dragging her back to bed there and then, but she broke away and said they should eat. She said this was the best breakfast she'd had in years, wolfing down everything on the table. He was tempted to take her there and then on the floor, but his watch told him Mei would be calling at any moment.

Chapter 12

"Can you talk?" Mei asked.

"Yes. Breakfast is over. She's getting ready."

"Zhang finished everything. He gave it to me when we left."

"You don't sound happy, Mei. What's wrong?"

"It didn't come out the way we expected," she said. "I don't think it's going to help. What do you want me to do?"

"Okay, we might need more time on that side. You know what those Americans say. 'Where there's some smoke there's a fire,' or something like that. Anyway, we'll find it. Go heavy on the other things. There's more to worry about there."

"Are you sure, Boss? They've still got friends in high places. They might bite back again."

'"Not this time. Friends and colleagues are one thing, but our all-seeing Party is a whole different matter. Anyway, listen to how Xin sees that side."

With that Wang Jun went over some talking points from his earlier meetings with Xin. She told him she would do her best, unless he wanted to wait.

"You're there. It sounds like we already have the edge over them with some of the things you've laid out. Show a few more and then press the offer. We'll see what we can do on the Lucy thing later."

"But she'll be leaving next week, won't she?" Mei asked.

He ended the conversation as Lucy came back into the room.

"Was that Mei?"

Wang Jun confirmed it was, that she had all the information needed to complete the deal, and one way or another ought to get a verbal that day. Lucy told him they should celebrate later, but he said there was no need, she was more important than any deal. He told her to finish getting ready, he was taking her sightseeing and to dress casual. She kissed him and left to finish dressing. He couldn't help but smile watching her act like an excited schoolgirl on her first field trip. He knew he was still in love with her. Was there any chance for him, he wondered, or was it too late?

◦◦◦◦◦◦◦

Mei and Zhang drove up to the Nanjing factory complex again. This time the security guards kept the gates locked. Mei was forced to get out of the car and fill out visitor forms, then waited impatiently to be told they could enter the facility. She knew they were being put through the full routine to irritate her; she was angry, but more determined than ever to crush her opponent in every way she could.

Mei walked from the security area back to the car. Zhang held the door open while she looked up at the main building. She suspected the leader was already looking down on them; she threw her bag of files on the seat ahead of getting in, looked up, and said to Zhang in English, "Fuck them and their factory. Fuck the lot of them!"

She climbed in and straightened her skirt. "Let's go, Zhang, I'm really ready for them now."

As Zhang pulled up to the front entrance another security guard came along, jumped in the front seat alongside Zhang, and guided him around the back, away from prying eyes. He apologized to Mei Rui and asked her to follow him. He was polite to her, so she returned his demeanor, thanking him for accompanying her. Once in the elevator she rode up to the private offices of the leader, wishing the results had been what she expected. She entered the leader's office and walked straight over to the easy chair and sat down.

"I have an offer here to buy the biomedical portion of your businesses," Mei said. "It's a good offer and your shareholders will approve it. I need your signature on this document accepting the offer and its terms before I leave."

"Are you crazy?"

"This offer is valid until two o'clock today. If you decide not to accept our generous offer—" she paused while extracting more papers from her bag— "then these documents will be made available in Beijing this afternoon to Party leaders, certain news outlets here, and the overseas press."

Mei's host rose from the desk, stormed over, and stood there, screaming in her face. "Just who the fuck do you think you are, bitch, coming in here and telling me what I'm going to do? I'll sell you and your asshole friends nothing! You think we slaved over building this company all these years to let some nobodies come in here and steal it away?"

Mei stood up, a document in one hand, the offer in the other, their noses almost touching. "Madame Li Buyun, you look at this document in my hand very closely, then look at this offer. If it were up to me I'd just have you fucked out of your job, period, and we'd take your goddamned business for a whole lot less."

"Like fuck you will!"

"For whatever reason, Wang Jun and his partners are being more than generous. Read this document carefully. We've worse ones incriminating you, and they're all ready to go. I'm walking out of this office and will ask one of your ladies to make me coffee. I'll be back in a half hour to settle this. If we don't, it goes public as promised."

"This is bullshit. It's illegal. It's blackmail. You think you can blackmail me? I've got as many friends in Beijing as your Wang Jun has, and don't you forget it."

"You mean these?" Mei said, pulling out a name list from her bag. "Keep it. These are all the names that will come out in the documents this afternoon. I've done some research for you and attached all their mobile numbers, just so it's easy for you to call them and tell them what's about to be released."

Li Buyun read through the list. Mei leaned over her trembling hand and pointed out one particular name. "Especially that one . . . he'd probably like to get to an airport as fast as he can."

"All this happened years ago. They've all moved beyond the crap in here. I don't think you have as much as you think you do."

"Well, that's your choice. Enjoy your reading; I'm getting my coffee. I'll tell them outside you asked not to be disturbed and to cancel all your other meetings."

"The hell you will," Li shouted.

"Watch me," Mei said as she left the room and slammed the door behind her.

Mei asked Li's secretary for a coffee, then both were startled by the sound of furniture crashing. Mei told the assistant Madame Li must have knocked something over, knowing the woman was likely having a temper tantrum over the documents. Another door opened and a younger woman came rushing through to Li's office. They heard the older woman inside screaming, "Get the fuck out of here . . . now!" The younger woman came out quickly, past Mei. She gave the assistant a worried look and a headshake, as if to say "here she goes again." She went off to her own office, closing the door with another slam.

"So who was that?" Mei asked.

"You don't know? That's her daughter, Zhao Wen. Next in line, she is. Not like her mother though; everyone loves her. She's smart like her father was, and if her mother stays out of the way she'll do something good for the company."

"How long before she might take over?"

"Tomorrow wouldn't be soon enough for most of us, but I think it's scheduled for next year. Don't say I told you that."

Mei thanked her and asked for coffee and a private area to make calls. She phoned Wang Jun as soon as she was alone. Now she understood everything, or thought she did.

Lucy was enjoying her morning, walking around Tiananmen Square and preparing to visit the Forbidden City. Wang Jun had told her of the extensive renovations and arranged for them to have a personally guided tour by one of Beijing's foremost experts on its history. Han followed the couple at a discreet distance, a security necessity for Wang Jun in public places. Whenever Lucy glanced behind her Han would smile, letting her know he was there to ensure their safety.

During the visit Wang Jun took an urgent call, leaving her with the guide and advising he would be back shortly. This time Han followed Wang Jun, leaving Lucy to continue listening to the guide's stories of palace events and intrigue, some largely unknown to the public.

Wang Jun made sure he was well out of earshot before responding to Mei. "What's up?"

"It's not at all as we thought, but you know what they say, boss, when one door closes another one opens, and I think one just has."

"You're not sure though?"

"Not a hundred percent, but this time I'd bet on it. " Mei described the situation in detail, Li Buyun's reaction, and the foul language she had put up with. They talked about their strategy, then Wang Jun said he needed some time to call Xin; he had another idea he was sure might swing it. He ended the call and got hold of Xin. They talked for a good fifteen minutes before he got Mei back on the line. She listened; surprised at their change in approach, resentful of anything that might let Li off the hook.

"I don't think we need to do that, Boss. I can get it done as we planned. These new ones might not work either. You don't know what she's like over this."

"I don't. I only dealt with her husband before, but Xin does . . . or so he says. Anyway, he wants us to take this route and he's the chairman. He agrees you should bluff your way through the other thing, but if you can get something to prove it, well go ahead since Zhang is there. I'm surprised we overlooked that Li was Zhao Chungang's wife before. "

"I know, but we were looking in the wrong place all the time. It was never Beijing. Zhao seems to have kept his wife out of everything until he died. I'm at fault as much as anyone for missing that completely."

"Don't worry, it's working out better than I could have imagined. Go to your meeting and put the revised approach to her. Xin is sure it will work.

"You're both sure?" Mei asked one last time.

"We are, and agree you're doing a great job. There'll be a nice bonus when you are all done."

"What about Lucy?"

"Great. She's still talking to our guide so I need to get back to her. We'll have to go over all this after the celebration and you're back." Wang Jun told Mei not to worry about Lucy leaving too quickly; he was already working on her.

"Okay, but I'll need her here for at least another week," she said. Wang Jun told her he wanted Lucy for a whole lot longer than that. Mei said she needed to ring off and get back to "that miserable bitch." Wang told her it was time to put her "nice" face on, to be as charming as he knew she could.

⸙

When Wang reappeared, Lucy was in one of the concubine areas closed off to the public and in the midst of renovation. Her guide was explaining how things worked during the emperor's times, that some of the concubines never met the emperor during their entire life living there. She'd heard and read those stories before, but the elderly guide brought everything to life in excellent English. Wang apologized for being gone so long, and Lucy asked if everything was going well for Mei.

"You remember what it's like here, Lucy. You always hit a few roadblocks along the way. Sometimes you have to change strategy, which she's going to have to do now. It should work out though."

Lucy told him if he needed to get more involved Han could take care of her the rest of the day, but he said everything was on track. He checked his watch, turned to Han, and pointed out it was time to get the car. He told the guide he was sorry to end the visit since his guest was enjoying it so much, but his driver would shortly drive the couple to a late lunch nearby. He slipped a red envelope into the guide's pocket, despite the old man's effort to stop him. After a prolonged to and fro, the old man accepted the gift with genuine appreciation.

Lucy told him it was the best tour of the Forbidden City she ever had, and asked Wang Jun to take a photo of them together. The guide then led them through a private alleyway to get them quickly to the north exit, where Han was already holding the car's rear doors open.

———⦀———

Mei walked back into the leader's office, quietly closing the door behind her. She could see an unhappy-looking lady at her desk, dejected, and not the brash woman she left earlier that day. This time Mei walked up to the desk and stood in front of her.

"Madame Li, could we sit down and talk? I may have something interesting for you to consider, perhaps a more attractive alternative than before." This time she let Li lead the way over to the easy chairs, waited for her to sit, then asked if she minded her sitting close by.

Li waved a hand in the air. "Do as you like."

"Madame Li, I talked to Wang Jun earlier today, and he and his partner have approved what I am about to offer you. They do understand how you feel about this company of your former husband, without mentioning some of the founding events, or your past activities. We also appreciate your interest in having the business continue and be passed along to your family, a daughter I believe, whom we understand is being groomed to replace you. Wang Jun's partner has heard very good things about her, by the way, and says you should be proud of her."

"Where is this going? What alternative offer are you making?"

"It's simple. We become partners with you, you retain the chairmanship for three more years, no more, and your daughter succeeds you. At that point our consortium takes full control of the entire business. If your daughter is as worthy as we have heard, she will be given a ten-year contract. If it's broken, other than for poor performance of course, there will be a hefty settlement."

"What about the shares I own in this business?" Li asked.

"You can retain all the shares you own, or trade them in, and receive more of them for your efforts in the coming years through the consortium. We will ensure that a sizeable gain in profit is secured for you as part of the transaction— if you choose to sell shares at that point. This is a little new, I know, but we can have people here next week to work through an agreeable settlement. This single sheet I have for you highlights the key points. Initial it and the documents we have will never be released." Mei watched Li's face stiffen when Mei added, "Nor will we be forced to give copies to your daughter."

"Is that it?"

"Not quite, we might ask you to fly to the U.S. to meet someone. We can explain that later. It's purely personal . . . private . . . a favor to someone."

"If I say yes to the deal, but no to that, what then?"

"I'm afraid our principals feel strongly about that; the documents will be released if you refuse. I assure you, however, it's nothing to worry about."

"Can I have longer than two o'clock? I need to talk to my daughter before I answer you. You can at least give me that surely."

"I can extend until four. There is one condition though."

"What's that?"

"I get to meet your daughter while I'm here."

Li Buyun assured Mei that, provided the discussions went as she expected with her daughter, it would be possible, but any discussions had to be away from any of the documents Mei possessed.

"Of course," Mei agreed. "After that I will leave for the day, but ask that you do me the honor of dining tonight in private. I have other things to talk to you about and I'd like to get on a different footing with you."

Li Buyun agreed, somewhat reluctantly, telling Mei she never left her mansion these days. She would have her picked up and they would dine privately at her home. Mei thanked her, saying she would be back by four, suggesting nicely that their car be allowed to enter promptly. It was the first time Li cracked a smile all day, telling Mei it would be taken care of.

As soon as Mei was in the car and on the way to her hotel, she phoned Wang Jun. The call lasted only ten minutes, Mei promising she would call back that evening with a full update. In the meantime she told him she was confident they would need their legal team ready for merger negotiations in Nanjing, maybe as early as Monday.

Chapter 13

Mei's car swept into the Nanjing facility past guards holding back vehicles waiting to pass through security. They were waved on to the corporate offices where Li Buyun's assistant stood waiting for them. Mei climbed out of the car, elegantly dressed as the day before, with new documents in her briefcase should she need them. The assistant told her they would be riding up directly to see Madame Li, and that arrangements had been made to pick her up for dinner that evening.

On entering the office she found a very different Madame Li, far less antagonistic, even shaking Mei's hand before leading her directly to the sitting area. Tea and coffee was already laid out for them.

"Miss Mei, I had a long conversation this afternoon with my daughter. I expect you and your principals to respect our discussions when talking to her, and in any public announcements. I have told Zhao Wen our companies are going to merge under favorable terms, that this is something I have been working on for two years, and that I will gradually retire over the next two to three years, maybe earlier. But she will replace me, providing she proves her worth. I have no doubt she will. This is of course subject to the final terms of our agreement and shareholder approval, but you can assure Wang Jun I will recommend acceptance. Is this agreeable?"

"Completely, Madame Li. Wang Jun has researched your daughter this afternoon and wants to compliment you on her reputation, in the industry. She will be welcomed into the group, as will you, and fully integrated into the business. Her compensation will be increased accordingly. I know Wang Jun and his partner will be very pleased to hear you have accepted our proposal."

"You mean Xin of course." Li said with a smile.

"You know him?"

"You are not the only one who knows certain things, Miss Mei. I just happen to protect my friends, which is more than you and Wang Jun seem to."

"What does that mean?" Mei asked.

"For him to say, and for you to find out. Now . . . what proof do I have that the materials will be destroyed?"

"You have our promise in that regard. There are some personal aspects of the non-political correspondence to talk about, but they are insignificant. We can discuss more this evening about that side, and the particular matter we need your help with."

Mei produced a basic memorandum of understanding. Madame Li looked at her directly while she signed her name as elegantly as she could.

"I may not like how this is being done, Miss Mei, but I will say Wang Jun's offer is more than I could have hoped for in today's market."

"I agree. To be frank with you, the whole offer was against my recommendation, but the merger idea was suggested by Wang Jun, and the revised valuation, apparently, by Chairman Xin."

"Xin is no fool, he does nothing without a reason."

"Interesting. With what you said earlier about knowing him, perhaps there's something else for me to uncover."

Li made no comment, but emphasized that anything more to be said was up to Xin, and Mei should tell him directly what she said in that regard. She then reverted to the things they needed to attend to if they were going to move forward. She asked Mei to invite Wang and Xin to her operations anytime they wanted, but emphasized the need to establish merger teams on both sides to get things started. The principals could meet later to resolve any differences that proved to be problematic. Her daughter would lead the SCNL team negotiations from their side; she also was insisting meetings be held in Nanjing, not Beijing, or neutral ground if necessary.

Li told Mei her daughter was waiting to meet her in the executive conference room, reminding her again of the agreement to say nothing of the documents in Mei's possession. Mei thanked her, told her she was looking forward to dining together that evening, and assured Li she would absolutely follow their agreement.

Lucy's back was fully arched, holding on to Wang Jun as tightly as she could, the rhythm and her moaning increasing. She was close to losing herself completely when the shrill sound of a cell phone shattered the moment.

"Oh, shit." He muttered.

"Let the damned thing ring. Please don't stop . . . not now," Lucy begged, still breathing heavily.

"I have to. It won't take long, I promise. Don't move. I'll be back."

Lucy watched him roll off the bed, cursing in Chinese as he left the room. Sweat was glistening on his back, the marks she made on him clearly visible. Perspiring heavily herself she left for the bathroom to towel off. Lying back on the bed she overheard a rushed conversation in Chinese, understanding only the words for "okay" and "that's good."

Wang held her again as soon as he was on the bed, saying how sorry he was. It was Mei, as Lucy assumed, and everything had gone well; they were now, potentially, an even bigger organization on the non-Global Industry's side. The two lay there for a while talking about it, the intensity of the moment lost. She knew Wang Jun would have to call certain people, especially Xin, so she told him to make whatever calls he needed. They would get back to it later.

"You sure you don't mind? I feel so bad," he said.

"I'm sure, but I need a hundred percent attention next time . . . no phone calls!"

The assistant led Mei into a large conference room where she introduced Madame Li's daughter, making sure they had everything before closing the door softly behind her.

"Miss Zhao Wen, my name is Mei Rui. I'm happy to meet you. We have been working on this for such a long time. Our leaders are very excited we can finally move forward. Your father's reputation goes without question in our industry, but we've heard good things about you too. We hope the upcoming discussions proceed smoothly, and quickly, so we can take advantage of the synergies our merger will bring." Mei paused allowing Zhao Wen to reciprocate.

"Well, Miss Mei, I must admit this is a bit of a shock for me. My mother really kept your discussions secret; we had no idea she had been working on this for so long. I'm afraid I've only had the last hour, since she told me, to do a little research on your group. I was well aware of the biotech side of your business, of course, but had no idea of the breadth of your associated businesses. I think there are opportunities beyond our efforts on the biotech side in a number of areas. I hope I can be a contributing party to them too."

"I'm sure you remember some preliminary discussions between our divisions. They were with your father over two years ago. Wang Jun was disappointed at the time we weren't able to agree to anything, but it did lay the groundwork for what we're about to accomplish. Your mother wasn't known to us at the time, but our research indicates she too is held in high regard by your management and shareholders."

"That's good to hear. I've been telling her these last months she needs to think about easing off, and let the rest of our management team take our strategy to the next level. I always thought she was ignoring me, but I guess not."

"Your mother is a wonderful lady. You should be proud of her. It must have been hard for her taking over from your father after his sudden passing. How about some tea or water, please? Let's talk a little about you; I'd love to know more about your background. If I can answer any questions about Wang Jun or the group I'll be happy to do so too.

"We can start there if you like."

"Oh, and I understand you will lead your team in the coming weeks. I doubt it will be me on our side, but at least we should know each other in case we need to talk on the sidelines."

Zhao Wen poured tea and began to describe her career to date with SCNL, her passion for the biotech industry, and vision for the future. Mei understood quickly that Wang Jun was going to be impressed with her, pleased she did not have her own or Lucy's looks to compliment her management capabilities. Mei was relieved no competition lay ahead in that department.

Mei asked for a napkin to wipe the tea she spilled. By the time Zhao Wen returned with a towel, Mei had gathered what she needed, and then indicated she needed to go back to the hotel and change for dinner. Before leaving she suggested it might be interesting for Zhao Wen to fly up to Beijing on Tuesday evening to be a guest at the celebration planned for their Chairman, if her mother agreed. The two ended the meeting cordially and Zhao told Mei to call her "Xiao" Wen in the future, as everyone did, not that Mei thought she was "little" by any means. She was taller than her mother by several inches.

The meetings had gone far smoother then Mei expected.

Mei sat in the hotel lobby, dressed in plain but classy attire for dinner. When Madame Li's driver arrived at the appointed hour, she left behind materials she needed Zhang to review, apologizing for having to leave him working. The drive to the mansion of Li Buyun took forty minutes. It was nestled in the rear of a very large and exclusive gated community. Compared to all the other properties, hers was monstrous. The driveway to the house itself meandered through a landscape of gardening masterpieces and ponds; it was most impressive. Finally, on the approach to the house, she saw Li Buyun herself, and realized she had come totally overdressed. The older woman was wearing a casual top, expensive blue jeans and sandals, her long hair hanging loosely over her shoulders.

As she got out of the car and Li walked toward her, Mei took off her jacket and unbuttoned her blouse to appear more casual.

"I'm sorry, Mei, if I can call you that. I should have told you to dress casual tonight. This is how I always dress once I'm home; the other stuff is just for the office and customers. Anyway, come on in. Please call me Li; everyone does."

"Mei is fine for me, or just Rui will do. Anyway, you have a beautiful home here, and the gardens are spectacular. I have a special visitor over from America who would love your flowers."

"Feel free to bring her along anytime. Now let's go eat. If you don't mind I'd prefer we talk after eating . . . let's first get to know each other better."

"That sounds great, I'm quite hungry myself. By the way, your daughter is impressive in her own right, a credit to you. I enjoyed talking to her. She will get along famously with Wang Jun."

"She appears to like you too. Thanks for maintaining our merger story. As much as it pissed me off yesterday the whole concept is growing on me. Now let's eat. I hope you like a kind of Korean barbecue. We'll eat out on the patio."

Li led Mei through her spectacular home. None of the furnishings were ostentatious, but could have featured in any architectural magazine. The patio itself was more than Mei expected, an outside room with kitchen and dining areas that could easily host several hundred guests. They sat in a small area off to the side, close to an expensive grilling area where two chefs were busy preparing food. Mei noticed Li was a woman who only picked at her food, which probably explained her gaunt appearance; on the other hand she ate most of the things the staff put in front of her.

"I like to see someone who enjoys their food," Li said to her, indicating her own daughter's eating habits were not as she would like to see them. "She's way too skinny for her height. I keep telling her to eat more, but she always throws the way I eat back in my face. I used to eat a lot more, you know, but these last couple of years since my husband died just haven't seemed the same."

The one thing Li hadn't given up on was good wine, and before long some of the finest French wines were lined up in front of them. Mei felt she was being tested again when asked to choose one. She was thankful that Wang Jun had sent her to a wine appreciation course, to educate her for entertaining important guests. Mei studied each bottle, made comments on them, asked Li's general taste preferences, then picked the one to be opened.

"I'm impressed. You've picked one of my favorites. You certainly have many talents, young lady, even though some of them I may not care for."

Li began to pour larger glasses of wine. Mei understood she was being tested in that regard too. Perhaps Li was thinking that enough drink would loosen Mei's tongue. But Mei knew she could stand up to that challenge. The first part of their conversation went over more of the pending merger discussions, before returning to the issue of the documents and where they came from.

Mei began the story of Lucy Summers, how she'd found computer drives in her father's office. She shared some of Lucy's background in China, except her intimate relationship with Wang Jun. Li showed no reaction, even when Mei mentioned that Lucy's father was John Wainright, as the daughter knew him, but was also known as Richard Towers, a false name he used in China. The expression on Li's face told Mei the woman knew far more than she was letting on. She decided on a different approach, including the bluff that Wang talked about using earlier that day.

"To be honest, Li, when all this started I assumed Lucy was the daughter of you and John Wainright, but she isn't, is she?" Mei waited for a reaction, but the woman said nothing. "On the other hand we now know your daughter Zhao Wen is the daughter of you and John, or Richard, whatever you called him at the time."

"That's a fanciful idea."

"No, not really. I'm sure your biotech knowledge will support me in our DNA reviews over the last couple of days. The amount of DNA in saliva that's deposited on cups or glasses is really quite significant, as you know, and can last for a long time."

Madame Li squirmed in her chair just a little, enough to tell Mei she was heading down the right track.

"Anyway, this Lucy Summers came to China a week ago, searching for answers regarding her father. Of course, she'd found references in communications to a Li Buyun. I missed resolving that part and finding you at first, assuming it was someone still in Beijing. It was only through the information we opened up on the drives that a company name led me to Nanjing. Then again, its always difficult here with women keeping their own surnames after marriage, isn't it?"

Mei took a few more sips of wine, then continued. "I told her one morning she looked sick and took her temperature. The thermometer gave me a baseline sample to work on my theory. Yesterday I took a sample when you were out of your office, and followed up just hours ago with one from your daughter. My chauffeur Zhang is not really a driver; he's one of our investigative specialists, and quite brilliant at it I might add. He handled Lucy's original analysis work and also made arrangements, at some cost I might add, to have your samples analyzed here right away. So there you have it. Zhao Wen is actually the daughter of you and John Wainright. I hope to unravel who Lucy's real parents are soon."

Li said nothing in response.

"This Lucy was told by her mother, John's wife, that she was a rescued orphan from Vietnam, the union of a Vietnamese and an American. She had a difficult upbringing at school, was called many names; slant eyes, Vietcong brat, and worse. I must say, though, she turned into a very beautiful girl who must have put every other young woman in her town to shame."

"What's this Lucy got to do with me?" Li asked, finally breaking her silence.

"I'm working on that. Certainly John Wainright has something to do with it. Our work on her DNA has produced some interesting findings, but we haven't told her anything about them yet. First of all, she is definitely not of Vietnamese origin, nor is her father American; quite the opposite. She is considered by experts to be the offspring of a Chinese male and an American female. An unusual combination for the times, don't you think?"

" I have no idea what you are talking about, I'm afraid."

"Actually I suspect you do. I'm not sure how yet, but I hope to find out. I wonder what Zhao Wen will say when she finds out about her real father? To be honest, with all the photos I've seen of Lucy's American father, I recognized his looks the moment I saw her in your office."

There was an uneasy silence between them, which seemed to last forever in Mei's mind. Li poured Mei a large glass of wine, excused the people serving them, and left Mei sitting alone while she went into the house. She returned some ten minutes later and set a large black album off to the side. Mei watched Li settle back into her seat, take a deep breath, and then slowly exhale as if about to relieve herself of whatever she was carrying around on her frail shoulders. Mei thought to herself, this is it, it's coming. And it did, as Madame Li gingerly opened the album.

———⁓———

Mei left Li well after midnight, wondering how she was going to handle what she now knew, and how they would tell Lucy. When they parted company it was as if they were old friends. Certainly Mei was now her confidante in many ways. The other testy moment had been when Mei told Li what they wanted she and her daughter to do. Li had reluctantly agreed for her own part, but refused to involve her daughter under any terms. That issue remained unsettled. Madame Li told her it was nonnegotiable, that Mei better talk to Wang Jun and Xin or the deal was off the table.

"Let me put it this way, Mei," she said, " I would rather end it all than have my daughter involved. Make sure Xin in particular understands that. Tell him I've held up my part all these years; he at least owes me that much. He can talk to Wang Jun about it; I'm not going to."

———⁓———

As Mei rode back to her hotel, still feeling the effects of the wine, her mind was still in high gear She couldn't stop thinking about all Li had revealed, and what she knew from the materials Lucy brought with her. She wanted to be back in Beijing as soon as she could, not so much for the celebration Tuesday evening, but to talk with Wang Jun and Xin about all she learned. Mei knew she had work left to bring the story to a conclusion. She had most of the keys, but the rest depended on discussions in Beijing.

She worried about how Lucy was going to react when she found out. Whether she was told everything was not up to her; it would be for Wang Jun to decide, and then only if she could fill in the gaps. She wasn't sure she could.

Chapter 14

The weekend flew by. Lucy knew she would remember this time with Wang Jun for the rest of her life. That she still loved him was in no doubt. Despite his pleas, and her own feelings, she still needed to return to the world of Blowing Rock and take care of Phil. Wang Jun promised he could arrange everything for her husband to never want for anything the rest of his life, if only she would leave him. It wasn't that Lucy did not want the same thing, but her upbringing would never allow her to walk out on Phil, especially with the problems he was facing. Wang Jun's promise to ensure that her husband had the best care money could buy was generous, but her marriage vows were sacred; she would not break them.

As the weekend drew to a close, they loved more passionately than ever, physically and emotionally. When Sunday evening was over they cried with happiness for their time together, but with the sadness of knowing they would soon part again. Wang Jun had to leave late that evening, to be in the office early Monday morning for merger situations. Mei was returning. He had to make sure arrangements were in place for the Tuesday celebration, and then they could spend Wednesday together. Thursday was her return flight day; neither of them looked forward to it. She was unsure when Phil was due back, but called Sarah at the flower shop to pass along her own updates. Sarah assured her that

Phil was fine. The men were having a great road trip, and Phil hoped to be back in time for her return.

———◦∞◦———

The call Sally Sweetland received from Lucy was a long one, revealing more about what was really going on in China. Sally listened, then told her it was time to do the right thing for herself, not to worry so much about Phil. She should do what she could for him, but not continue suffering in a pointless marriage.

"You love this guy, don't you?" Sally asked.

"More than anything in the world . . . always have really."

"Then who are you kidding? Take the chance you've been given for real love, not to mention a life most of us can only dream of. You're a fool if you don't, and you'll regret it for the rest of your life."

"I can't."

"Goddamn it, Lucy, are you nuts?"

"You're right. I know you're right, but I still can't. I'll be home Thursday, late. Can you pick me up over in Greensboro? Sarah has the flight details, I'm not sure if Phil will be back in time, but I can't face him right away off the plane. Please come."

"Of course I'll pick you up, but think again about what you're doing to yourself. I wish I was there to knock some sense into you."

"I wish you were too," Lucy said.

As Sally waited to hear more, the line went quiet and she could hear Lucy's whimpering develop into sobbing; then the call went dead.

Sally turned to her husband, who seemed to understand what the two were talking about. She shook her head in despair.

"Honey, you tried. And you're right . . . from what I can gather . . . she ought to ditch Phil and stay where the hell she is. You can't make her though, Sally. There's her father to worry about too, you know. It's not easy for her."

"I know that. It just doesn't seem fair. She's my best friend, and I'm sure she'd be happier over there."

Sally wiped some of her own tears away, gave her husband a hug, and told him how lucky they were to have each other.

———— ✸✸✸ ————

Lucy finally fell asleep around two in the morning, after making calls to Sarah and Sally. She knew Sally was right, but it wouldn't change anything. Her mind drifted back and forth, from staying with Phil to leaving him for Wang Jun. She was also anxious to see Mei Rui back in Beijing, for them to continue looking for Li Buyun. Time was running out. She wanted to stay longer, not just for Wang Jun, but to find out more about her father.

Lucy awoke late in the morning, unusual for her in Beijing. Perhaps the jet lag was easing, not to mention the benefits of the exercise in and out of bed with Wang Jun over the entire weekend. She reached over to the bedside lights and flicked the switches, but nothing happened. She glanced at the electronic clock and noticed the time of three forty a.m. flashing, even though it was light outside. Mei had warned her of occasional power cuts, but so far there had been none. She assumed there was an outage at the hour the clock stopped at.

She made her way to the main fuse box Mei had shown her, flipped the fuse switches back and forth as instructed until the lights came on. She went off to make herself some coffee, planning to venture out later for the breakfast she liked so much out on the street. Wang Jun had said he could have it delivered to her again, but she insisted on the full experience, eating outside with the locals.

She soon noticed Mei's bedroom door ajar, but remembered shutting it the night before. She went over to close it again, soon noticing several of the drawers open. Concerned, she started to check them; all of Mei's clothes were neatly laid there, but the upper drawers, where she had seen Mei removing her jewelry, were empty. It was then she noticed the faint footprints on the carpet and panicked. More small marks on the carpet led into her bedroom also. It took a matter of seconds for her to realize her purse had been emptied too. Credit cards, cash, airline tickets, a few pieces of jewelry, and her passport were all missing. She immediately rang Wang Jun, to no avail, tried to get in touch with Mei Rui, who was not answering either. She was probably on her way back to Beijing.

Within minutes of the call Wang Jun was on the phone, trying to calm her down and understand what happened. She told him as best she could about the power cut, and about everything that was missing.

"You're lucky, Lucy, not to have been harmed. Thank the gods for that. I can't get away right now, but I'll send Han over to protect you. He'll contact the management and police. I'll get to the bottom of this somehow. When I do security over there is going to regret they ever let this happen."

"What should I do?"

"Lock the door and sit tight. Call me as soon as Han gets there, or you hear from Mei. I'll talk to Han right away. Better let him warn Mei what's happened. I hope she hasn't lost much."

"Me too. What about my passport and tickets though? How am I going to get them back in time for the flight?'

"Look, you're safe; that's the most important thing. We have good relations with the embassy in Beijing; we'll have someone there work with you on it. I'm sure you can have everything ready to leave here in a week, maybe less. Anyway, you'd better call your husband and let him know you'll be delayed."

"He's not going to be happy."

"I guess not. Look, if he wants to wait for you here we'll pay for a ticket for him; that way maybe you can both stay longer."

Wang Jun had to ring off and get back to his meeting. Lucy waited for Han to arrive. As soon as he did she felt much safer. Within minutes the police appeared too, along with the manager of the complex. They checked what they could, and promised to come back when Mei Rui returned for more details of what was stolen. They gave Lucy an official stamped notice confirming what happened to her lost passport for embassy formalities. They also pointed out marks on the outer door where the thief, or thieves, used a card and pointed instrument to work the door open. The chain, which Lucy was sure she secured before going to bed, had been cut and rejoined with extra links, allowing an intruder to exit without too much trouble. Lucy told them she hadn't noticed the longer door chain when opening the door for Han.

The manager, who spoke broken English, apologized for the break-in. He explained that such thefts were not uncommon. They would check their security videos for the police right away, and he hoped for a quick resolution. After they left, Han shrugged his shoulders as if to say, "these things happen." He called Wang Jun, who talked to Lucy again to calm her, leaving Han to contact Mei as soon as he could. Thirty minutes later she heard Han talking to Mei and could tell by the shouting going on she was also in a panic— and angry! It was another hour before Mei arrived from the airport, rushing past Lucy and straight into her bedroom.

"Oh my god, Lucy," She screamed. "The fuckers have taken everything in here. Shit, shit, shit! What am I going to do?"

Lucy was holding her within seconds. "I'm so sorry, Mei. So sorry."

"What am I doing? Oh my god! At least you're safe. Thank goodness for that. Fuck, fuck, fuck."

Lucy had never heard her swear so vociferously.

"What about you? Anything of yours?" Mei asked.

"Nothing as important as yours. They emptied my purse and a few cheap trinkets are gone. They meant nothing, but my credit cards, the passport . . . that's different. I don't know what I'm going to do."

"That we can do something about . . . the passport I mean. We'll get to work on it once I calm down. Meantime I need to report what's missing. Fuck, fuck, fuck, and fuck again. I should have kept all my jewelry in the safe deposit box, not just a few things."

"Can it all be replaced?"

"Sure . . . not my mother's pearls though; they're priceless to me."

Lucy felt terrible. There she was worrying about an easily replaceable passport, and Mei was losing a precious item from her mother, not to mention the expensive jewelry. There was soon a call from Wang Jun; he asked to be put on Mei's speakerphone so they could both listen in. He told them how sorry he was. He had called the chief of police about the incident, and wanted Mei to know there was full insurance on the apartment and any contents. She told him about her mother's pearls, which nothing could replace, and he was especially sorry for their loss. He told Mei to take care of everything at the apartment before coming back to work, and he urged Lucy to contact her husband right away.

Mei told him it was critical she come to the office then and there to discuss the merger situation. He suggested they go over the key parts on the phone, that she needed to get her matters straightened out in the apartment first.

"No, no, Boss, absolutely not on the phone. I can make the list of what's missing for Han to handle, and head over right away. We need to talk."

"What about Lucy's issues?" Wang Jun asked.

"Lucy, would you be okay if I disappeared for a couple of hours, then get back with you on the passport thing?"

"Of course," Lucy said. "I feel awful about what's happened, that somehow it's all my fault."

"Don't be stupid. Try to call the States while I'm gone. It's late, but they might be up. I'll be back as soon as I can. Han will take care of you."

The two women gave each other a reassuring hug before Mei left, Han asking where the list was she was supposed to give him.

"Later, Han, later," she yelled, as she ran out the door.

Lucy got through to Sarah and explained what happened. She asked her to get hold of Phil and tell him to call her when he could. She thought she would be delayed a week, but the company was offering to fly him out to Beijing if he was concerned. She told Sarah to assure him she was okay; the apartment block was under heightened security, and she was no longer concerned about her safety. Sarah told her Phil seemed fine the last time they talked. The business was doing well, and their monthly regular, Don Roberts, had been in for his usual flowers. He'd been surprised his favorite flower girl was not there and sent his best wishes to her. Sarah assured Lucy she could manage easily until her return, to take as much time as she needed.

The call to Sally was very different. After Lucy went through everything, Sally told her she was pleased to hear about her trouble.

"I'm sorry about your friend's loss, of course, but happy for you. Maybe a few days will give your man a chance to knock some sense into that thick skull of yours. John agrees with me that you're stupid to let this chance go by. We'd both like to meet this Wong guy of yours someday."

"It's Wang, Sally, not Wong. Wang Jun."

"Well, he sounds like just the thing you need. Of course, I'm happy you didn't get hurt or anything in the apartment."

Lucy eventually rang off. Apart from feeling bad for Mei, she was growing more relaxed, a part of her glad she was robbed and had to stay longer. She did not need to lie to Phil now about staying longer, and maybe she could find out more about her father.

When Mei got to the office she was visibly agitated and the other staff steered clear of her. Admired by her peers, popular with other employees, they knew she could be moody and explosive at times. No one knew about the robbery at home, nor did she tell anyone, preferring to see Wang Jun as soon as she could about the merger and Li Buyun meetings. As soon as she approached his office he came out to greet her, put his arm around her, and led her inside. He returned to his desk and motioned for her to sit across from him.

"I can't believe it. I really can't," she said. "All these months living with all that security, and we still get burgled . . . while Lucy is sleeping! Heaven forbid what they might have done to me if I'd been in my own bed last night. Shit, Boss, they only took jewelry and Lucy's things. They never touched the computers, or anything else expensive in there."

"I'm so sorry, Mei, really."

"I don't care about most of the jewelry. It's worth a lot, but it's my mother's pearls that meant the most to me. They can't be replaced. My father gave them to her when they married. How could I lose them after all these years? Will he forgive me?"

She could see that Wang Jun was sympathetic to her situation, and accepted the napkin he passed over to wipe her uncharacteristic tears away.

"Mei, take a look at this," he said, "and please forgive me."

He slid a briefcase across the desk, opened the lid, and motioned her to look inside.

"You son of a pig farmer!" she screamed. "You did it! All along it was you. Why the hell didn't you tell me?"

Wang came around the desk and put his arm around her, holding on as she tried to shrug him off. "I'm sorry, Mei, I couldn't tell you before. I needed you to react as if you really had been robbed. I couldn't afford to have Lucy think otherwise."

"Well, you accomplished that."

"Look, I didn't think she would stay if she thought it was a set-up. You said yourself you needed more time to help her. Don't worry. It's all there . . . your pearls and everything."

"And I suppose I still have to go through this charade with the U.S. embassy, right?"

"Mei, I can't let her go yet. Take as long as you can with the passport . . . please. I really am sorry to have upset you so much."

Mei began to calm down, angry with him, but overjoyed her mother's pearls were still there.

"That's all fine, but what am I going to wear to the celebration tomorrow evening? I can't trot out any of these things until she's back in the U.S. Not that she'd remember what stuff I had."

Another jewelry box was slid across the desk to her.

"Compensation for pain and suffering," he said.

She opened the box, looked at the necklace, earrings, and bracelet, then scrambled around the desk to kiss him. "You nasty man you. You're adorable. They're gorgeous. I won't say you shouldn't have because you absolutely needed to."

"Glad you like them."

"Any time you want to break in again like this, be my guest. Does Han know?"

"No. I had Zhang organize it, if you must know. I needed Han to act surprised too. I'll let you tell him the next time you see him. You better keep your old stuff in the safe here for now. You've got an appointment with the embassy visa section tomorrow at eleven in the morning. That should give you both time to get things started before the evening events."

"Who is it with this time, Joe or Michael?"

"With Michael. He's promised to move it through as slowly as he can."

"You really are an evil man, Mr. Wang Jun. If only she knew about your devious ways . . . wonder if she would still love you."

"Of course, Mei. Maybe more. Now let's have some tea. We need to talk about Nanjing and where we go from here. I'm sure Lucy is anxious to follow up with you on her father too. At least now you'll have another week, thanks to yours truly."

"Who was in my bedroom by the way?" She asked.

"Your hacker friend of Zhang's, young Li. He tells me you have some really nice underwear there."

"As if you didn't know," Mei said with a mischievous smile

Chapter 15

Lucy received a message from Sarah; Phil had been told about the robbery and was relieved she was all right. He wanted Lucy to thank her hosts for offering to pay for his ticket to come over there, but reminded her there was no way he would fly. He missed her, but was having a good time on the road trip; with her delay he was planning to stop off on the way back, and spend a few days visiting an old army buddy.

Sarah passed along a number Lucy could use to try and to reach Phil if she needed to. His friend's name was Ralph, she passed on, but if the men weren't around, she could talk to his wife, Peggy. The last part of the message was to bring him back something nice. She was relieved he was all right with her delay; as much as she disliked his friends, it appeared they were helping again.

Mei had taken an earlier call in her office from Lucy. She was feeling happier now that her husband was not pressing for her to return right away. Later she headed for a meeting with Wang Jun, who asked right away if Lucy was okay.

"She's fine, "Mei told him. "You'll be happy to hear her husband is okay for another week, especially that he declined your kind offer and won't be coming over. She needs to find him something nice to take him back though. I said we'd take care of it for her. Any ideas?"

"Yes, actually. Get him a nice Harley Davidson rider's leather jacket with a Beijing logo on the back. I bet he'll like that. Charge it to the evening. Xin won't mind."

Mei thought it a great idea, stepped out of the room, and called Han. She asked him to head out and buy three sizes of jackets for Lucy to choose from. With that in process it was time for Mei to get back to the events in Nanjing. The first part of their discussions was to be the merger, then a strategy for it. Chairman Xin was called in briefly to join the meeting, which also included their top legal and financial managers. The immediate task was to appoint a project manager, then get a team in contact with Li Buyun's daughter and start the process.

The media chief and legal people were delegated to draft a public announcement to submit to Madame Li in Nanjing for review. Xin agreed to personally oversee its preparation. Wang Jun asked if he was willing to stick around beyond retirement to help see the process through for them. Xin initially declined, but Mei supported Wang's request, intimating she thought that perhaps he had some prior association with Li, something that might help things go smoother. Mei could sense Xin's discomfort at their request, but with Wang Jun pressing him to agree he relented, committing only to involvement on an as-needed basis.

Once everyone left the room, Wang Jun stayed back to talk alone with Mei about Lucy. His assistant came in to clear everything from the conference table, but Mei stopped her and asked for everything to be left where it was.

"Is our Mr. Zhang waiting outside?" she asked.

"Yes, Mei Rui, he's been sitting there for over an hour, poor man."

"Can you send him in and leave us alone for a while, please?"

Puzzled, Wang Jun nodded to his assistant to send Zhang in. "What's this about, Mei? Nanjing? The theft? Or your underwear?"

Mei told him it was nothing to do with that. She motioned Zhang over to the conference table as he came in, checking again which cups Wang Jun and the chairman had used.

"Okay, Zhang, take these two and have them analyzed as fast as you can, please. Oh, and by the way, tell young Li if he, or you, say anything about my underwear I'll have Han cut your balls off."

Zhang quickly bagged both cups and spoons separately, and apologized for the intrusion. After telling Mei he'd heard her red thongs were the sexiest, he left as quickly as he could. Wang Jun's amusement with Zhang quickly turned to anger.

"What are you checking, Mei? And what the hell do Xin and I have to do with this? You're checking our DNA against Li Buyun? Or is it Lucy's? Are you going to tell me we're all related or something?"

"I'm just ruling out everything, Boss. I'm sure there's nothing there."

Wang was annoyed, tempted to call Zhang back in, but after what he had put Mei through of late he figured he would let her go ahead with the tests. He was sure neither he nor Xin had any connections with Madame Li or Lucy. And if it turned out Xin was his father, well, that would not be an unwelcome revelation. Then again, everything he knew about his parents told him it was impossible, or so he thought.

"Okay, go ahead, but the information stays between us, and Zhang keeps his mouth shut, unless I approve it. Understood?"

"Of course. I'm more interested in Xin and Li anyway based on what she said to me," Mei said.

"Walk me through everything you heard down there. Don't leave anything out."

Mei left Wang's office after two hours. The discussion about Madame Li had gone on far longer than expected and Lucy's situation remained a mystery. The father's connection was the key to it, but she knew there were still pieces missing. Wang Jun suggested they do more digging and meet the next day, that Mei take care of Lucy in the evening as he had too much to catch up on; he needed to work on the merger. He suggested Mei take her shopping for jewelry to wear at the celebration, something to go with the chipao he bought her.

"How much do you want me to spend, Boss?"

He walked over to the safe in the corner of his office, opened it, and threw Mei a large pack of hundred yuan notes.

"Do you want something cheap or classy?" Another thick wad of notes came her way.

"This is my own, by the way, not the company's."

"Elegant it is then . . . do you need the change?"

"After what I spent on yours, absolutely."

Mei headed back to her apartment, leaving Wang Jun to think about how much of this to tell Lucy. Mei recommended the whole truth, the fake robbery too, but Wang was against shattering Lucy's image of her father, or her dead mother. He was also worried about how she was going to react to finding out that Mei had been with Li Buyun. He was desperate to please her, but would all of this turn her against him? Should he call Madame Li direct about what they knew, or talk to Xin? He finally decided to mull it over, see what more Mei came up with, and then decide after their evening's event.

There would be important businesspeople at the celebration— city government personnel and a number of key Party officials. The crackdown on corruption and lavish spending forced them to put together an event that was considered appropriate and would in no way draw unwelcome attention to him, the chairman, or their businesses.

Xin told him there was no need for any of it at all, preferring to retire quietly, but Wang would have none of it. They had accomplished great things together, and Xin as his mentor was like a father to him, their association bringing him personal wealth. He felt it his filial duty, like a true son, to honor Xin as meaningfully as he could. He was grateful to him for inviting Lucy to China to commemorate their beginning, a request he had been happy to arrange. The trouble was, his loathing for his own marriage deepened every minute he spent around her.

Lucy enjoyed her evening with Mei, despite missing the opportunity to spend another night with Wang Jun. They had dinner at an Italian restaurant alongside the lake in Chaoyang Park, then went shopping for jewelry to wear at the celebration. When told this was to be another gift from Wang Jun, Lucy was adamant they find something nice, but not expensive. Mei tried to push her towards an expensive bracelet and earrings, but she insisted on choosing a cheaper alternative, though Mei could see they would look great with the chipao dress.

When they got back to the apartment Lucy tried again to call Phil. It was early morning in the U.S. and she could only find his friend's wife, Peggy. She sounded friendly, telling Lucy the boys, as she called them, were already off fishing. They were having a great time, and most importantly Phil was a tonic for her husband. The more Peggy opened up about her own problems, the closer Lucy felt to her.

Peggy talked about experiencing many of the same difficulties with her husband, even though Lucy could tell he had not suffered as much in the war. By the time Lucy ended the call they decided to stay in touch and encourage their husbands and families to get to know each other better. Lucy promised to contact her again when she got back to Blowing Rock, and thanked her for taking care of her husband while her passport problem was resolved. Peggy told her to stay as long as she liked. Phil was a real boost for her husband's state of mind, and she was grateful for him being there.

—⸺—

Wang Jun was busy making sure his assistant and marketing people had all the arrangements in place for the celebration, trying to balance a memorable evening without the impression of undue excess. They avoided using top-flight hotels that had been used in the past for such events, but still selected an elegant Crowne Plaza hotel for the event. Located in the Lido area, it was within easy reach of the airport for people flying in. A large block of rooms and suites were reserved for certain key people. It was likely most would pay their own bills to avoid any hint of impropriety, but the company would still pay for any guests if asked.

The evening's food would be first class, featuring dishes originating from Xin's hometown in Shanxi Province. For the table toasts Wang's people traveled to Shanxi to buy a large quantity of Xin's favorite local baijiu. Guests would be given bottles to take back as mementos, with labels commemorating the evening. Wang had elected not to serve the Maotai brand of white liquor. Although renowned by many as the best baijiu in China, it was expensive and might have raised eyebrows. In any event, once the heavy toasting was under way, he was sure no one would notice the difference. The main expense of the evening would be the entertainment, along with a specially prepared video covering Xin's career and the rise of their businesses.

Xin was an avid collector of Buddhist artifacts; Wang Jun obtained an ancient jade Buddha dating back to the earliest days of Buddhism in China as his special retirement gift. The video was expensive to make, but could easily be modified to promote the group companies later. A number of Global Industry executives were invited as a matter of courtesy, since they too had benefitted from intra-company business with Xin's group.

The one thorny issue in some respects was where to seat Lucy; despite wives being invited it was likely to be a male-dominated evening, except for the chairman's family. Wang Jun's wife, to his relief, refused to give up her mahjong evening with friends to attend any event with Xin. She always complained to her husband over what she felt was undue influence by the chairman, especially when it came to his share of the businesses. Wang knew he could not seat Lucy next to him; that was too obvious. He couldn't put her by Xin, since the two leaders would have to be at the head table with their most senior guests. Instead, Wang decided to put her with Mei at a table near Xin's family along with other foreigners, primarily those from Global Industries where she had worked all those years before.

At eleven Mei arrived with Lucy at the American Embassy for their passport meeting. They were met separately from the crowd and led to a special room. The guard left them alone until a young Chinese-American came in, loaded down with files, to welcome them.

"Mei Rui, good to see you again." The two hugged warmly. "How is business these days? Our commercial people are most appreciative of the good relations they have with Wang Jun's group. This must be Mrs. Summers, I presume."

"It is indeed, Michael. Let me introduce you. Lucy, this is Michael Song." Lucy rose and shook his hand, sitting back down across from him.

"She's had a harrowing experience, Michael, like me I might add."

"I was sorry to hear about it, Mei. I can certainly take care of Mrs. Summers issues, but can't do much about yours I'm afraid. What happened?"

Lucy went over the details and provided Michael with a copy of the police report.

"Ah yes, this is fine, Lucy, if I can call you that. I do need to contact the police to verify the notice. I'm sure it's authentic, but fakes are so prevalent here I have to follow protocol. That part should only take a couple of days. I have the paperwork here for you to fill out, and we'll need photographs. Is there an emergency at all? Do you have to get back to the U.S. right away?" Michael asked.

Mei glanced at Lucy, who shook her head. When Lucy was distracted Mei glared at him, but was relieved to hear Lucy repeat it was not urgent and another week would be fine.

"Sorry, I have to ask these questions. We have a lot of people coming in saying everything is an emergency; many times it isn't. We like to go through hoops only when it is life-threatening. Be assured, though, we'll move things along as quickly as we can. I may need to see you again. If I do, I'll call Mei. Meantime. if you would complete all these forms for me we can get the process moving. I have another interview right now, but I'll be back later to finish with you."

Lucy thanked Mei for everything after Michael left. It all seemed less complicated than she had thought it would be. She completed all the forms and the two waited for Michael's return. Once the forms were reviewed he told Lucy not to worry, he would personally follow the application through. They would need to exchange e-mails with the U.S. to check various things, but he anticipated no problems.

"Unfortunately, Lucy, you would be surprised if I told you some of the things people have done to obtain U.S. passports. I know it doesn't apply to you, but it has made the process more difficult lately. We used to be able to process these things really quickly, so please don't call me too many names if it runs longer than a week. I doubt it will, but you never know, and all we need is our two governments to have a little visa tiff to slow things down. Use your extra time here to enjoy everything Beijing has to offer. You couldn't ask for a better guide than Mei here."

"You're right about that, Mr. Song."

Mei smiled. "Michael, please. If I can help at all, here is my card and cell phone number," she said.

Lucy thanked Michael for his help and headed to the door, Mei turned back, with a look that said, "Are you trying to hit on my friend?" Michael grinned, mouthing to her, "She's gorgeous."

———⚬⚭⚬———

That afternoon Mei took a number of calls, one from Zhang asking her to meet him the next morning. She told Lucy they were in for a treat that afternoon, thanks to the boss, at a nearby spa and beauty parlor; the two would relax in luxury before being getting ready for the evening. Lucy was pleased to hear she would be at a table with the Global Industry people, thankful Mei would be with them too. Lucy said she knew none of the executives coming from Dallas, but recognized the one named Dick Humphrey whom she called when tracking Wang Jun down. Mei could tell Lucy was relieved to hear that Wang Jun's wife would not be there. Mei was more blunt and said she was happy "the bitch" was going to be nowhere near them.

———⚬⚭⚬———

By five the two women were ready to be picked up for the celebration. Han was occupied with the arrival at the airport of a senior official, so they were to be taken by another limo service to the hotel. Each complimented the other on their looks and dresses; Mei was not as beautiful, but oozed a sensuality that even Lucy admired and could see would draw men to her. Mei envied Lucy's long hair, slim figure, special dress, and the way she carried herself.

Lucy seemed nervous about the event and put it down to having been away from the business world for some years. Mei poured them both stiff gin martinis, pleased to see Lucy becoming more relaxed and gregarious about the night ahead as they drank.

The celebration was to start at six thirty, with an hour long reception before everyone was seated. Wang Jun asked them both to be there ahead of time for introductions and helping to welcome his special guests. When the two walked in Wang Jun's jaw dropped. Mei looked gorgeous, but Lucy's appearance was stunning and left him speechless for a moment. He gave them both a warm embrace, whispering to Lucy that she looked marvelous and he loved her, then complimented Mei on how pretty she looked, especially the jewelry she was wearing.

"Glad you like it. An old boyfriend bought it for me. After losing everything the other night his timing was perfect."

Lucy nudged her, demanding to know when she would get to meet him.

Mei smiled back mischievously. "I'm afraid he's a married man, so I doubt you will see him with me anytime soon."

Wang Jun asked Mei to put her company hat back on, to go around and make sure nothing was amiss with the arrangements. He also took her aside and advised her there was to be no announcement of the Nanjing merger discussions during the evening, and certainly no one was to talk about Li Buyun with Lucy around. He asked Lucy to get a drink and visit with his assistant until the Global Industry people arrived; then she could join them for the evening. He told her they were looking forward to meeting her, especially Dick Humphrey, who remembered talking to her on the phone and would enjoy reminiscing about their old boss, Bob Jenkins.

Chapter 16

The evening proved to be a success. All the planning and organization made the event especially meaningful for Chairman Xin. He gave an emotional speech after Wang Jun presented his retirement gift. The video itself drew applause for demonstrating all Xin and his companies had achieved. Wang Jun played down any role in their success, but Xin remedied that in his own remarks. His Shanxi family members had been flown in for the event, and their pride in their patriarch's achievements was evident to all there.

As the evening progressed to the entertainment, the toasting activities began in earnest, with Xin circulating the room to toast every table of guests as tradition dictated. Wang was careful to provide Xin with an attractive girl, dressed in traditional Shanxi style and armed with a bottle of low alcohol baijiu and water. She poured small shots for him to toast as he circulated, often substituting water when no one was looking.

Lucy was enjoying the evening with the Global executives, even though she didn't know any of them. She talked about her old boss, Bob Jenkins, and told everyone stories of their early negotiations with Xin. Dick Humphrey seemed overly attentive to Mei, who was keeping a protective watch over Lucy. The liquor flowed heavily at their table, but Mei could see that Lucy was handling it well.

Humphrey, however, was clearly not used to the white baijiu and became too forward for her liking. She decided to put a finish to any potentially embarrassing situation, and made the man "gambei" two glasses of baijiu with her — very large ones. Humphrey became more intoxicated to the point that his directors quietly advised him to give it a rest and leave. But aside from that Lucy was a hit with everyone who met her. She had to repeatedly assure everyone she was of Vietnamese origin, not Chinese, an American father for sure. "American as apple pie," she told them.

Mei saw how Xin looked at Lucy from time to time; she particularly noticed how the family was introduced to her, many of them touching her in a way Mei thought unusual for Chinese. It told her everything she needed to know, or so she thought.

By the time the evening came to a close Lucy was somewhat intoxicated, but seemingly in a comfortable way. Mei knew she had drunk too much herself, and that putting Dick Humphrey out of action might not have been her smartest move. She was feeling no pain when the Xin family party announced they were leaving, well before the evening was scheduled to end. Along the way out, guests came up to shake Xin's hand and wish him well. He stopped by the Global table in particular and thanked everyone for coming, especially Lucy. Mei watched the family hugging Lucy with obvious affection, then pulled Xin to one side, later worrying she had overstepped the mark by what she quietly said next.

"Chairman Xin, forgive me if I offend you in any way, but I know that Lucy is your daughter . . . and I'll prove it. She is a wonderful person and you can be proud of her."

Xin stepped back, continued to smile, then leaned over and whispered, "My office, nine o'clock sharp. You may not be as clever as you think you are, young lady."

Mei's face drained at his words, but he patted her on the shoulder. "Now enjoy the rest of your evening. Don't worry about what we just said to each other; it's okay. Really. We will talk in the morning. Make sure Lucy is okay, will you?"

"Of course, and thank you, Chairman, I'll take care of her."

Mei turned to see Wang Jun and Lucy departing by a side door, pausing for Wang to wave as the two left for her apartment and away from prying eyes. Wang had booked a room at the hotel for Mei to stay the night, but she didn't want to spend it alone, especially after her words with Xin. She began looking around to decide who was going to share her bed; it would have to be a short night if she was to meet Xin as planned in the morning. She was already organized for the evening, her overnight bag stored in the hotel, anticipating what her boss planned for the night with Lucy.

When they arrived at the apartment building, Wang Jun thanked Han for bringing them, then told him to head off to the party if he wanted to. He passed along a key and told him to use his suite, rather than drive after drinking.

Wang Jun told Lucy that Han would definitely be headed back to the hotel. More than likely he was going to end up with Mei. He could see Lucy's expression, but told her the two understood each other very well, and Han was as much her protector as anyone. While there was great affection between them, he said, neither one had any doubt each was using the other for pure pleasure.

As they rode the elevator, Wang told her he only wanted to talk to her that night, hold her close, and sleep with her until the morning. He answered her puzzled look by asking her to understand their relationship wasn't about sex, and he wanted to prove it. She said there was no need. What they felt for each other went way beyond that, but it was up to him. There was little sleep that night for either of them as Wang Jun tried to convince Lucy her future was with him, that he would divorce and marry her the moment she agreed. It was the one thing he wanted most, and lamented how this was the one thing his money couldn't simply buy for him. They talked for hours about Phil, his wife, their own problems, the past, the last few days together, and especially the joy in finding each other again. They laughed a lot, held each other close, and cried together.

As much as he tried, Wang Jun couldn't get around Lucy's commitment to her husband. She told him they could enjoy the few days left, and hope that somehow in the future things would be different. Wang suggested an imaginary position for her in his U.S. operations, something that would require her to travel to Beijing occasionally. She was sorely tempted, but told him she would continue with the shop and taking care of Phil.

———— ∞∞∞ ————

At five in the morning Wang awoke to find Lucy climbing on top of him and throwing the sheets back. "You've proved your point, John, but enough of it. We only have days left. I'm not going waste a moment of it. I love you, and will until the day I die."

He felt himself stiffen as she reached down to hold and guide him towards her. She told him to do nothing, to just lie there, then brushed his eyelids down with her fingertips and pulled the sheet over his face. Was the way she chose to make love to him so passionately her expression of love and caring for him? Or a hunger inside her she still had not satisfied?

He tried to control himself for as long as he could, until he heard Lucy begin to moan, which only accelerated the ending he had struggled to delay. The two climaxed together after he rolled Lucy onto her back and took control. They lay for another two hours and slept peacefully until Wang Jun climbed out of bed and told Lucy he had to get to the office.

He had many things to get moving on the Nanjing merger and would be meeting with Mei and the chairman. He suggested Lucy rest for the day, or meet up with the Global Industry people for the tour and shopping that Mei had arranged. Lucy said she preferred to have a lazy day, perhaps walk across to the Chaoyang Park and spend time there on her own. He told her he was obligated to dine with the Global people, but that he would see her later.

When he was ready to leave, Lucy followed him to the door naked. She held him close and tried to persuade him to skip his meetings. He was sorely tempted, but there was no way. He caressed and kissed her one last time, waited for her to become aroused yet again, then promptly opened the door and left her pouting and swearing at him.

———— ∞∞∞ ————

Mei was sitting outside Xin's office at nine in the morning waiting for him to arrive. She felt surprisingly refreshed after the evening's events, the drinking, and especially the rest of the night trying to keep up with Han. She couldn't help but smile to herself at some of the things they had done to each other. It would keep her going for some time before she needed it again. She straightened her blouse and continued chatting with Xin's assistant. Xin was on the way, but stuck in traffic.

Mei took a few calls on her cell phone, gave out some project tasks to some of her other people, and then took an urgent call from Zhang.

"Is there anything wrong, Mei?" the assistant asked.

Mei knew her face had reddened. The lady had seen her obvious concern. "Is there a problem," she asked again.

"Nothing, it's fine. Just something I need to attend to right away. Please excuse me. Tell Xin when he arrives I was here, but had to take a call." Mei left the area and called Zhang right back.

"Are you sure? I mean a hundred percent?" she asked, and listened intently to his response. "Okay. I have to go. Xin is on his way and I promised to be there when he arrives. Can you do another check on this for me today, please?'

"It won't be different, Mei. You know there's no point."

"For me then, and call me if you find anything different."

"Only for you, but it's a waste of time." Zhang rang off.

⸎

Mei walked back to Xin's outer office to find the assistant explaining how Mei had already waited for him but was taking another call.

As she came up behind him he turned to greet her. "Ah, Mei, I'm so sorry to be late. The traffic was terrible. Come in. Come drink some tea with me."

His assistant headed out to make tea, as Xin led Mei into his inner office. They talked about the evening and how pleased Xin's family had been with everything. Once the tea was served Xin went right to the point.

"So, investigator Mei, you think Lucy Summers is my daughter, heh?"

"I'm sorry, Chairman, if I offended you. It's just that I really like Lucy, and I'm trying to help her figure out what's really going on with her father."

"And what does she know?"

"Frankly, I know a lot more than she does at this point. I'm worried she might hate me when she finds out what I've been doing."

"That's something we won't know until you tell her. Assuming I am the father of Lucy, as you think, why don't you tell me everything you know?"

"Shouldn't we have Wang Jun with us for these discussions?"

"Later, Mei. Let's figure out what we do and do not know before we decide on that. Don't hide anything from me. I'm not annoyed with you, but if I find you haven't told me everything you may not like what I can do to your career here."

Mei felt stung. He had said it calmly, but she had no doubt how serious a situation she could find herself in if she lied or left anything out.

———— ✦ ————

They talked for over two hours. Xin blocked all incoming calls and instructed his assistant to keep well-wishers away while they were in conference. When they finished Mei suggested it was a good time to talk to Wang Jun, but Xin thought it better that the three of them got together after lunch. He had a number of things to catch up on for now. As she rose to leave, Xin came around his desk and hugged her, the way she remembered her grandfather had as a child.

"Don't worry, Mei, it will be fine, trust me. This is long overdue . . . some of us have kept things hidden for far too long. I only hope Lucy finds some peace in this, and happiness, with or without Wang Jun. She's strong willed like her mother. I can see that now."

"You're right about her being strong willed. What time do you want to meet?"

"Call Wang Jun and set us up to meet at three."

Mei left for Wang's office thinking about everything they had uncovered and what Xin had told her. Wang's assistant told her he had already left for a lunch meeting and wouldn't be back that afternoon. She phoned him direct, outlined Xin's request for a meeting, and what it was about. He suggested they meet at two; he would cut his lunch short to listen to what she had uncovered.

⚬⚬⚬

Li Buyun was surprised to hear that Chairman Xin was calling to talk privately. She hadn't seen or spoken to him in years. Whenever they had been near each other they avoided contact. Curious at first why he would be calling she took the call, but within seconds her emotions got the better of her and she swore at Xin. Eventually, when she had vented her rage and could think of no more insults, sat back and listened. Her screaming had been so loud that an assistant came in, leaving abruptly when Li cursed at her too and threw an ornate vase off the desk against the wall. She finally willed herself to listen to Xin.

"Okay, Li, you can calm down . . . listen to me for a change."

"What the hell for? You weren't the one that suffered."

"I understand how you feel, but this has to stop. You and I are older now. What happened before is over and we need to put it behind us."

"That? Or is this just about getting your hands on our business as well?"

"The merger is good business for both our companies, and you know it, especially for you and your daughter; I've made sure of that. On the other side it's time to put the past behind us, Li, and for others to know the truth. I think you might be surprised how much good it will do for your soul. We will pass from this life at peace with ourselves, at least I will."

"What truth is it you want to tell her?" Li asked.

She listened to Xin relay all Mei Rui had uncovered, some of which she knew from her own discussions during their recent meeting. Xin filled in the gaps, especially concerning Lucy's real mother and father. She tried to convince Xin they should not discuss any of it, especially with her daughter, Zhao Wen. He warned her Lucy was going to be told everything, that she could be a part of it or not. He recommended she put aside any fears and let the truth be known.

She went silent. When Xin had asked several times if she was still on the line she finally spoke, chuckling as she responded, " Xin, you never change, do you? As big a rogue as you can be in business, you are as honest as they come in other ways. No matter what I say you are going to tell this Lucy Summers everything, even if I kowtow to you and beg you with all my heart not to. Am I right?"

"Yes, but you can help," Xin said.

"Look, I'll help, but only as much as I agreed to with Mei Rui. My daughter has to be left out of it. That's my condition. Period."

"Li, I understand how you feel, I really do. From what I hear of your daughter she can handle it. What do you think is going to happen anyway when she moves into the top position and takes on a leadership role? This is a global world we're moving into. You don't think one day Lucy is going to read about a Li Buyun, who she's been searching for, giving up the reins of her company to her young daughter? A daughter who looks like this girl's own father? Come on Li, it's going to happen. Lucy is a very smart young lady."

"So is your Mei Rui, unfortunately," Li said.

"Not entirely, but yes she is a good investigator, and she is not going to keep quiet over this. She's grown attached to Lucy, and I might add she speaks highly of your daughter— even you, once she got beyond your foul mouth."

Li laughed. "Give me twenty-four hours to think about it. You can do that, can't you?"

"Only until my meeting with Lucy this afternoon. It's at three, so call me an hour before. Lucy, Mei, and Wang Jun will be there to hear what I have to tell them."

"You really are an old bastard, Xin. There was a time you could have been Zhao Wen's father yourself . . . do you remember?"

"How can I forget? Call me back as soon as you can. Whatever happens let's get together some time. We've been through too much not to be friends again."

"I'll think about that too. I have to go now, I'll call you when I'm ready."

After the call she had to admit feeling better. She already knew what her answer was, but decided to keep him waiting until the last moment.

Chapter 17

They gathered in Xin's office as planned. Mei had brought everything she had discovered into the meeting; the material from the hard drives Lucy provided, as well as separate reports from Zhang. The discussions concerning the merger process went quickly, and the release to the public was approved with only minor changes. It was to be sent off to Li Buyun right away for her lawyers to review and approve.

The situation with Lucy was more complicated. For some time there was conversation about what she would, or should be told. Mei was concerned about how it might affect Lucy's trust in them, and how she was going to look at her father once she knew everything. The look on Wang Jun's face told Mei he was more worried about how it might affect Lucy's feelings for him. In the end Xin insisted she be told everything. If it affected her view of any of them, then so be it. He told them he could not go to his grave with a clear conscience unless he made sure the truth was revealed.

Deciding where they would meet and how they would tell her was an issue brought up by Wang Jun. Should it be separately, together, in a social gathering, at Mei's apartment, or in Xin's office? They settled on meeting in the board-room later that day. Xin indicated there was something he needed to discuss at the meeting that required him to go home briefly. It was agreed that Mei should phone Lucy and tell her of a meeting to discuss her search for Li Buyun, that she and Han would pick her up, and they were invited to Xin's home for dinner afterwards.

———

Lucy received the call from Mei and was excited to hear there was news of Li Buyun. She was a little frustrated by Mei's reluctance to explain what the news might be. When Mei arrived, Lucy was eager to question her more about Li Buyun. The celebration and her recent days with Wang Jun had been special, but finding the key behind her father's withdrawal into himself was still paramount. Mei refused to tell her anything, asking her to be patient until everyone was together.

———

This was the first time Lucy had visited Wang Jun's group headquarters. She had been to his "black factory " in a poor section of Beijing, but this was totally different. The office complex was ultra-modern and fit Wang Jun's image perfectly, but Mei also pointed out the chairman's heavy influence in the design. Lucy could sense the longevity in the architecture and Chinese classicism; the power of the company permeated the lobby area and beyond. She was impressed as Mei walked her through the security areas to the private offices where Wang and Xin held court. The building had an open feeling to it, allowing the two main leaders to wander the rest of the organization as they often did, but gave them privacy when needed.

Lucy sensed the loyalty and respect in employees as she was introduced to them, but she felt everyone was scrutinizing her as she followed Mei into the boardroom. All she could think was, "I'm being checked out. How much do they know?" She looked at Mei, as if to say she knew what was on everyone's mind, then told herself not to be ridiculous.

———

In the boardroom, Xin was seated at the head of the table, with Wang Jun to his right. They both rose right away to greet her, their look more serious than before. She still felt their warmth, but wondered why everyone in the room seemed uncomfortable. Wang Jun positioned the four of them at a smaller table, away from the large windows of the boardroom. He placed Lucy to the right of Xin, according to Chinese custom, signifying her as the most important guest. Instead of sitting on the other side of Xin, he sat next to Lucy. Mei was asked to sit directly opposite; a number of binders were already on the table.

As they settled down, Mei got up to pour tea for everyone. Xin walked back to his desk and opened a case, remove some old papers and an album, and laid them on the table too. Lucy noticed a slight look of surprise on the other two's faces. Was this something they were not expecting? She began to realize this whole meeting had been planned and orchestrated by Xin; something was coming, but what? She tried to appear calm, waiting for someone to get things started.

Finally Xin opened the discussions. "Lucy, my dear, we are very happy to have you here. I know you are anxious to hear what Mei Rui has discovered. She is quite an impressive researcher, as you know." He glanced at Mei before adding, "Not always perfect, but very good nonetheless. We'll start our story for you by having Mei tell you what she has been up to these past days."

"Up to, Uncle Xin? What do you mean, up to?"

Wang Jun reached over and held her hand. "Lucy, you need to understand you're loved by everyone at this table. Whatever we've done was for you, it was with the best intentions. We want you to feel like one of our family here. Please never forget that."

Lucy wasn't sure how to respond. What were they about to tell her?

———— ⁂ ————

Mei was uncomfortable. This was not how she wanted to handle it, but everyone sat waiting for her to begin, especially Lucy.

"As you know, Lucy, finding your Li Buyun was our main concern, and what was behind the correspondence with your father. You discovered two identities for him, a Richard Towers and the other, John Wainright."

"That's right, go on."

"You brought along two hard drives you'd found of your father's, which you allowed us to try to open. As you know, we told you we had limited access, and showed you everything we said we could get into."

"Yes, that's all true. But where's this headed? Have you found Li Buyun?"

"We'll get to that. I'm embarrassed now to tell you we accessed both your hard drives, and we lied to you that we couldn't."

"What? Why would you do that? Why didn't you tell me before?"

"We're going to tell you now, really we are. Please be patient and forgive me if you can. I'm also ashamed to tell you that what you brought to us proved very useful to our own businesses." Wang Jun and Xin nodded to Lucy at that remark.

Mei continued. "The information we showed you on the one drive was only part of the data on it. The other drive was highly confidential. Top secret is probably a more accurate statement. Anyway, we copied all the information; it's here for you to read, keep, or destroy if you want to."

"Mei, you're starting to frighten me. What the hell's in those files?" Lucy asked.

"I'll get to that later. I think there's other information you're going to be more interested in, if you'll just let me explain."

They could all see Lucy was becoming angry and Wang Jun interrupted. "Lucy, there's a lot to tell you. I know it's difficult, but you'll be wise to let Mei tell you everything she knows. We have the whole week before you go back; we can go over everything later, as much as you like."

Lucy promised she would try to listen to what Mei had to say. None of them thought she was going to stay quiet for long.

"When you talked to me first, Lucy, I assumed that this Li Buyun must have been your real mother. I know you said to me you were part Vietnamese, but to me you could just as easily be Chinese."

"I'm part Vietnamese, like I told you already!"

"So you said. At any rate, I quietly took a glass from you one day, and Zhang had a DNA analysis done to establish a baseline on you, in case we ever found your Li Buyun. We looked for him, or her, in Beijing. There were only a few, which we already talked to you about, but no viable candidates. What we found on the confidential drive, however, was a useful clue, one particular company and reference that led me to the real Li Buyun."

"A man or woman?"

"A woman"

"You've found her?"

"Yes. As you know, here in China wives don't take their husband's name, so initially I didn't spot that she was Zhao Chungang's wife, until I saw the reference to him dying and his wife assuming control of his company."

"So where is she then?"

"She owns and runs Sunrise Chemicals in Nanjing."

"You were there last week, Mei. You said nothing about her. Is this whole thing only about your merger?"

"Not directly, Lucy. But yes I was there. The information you brought helped us . . . how to put it . . . persuade Li to agree to a merger they would never do before."

"You all used me?" Lucy turned to Wang Jun in disbelief.

Mei cut her off quickly before she could say anything. "No, not really. It may seem that way to you now, but hear us out. Then you can make up your mind if what we did was worth it to you or not, okay?"

Lucy looked hurt and confused. She pulled her hand away from Wang Jun's, as if separating herself from everyone at the table.

Mei could see how uncomfortable she was with her too. "You might as well know, Lucy, I also bagged a glass from Li Buyun's office. Zhang had her DNA analyzed too."

"And, I'm her daughter. Is that it?"

"No, Lucy, you're not. In fact experts have reviewed the results and this report confirms you have no Vietnamese in you at all. It won't say it categorically, only that it's highly probable you're part American and Chinese," Mei said.

"That can't be. My father told me I was an orphan, brought from Vietnam. I had an American father, and my mother told me the same thing."

"There's more. Li Buyun has a daughter; I got a fleeting glance of her in Li's office. My instincts told me to play a hunch and see her reaction. The young woman bore a striking resemblance to the photos of your father, so with all the other documents I have, I lied, said I had DNA evidence that John Wainright was the father of her daughter."

"And is he?"

"Yes, Lucy, he is. She finally admitted it too. I tried to get her to agree to meet your father along with her daughter, but she's only agreed to help you herself. She refuses to allow her daughter to become involved. I tried to use some of our information to persuade her, but she still wouldn't change her mind."

"What else did you find about out about my father?' Lucy asked, pointing to the pile of documents by Mei.

"Your father's real name is John Wainright, yes, but Richard Towers was the name he used in China later working alongside Goldman Sachs. As John Wainright, he was in China in the early eighties, when the country was opening up. He posed as a commercial specialist with different companies, but actually worked for your State Department.

"A spy?"

"I found nothing to say he was with the CIA as a spy, but the correspondence does show him obtaining and passing along a lot of information."

"You mean military stuff . . . state secrets?"

"Some of both, a lot more economic and political material though. At the time it would have been more serious than today, but given the years that your father was involved over here, it's obvious he led a dangerous life."

Lucy interrupted. "What about with Goldman then?"

"That's different. He was working with them for sure, but also spent more time on political and economic work, much of it dealing with the Party as before. He probably kept those secret files for future protection."

"So what was the connection with Li Buyun? How old is his daughter? Is she my sister or something?"

"Her name's Zhao Wen. She's about your age, a bit younger, not as attractive as you, but certainly very smart. And your father's looks are readily apparent if you meet her."

"Does she know?" Lucy asked.

"Not yet, but we hope Madame Li will see the light, that you two can meet and talk, especially about your father."

"How is that going to help?"

Mei pointed to some of the documents on the table Lucy had not seen. "Your father was begging Li to allow him to see his daughter, especially since your mother passed away and he learned Li's husband was dead too."

"You think that was all it took to throw my father into his state of withdrawal? Sorry I don't buy it, Mei."

"I don't understand that either. She was certainly angry your father didn't arrange for the child to be smuggled out of China. She hated him for what she and her daughter endured when he left."

"Endured what?" Lucy asked.

"They were shipped to a remote part of Inner Mongolia. She was accused of being a traitor, her daughter ridiculed for having foreign blood. A lot of bad things happened to them. She was considered a whore, you know, and I'm sorry to tell you, raped mercilessly while she was banished."

Lucy was visibly shaken," That's terrible, how were they saved?"

"This Zhao Chungang was running the camp out there, a prisoner himself at one time, a very smart chemistry professor before. He saved her. He fell in love with her and the baby, protected them until everything changed and they were rehabilitated. With his former connections and the opening up under Chairman Deng, they were somehow able to develop a small chemical operation near Hohhot, right there in Inner Mongolia. They were successful, expanded the business, and moved to Nanjing. Later they took over Sunrise with government help and some old friends in high places. It was all part of the privatization effort."

"Is that it? Anything more? What about me?"

"Nothing, I'm afraid. I hope you forgive me for not telling you before." Mei glanced over at the chairman. "What I will say is that Li Buyun told me she'd kept quiet about certain things, and that I should speak to Chairman Xin about that. I did wonder if he might be your father after that."

"Uncle Xin? You must be kidding. You want to get yourself fired?"

Xin sat back and laughed. It was the first time any of them had smiled since the meeting began.

"Don't think I invaded your privacy and Li's only," Mei said. " I made sure I had a sample from the daughter, Chairman Xin here, and Wang Jun too." Mei explained how she had watched the Xin family's reaction to Lucy at the retirement evening, and seen what she herself had been missing all along— a family resemblance with Lucy.

"That's crazy!" Lucy shook her head in disbelief.

Mei went on. "But when they compared the DNA of your sample with the chairman's, I was assured he is not your father." Before she could continue, Xin rose and told everyone it was his turn to speak. He told them to take a fifteen-minute break, and give Lucy time to take in what she had heard. Wang Jun tried to take her hand in his again. She allowed him to give a reassuring touch, but then withdrew her hand. Mei stood up and said nothing. She looked straight at Lucy and whispered how sorry she was, then headed to the ladies room.

Lucy rose, walked over to the window, and gazed out over the ornate Chinese gardens behind the office. She wondered who she really was, and how her father could have done what he did to this woman. It was no surprise this Li woman had told him so succinctly to "fuck off." Then again, maybe her father never knew what happened to her. What if he'd truly loved her? Could the truth have indeed driven him to despair? Had he been a liar all along to this woman Li? To his own wife? Or was he only doing what his country wanted him to do? She was more confused then ever.

Lucy walked over to the stack of documents where Mei had been sitting. She began flipping through the binders of correspondence and other documents; it was going to take a long time to read through them.

Chapter 18

Lucy was still reading files when Mei returned, and Wang Jun had never left. Chairman Xin went over to his own desk to busy himself with some paperwork, took an outside call he needed to answer in private, and left the room. When he came back Mei was already seated reading, while Wang Jun was trying to reassure Lucy they had not used all this for their own gain. Xin could see the atmosphere was tense as he walked to the table and sat down across from Lucy this time.

"Okay, Lucy," he said. "It's a good time to continue. I talked to Mei this morning, and to Wang Jun here, I had some things to say this morning but decided to wait until we were all together. I also needed to have one important call, which came in just now. I think, Lucy, I can clear some things up for you today."

"I really hope you can, Uncle Xin," Lucy said with reverence.

"Ah yes . . . Uncle Xin . . . That name has always been special coming from you. Mei discovered my own DNA sample is close to yours, but not close enough." Xin rose and walked around the table to look down at Lucy. "But it's close enough to tell you I am your real uncle. My brother was your father." He paused, and waited a few seconds for the words to sink in.

"You, mean . . . you're my uncle . . . really?"

Wang Jun looked stunned.

Mei reacted quickly. "I knew I was close, Chairman, very close. I didn't know you had a brother though." Xin could see Mei was pleased to hear she had not been that far off.

"My brother is long dead, I'm afraid, and there is more to tell Lucy in that regard."

"What happened to him? Who's my real mother? Tell me . . . please."

"Lucy, I'm afraid both of your parents are no longer with us. They were killed at the same time."

"Killed? Both of them? How? Who was she? Please, for god's sake tell me everything."

"I intend to Lucy. Your father and mother were lovers in a difficult period of our history. She was American, very beautiful, who fell in love with my brother under difficult circumstances. In those days associating with foreigners was strictly forbidden, especially for someone in my brother's position. You were the result of a relationship in a time that spelt grave danger for any offspring of our two cultures."

"Who was she then? How did she die? How were you involved?"

"Your mother worked with the first U.S. companies doing business here in China after we opened up to the West. My brother was part of the government department dealing with foreign transactions; he met your mother on many occasions before they fell in love. I tried to get him to stop— it was so danger-ous— but he insisted on continuing to see her. You were the direct result of that love. She wanted to change the world, just like he did, insisted on carrying you through to birth. I told my brother he was crazy to allow her to do that, but he said she was adamant that the baby, you, would be born here."

"How could that be, Chairman?"

"What do you mean, Mei?"

"Well, she would have shown to the world she was pregnant. You don't hide that. How could she have a child without all those people at that time watching and reporting on each other? She was either very brave, or stupid." She turned to Lucy. "I'm sorry, I mean she must have been really brave if that's what happened."

"Oh, it happened that way all right. There were several others who were very brave for those times," Xin added.

"Who are the others?" Wang Jun asked.

"I'll get to that later. Anyway, Lucy, your father was my brother, your mother was a Christine Meyer. I have some things I managed to save here for you to look at."

Xin opened the old file he had by his side, and laid out first the photos of his brother, then those of Lucy's mother.

"This is your father, taken just before he died. You can see he was much more handsome than me, and here is your mother, a very beautiful lady, as are you. These here are group shots from the photos taken at the signing ceremonies of the contracts they worked on . . . here is your mother . . . and over here my brother."

"He's very handsome, I can see that. And my mother, I see a resemblance."

"You really have your mother's features and the looks of my brother. My wife saw the resemblance right away at the party. Others in my family have known the story of my brother and the American girl, but we kept it secret all these years. That is why they were excited to meet you."

Xin watched Lucy lovingly touch the photos of her parents and ask if there were any personal photos of them together. There were none, except for a crude one showing them with a baby.

"This is the only one. You were born at my aunt's home. Your mother endured much prior to your birth. She was tiny, as you can see. She bound herself to hide the pregnancy. My aunt loved us boys. Without her I don't know what they would have done. She managed everything and kept you there for a few days, but they both knew you could never have stayed there. They had to find a way to get you out of China, along with my brother. Your mother made all the arrangements. My brother told me everything that was going on. I was to take care of the family if anything happened to him. We were worried if the authorities found out anything. That she was never reported by the neighborhood watch was a miracle."

Lucy's voice lowered. "How were they killed?"

"They were out late one night to walk in a park. You were with my aunt, and they were finalizing plans to get you out. Your mother was always worried how the authorities would treat the rest of the family; we knew we could be jailed, maybe even killed. The idea was to get you and your mother out first, and then try to get my brother out later. We had no idea what would happen if we didn't get you out. You might have been taken away and someone would conveniently say you died. Many people disappeared back then to the country; they never came back."

"Were they arrested or something?"

"No, your parents were walking back to our aunt's small home when a military truck hit them. It was dark, the truck carried on, never even stopped. Was it arranged? We never found out. A neighbor recognized my brother's body but not the female's. I'm afraid she took the brunt of the accident." He paused.

"What happened afterwards?"

"We bought the silence of our neighbor, then carried my brother's body to my aunt's. There was nothing we could do for him. We took his body on a cart and set him free into a nearby lake. He was declared dead by drowning the next day. An accident, they said. We made sure he was not labeled with the stigma of suicide. We also needed to keep your mother and you out of it."

"How did you do that?" Lucy asked.

"We moved your mother, with as much dignity as we could, to a back road near the Beijing Hotel where her delegation was staying. They found her in the morning . . . here, this is a report."

Lucy was shown a Chinese news article, which Mei translated for her.

"It notes an American delegate wandered outside of her hotel illegally, without supervision, only to be killed in a road accident. The police report indicates the accident could have involved a large military or construction vehicle. It states the accident was the result of the individual walking along a poorly lit road, and that the victim was in an area she should not have been in. It reports the injuries were extensive and death would have been instantaneous. Furthermore the authorities are arranging, with the help of the Communist Party, to ship the remains back to the victim's parents along with the Chinese people's condolences for the family's loss.

"And me?"

I contacted your mother's associate, who my brother had been working with, and he agreed to continue with whatever was planned to get you out," Xin said.

"How did they do it?"

"He refused to tell me. He said it was better that none of us knew anything about it. He was a good man. We never did find out how it was arranged. He came to my aunt's house one night where you were hidden and took you away. That was the last time I saw you, until you came to China with Global Industries. You cannot imagine how I felt when you called me "Uncle" after that one banquet."

"I'd had a lot of baijiu. The old lady with you told me I should call you that as a term of endearment, said it was very Chinese and you would like it. "

"I know. I told her it would be a nice thing for our negotiations. Maybe you understand now why it meant so much more."

"But who got me out?"

"Who else? John Wainright."

Lucy stood up, staring at her newfound uncle, stunned by the news of a family she never knew, relieved to find her father was perhaps not as wicked as she had begun to think. She held the few articles and photographs before her and began to weep again, soon finding herself in the arms of her uncle. At last she felt a connection to her real biological parents. Xin let her continue to cry for them, until he released her. She turned to face the others, and looked at them, bewildered by how everything had turned out. She opened up her arms to Wang Jun, and mouthed a silent thank you to Mei Rui, who was wiping tears from her own eyes.

Finally she broke away from Wang Jun and sat down. She could hardly believe everything she'd heard. Her next question would need more answers. "What was the connection between Li Buyun, my father, and the others?" she asked.

Wang Jun and Mei looked to Xin for the answer.

"Lucy, we were all young and more idealistic in those days. Li Buyun and my brother were good friends. They knew each other through their school years, all through the Cultural Revolution and beyond, I knew her through hanging around my brother. He was always my protector, kept me straight and pushed me to make something of myself in life. I think the two of them might even have been lovers at one time, but all that ended when he met your mother."

"How did they meet?"

"Li worked in the electrical component business, actually right there in the Beijing Art District, you know. It's called the 798 now. She worked there when it was the factory 718 complex. She was successful and rose to a senior level. The Party often used her as an expert in technical negotiations with overseas countries, especially with her other major in chemistry before going there. They also involved her in commercial agreements, sometimes in military discussions. She was especially busy during the years we began to open up. If you look at some of the official photographs, like this one with the Boeing Aircraft Company, you will see her. There she is . . . and over there is my brother. He was with the Foreign Trade Ministry at the time.

"I knew nothing of this," Lucy said.

"John Wainright was also involved in the negotiations, but in the background, along with your mother. What is clear today is your real mother, and John Wainright, were there to find out all they could about matters other than those contracts. Your mother seems to have pursued the economic side of things while Wainright was trying to understand the military and political aims of our leaders."

"They were both spies?"

" I always thought they were CIA agents but my brother claimed otherwise, certainly in regards to your mother. Anyway, you know firsthand, Lucy, how intensive our negotiating practices are; well, they were much worse back then. They spent a lot of time together, all four of them. Sometimes I wondered if Wainright and your mother were a team working on this." He paused.

"But how come they were able to get together? My understanding is that would have been impossible back then. I've read where they were monitoring all foreign contacts closely. Weren't they all being watched?"

"They were, but the Americans were lucky. They happened to latch on to two people who were disgusted with how the revolution was going, and enamored with all things American. My brother thought sharing what he could with your mother might help move our countries closer together in some way. He never looked at himself as a traitor, nor did Li Buyun."

"That sounds like wishful thinking on their part."

"They shared the same ideals. According to my brother, they were trying to form an underground group to help the outside world understand what was going on here. I wanted to help, but he told me to stay out of it. They all took a huge risk in seeing each other, usually late at night. Somehow they all managed to avoid getting caught . . . for a while anyway."

"But it all came to a crashing end. How did it happen?" Wang Jun asked.

"They never did connect my brother and Lucy's mother. They would have if she had not been moved. Wainright took care of that. Li Buyun was not so lucky; once she became pregnant too the situation was more difficult than ever. She always claimed there were promises of a way in exchange for the information they provided. Li knew what happened with your mother, so was expecting to be smuggled out too. It never happened."

"Do you know why not?" Lucy asked.

"You need to ask your father that question, Lucy, and how the authorities found out and arrested Li and her daughter. The one thing I do know is the Party never knew exactly what she was feeding to Wainright; if they had, she would have been executed as a traitor for sure, the daughter gotten rid of. As it was, your father had left the country. All the authorities could prove was they had an illicit love affair resulting in a child. Li's friends and managers stood up for her, basically saved her life, but in the end she was shipped off to the country for reform."

———⬥———

As they talked, Mei pulled another folder of downloads from the hard drive Lucy had brought with her. "I think I have an idea now of what's been going on with your father, Lucy. Especially after what Chairman Xin has told us."

"What do you think happened, Mei?"

"I can't say with absolute certainty, but if you read this correspondence it helps. Some of it's missing though. Look at these. It seems your father's efforts to see his biological daughter began right after your mother in the U.S. died. I suspect he knew nothing of the horrors he put Li and her daughter through. In fact she referred me to a secret memo in her arrest file that she was shown in her interrogation that had your father's signature on it. In it he admitted to being the baby's father and that he was receiving information from her on the negotiations they were involved in.

"From my conversations with her, and studying the document with our Mr. Zhang, we both believe it was a forgery. Likely the interrogators used it to try to get her to admit to being more than a love struck young woman enamored with an American. She believes it caused her downfall, and that John Wainright left her high and dry to save his own skin. She was fuming when I was with her over how he arranged to smuggle you out, when you weren't even his own daughter. Maybe for him, as I said, it was the shock and horror of finding out what he actually did to them. I honestly can't say. I think you have to confront him with Li to find out."

———— ❧ ————

Lucy sat looking at the documents, wondering how her father had continued to go back to China as Richard Towers, especially after what had happened. Was he still looking for his daughter at the time, or just trying to find Li? Surely that would have been too risky, she thought. Was that why he was using another name? Was he still working for the government? How did he get to work for Goldman Sachs as Richard Towers? Was that going on inside the office she was forbidden to enter all those years at home?

"Uncle," Lucy said, looking straight at him, "I'm more sure than ever I need to get Li Buyun and her daughter in front of my father . . . er, John Wainright."

"It's okay, Lucy, I am not offended by your referring to him as your father. That's natural, but I hope you will learn more in the coming days about your real family."

"Thanks. I want to learn more, but it's confusing right now. I need to learn the whole truth. I think the only way to shake my father out of it is for both of them to visit him. I know that's not easy, but we have to do it."

"Lucy, Li will never agree to her daughter being involved; she's made that absolutely clear. Don't you agree, Chairman?" Mei said.

"I'm not so sure, maybe. If we can get Lucy to talk to her, as another daughter to a mother, that might convince her to help."

"I doubt it," Wang Jun interjected. "We might be better using the information we have here to force it. Maybe we should talk to the daughter directly, let her see the truth? What do you think?"

"No! Absolutely not," Lucy said. "With everything that my father did to her, and everything that's happened since, I won't allow it. If we can't persuade Madame Li to involve her daughter, then we'll just try to have Li Buyun come with me to see my father."

"Well said, Lucy. My brother would have said the same thing. There is still something of him in you. I can see that."

Xin gave Lucy another reassuring hug. "I should talk to her and see if she can come to Beijing to meet us, and you. She needs to come anyway to review our merger."

Lucy wasn't sure Madame Li would cooperate, but Xin assured her he thought he could arrange it, without involving the daughter at this stage. They would have to move quickly with Lucy leaving in days. She told everyone she could not delay beyond the weekend. She saw the disappointed expression on Wang Jun's face at the comment, but her uncle merely shrugged his shoulders in regret.

It was getting late; they were already late for the dinner gathering at Xin's home. Her uncle told her he was pleased so much was out in the open now, and that she should not be surprised to be questioned at length by the family that evening. Wang Jun and Mei were told they were welcome to join the party, but Mei decided she needed a rest; she also had work to do on the merger. Wang Jun decided it was better to leave Lucy with her newfound family, but would pick her up at ten o'clock to take her home. Xin told Lucy the family album and photos he had shown her were hers to carry back, as were the materials Mei had gathered.

There were final embraces among all three of them as Xin and Lucy prepared to leave.

"This has been incredible," she said. "Whatever happens, from now on I have a real family. I can never, ever thank you all enough. Leaving is going to be hard, but I've no choice. I have to go back."

"We all have choices, Lucy," Xin said. "Whatever you finally choose to do, remember you are still young. You have a long life ahead of you; make sure it is the right thing for you, not somebody else. Always remember you are a Xin, and we are here to help you, whatever happens."

The chairman phoned his driver to take them to his home. Wang Jun kissed Lucy on the cheek as he left the boardroom. Mei gave her another hug. Lucy thanked her again for all she had done for her, smiling as she left to meet her new family.

Chapter 19

The evening with her uncle's family was a night she would never forget. His home was a renovated courtyard-style dwelling from the Qing Dynasty, bought from an industrialist who had fled the country. Xin told her the man had been very rich, but unscrupulous. He made millions in the forties off the backs of his low paid workers, from supplying arms to the Nationalists, and even working with the Japanese invaders back then. Xin had purchased the home some years earlier, without explaining to her how it exactly came into his possession. He told her he had the complex rebuilt to its original splendor. Lucy could hear in his voice the obvious love and care he'd taken preserving a piece of China's heritage, to say nothing of the millions of yuan it must have cost to improve the home.

As they entered the main courtyard area, the whole family and several of his staff were waiting to greet her. There was a festive atmosphere to the whole affair, with streamers and character banners hanging in the large entryway. She asked what the Chinese characters meant and was told they were to welcome their lost relative back to her roots. Despite the lavish surroundings, Lucy was surprised how down to earth the Xin family was, receiving her warmly. They were as anxious to learn about her as she was about them. Xin was the clear patriarch; the rest of the family openly showed their respect and adoration for him. His wife was especially attentive to Lucy. She had not known Xin's brother, but heard from her husband many times the story of his lost niece in America.

There were sixteen members of Xin's extended family at the gathering; many more could not be there. Lucy was presented with many gifts from the family, the most touching a small package, very old, and split on the corners. The family stood around her as Xin presented it to her.

"This is something my aunt gave me before she died. I have never opened it, but she asked that one day I should give it to you. Please open it now."

Lucy hesitated, the wrapping seemed so fragile, but she was able to carefully undo the faded red ribbon and gently peel back the wrapping, exposing a small jewelry box. The family edged closer to see what was inside. Lucy laid the box on the table in front of her and removed the objects. There was a small ring and three envelopes, along with a note she could not read. "What does this say?" she asked her uncle. "Please read it aloud."

"Are you sure?"

"Of course, it's from your aunt."

"It says, 'To my grand niece, I leave you these precious gifts I saved for you all these years. Your father gave this ring to your mother. She wore this the night she died, and my dream was to one day hand it to you myself. The small envelopes contain three clippings. The black hair is my nephew's, the auburn your mother's, and the blond hair is the first clipping I took from you days after your birth. Your father's brother has sworn to find and protect you. For that I am grateful. You were a beautiful baby. Honor your mother and father as long as you live."

Lucy was overwhelmed and touched by it all; several females in the group were as tearful as she. Xin's wife eased the small ring onto lucy's finger; it fit perfectly. She held the remnants of hair in her hands.

The dinner that night was formal, but presented in a casual atmosphere. Lucy spent much of the night asking about her father, and listening to many other stories the family had to tell. The dishes brought out were not only delicious, but elaborately laid out, each one presented to her first as the guest of honor.

As the evening wound down, Xin asked Lucy to follow him. He had something else to show her, and someone he wanted her to meet. Intrigued, she followed him through other small courtyards in the complex to what had evidently been a small family temple during the Qing Dynasty. The hum of chanting told her that the Xin family was still using it as their private temple, and that someone inside was reciting a Buddhist sutra. As they approached the temple, the sound of the rhythmic sutra grew louder. Xin stopped and turned toward her. "Lucy, are you religious in any way?"

"Afraid not, Uncle. Mother brought me up as a Catholic, but I never found it satisfied the questions I had about life. She was never happy when I stopped going to church."

"I was not brought up with strong beliefs either, Lucy. There was too much hardship in our lives, which lasted for a very long time. A few years ago, while the loss of my dear brother still bothered me, I finally began to search for more meaning in my life, and I found it. One day I wandered into a temple near Houhai, you may have passed it yourself as a tourist sometime; many do. It was during a dark period in my life, both personally and professionally, that I found great peace there. I never experienced that before then."

"I think I know what you mean, Uncle. Wang Jun took me to some of the temples years ago. They were peaceful places for me too. I always thought it might be something to look into further, but I never did."

"I can only tell you that it changed my life, Lucy. I want to introduce you now to the monk that I met those years ago, and who has been my teacher and spiritual guide ever since. He is the one who encouraged me to find you again."

"Again?"

Xin explained that he had known she was coming to China with Global Industries; how her father had contacted him out of the blue and begged him not to reveal her true origins to her. That was why he never acknowledged who she was at the time, but welcomed her calling him "uncle" as a term of endearment from her. That was very special to him.

"But why would my father do that?" She paused for a few moments then added, "Now I think about it though, he was anxious at the time I told him I was going to China. I thought he would be happy about me treading in his footsteps, but he wasn't. He said he was worried for my safety, but never said I shouldn't go . . . I guess he knew he couldn't stop me."

"He was curious about your trip when you returned?"

"Mm . . . I do remember when I came back he asked many questions about who I met, what was said, and where I'd traveled to. I just thought he was interested in my trip at the time; I know I mentioned our meetings with you. He must have been afraid of me meeting you, of hearing the truth. Was that it?"

"Maybe. Who knows?" Xin said. "The excuse he gave me was they told you for so long you were of Vietnamese origin, your father an American, that neither of them wanted you to know otherwise. He told me I needed to honor that; for my brother's sake, I should not have agreed."

Xin led Lucy inside the temple; they waited in silence for the monk to finish chanting. She stood there with her eyes closed; the hum of the sutra, the aroma of the incense, and the peacefulness of her surroundings calmed her. She thought about all that had occurred over the past days, never imagining she would be standing next to someone who was directly related to her. The monk finished his prayers and rose to greet them; his serene look and calm demeanor made her feel relaxed. The old man bowed and welcomed her, his large hands gently enveloping hers.

Her uncle translated all that the monk told Lucy, starting with how her uncle had found peace in his temple. He described how Xin had finally decided to put his life in order and seek peace in his heart, "before the final journey that comes to everyone in this world." Through their discussions, Xin had revealed all that he regretted in his life, his errors, and the desire to right any wrongs he had been party to. The monk explained that the fate of his brother's child had left a mark on her uncle's soul, especially since he had met her but hadn't revealed the truth to her. It was the monk who told him he needed to seek her out, and watch over her. Until he did, he would never find the peace he was looking for.

Lucy told the monk she was glad he had, then Xin led her to a small room in the temple. "Lucy, I want you to come in here with me and pray. This is the memorial to my brother."

As she walked into the darkened room, the monk lit candles all around. Xin led her quietly to a statue of Buddha on the main altar; there, cradled in its hands was a larger copy of the photograph of his brother that she saw earlier.

Her uncle led her to two prayer cushions, and the monk moved to stand beside her. Holding a metal bowl he began to ring it several times. Xin began to pray to his brother in Chinese, bowing, kneeling, and laying his hands open to the Buddha, before rising again as the bowl was rung one final time. When he was finished he spoke to the monk, then told Lucy he would now pray in English.

As Lucy watched and listened her uncle expressed in English his love for his brother, how their family missed him, how his honor was being upheld in spite of everything. He thanked Buddha for the riches that had come their way since his brother's death, but above all for the chance to introduce Lucy to him. "From now to eternity I will assure her happiness and security, no matter what it might take to do so. Dear brother, you have a beautiful daughter before you. She honors your memory. Lucy has developed into a young woman of high moral standing; she is here at last to offer you a daughter's love and gratitude for bringing her into this world."

By the time Xin had finished Lucy was in tears. The monk motioned Xin to step back. He motioned for Lucy to kneel, demonstrating how she should pray. He placed his hand on her head and recited a prayer, before ringing the bowl and indicating she could rise. She was invited to say whatever she wanted, then kneel again in the same ritual she had watched Xin perform. At first she didn't know what to say, but Xin looked over and told her to say whatever she was feeling. From somewhere within, all that had been locked inside her, about wanting to know where she came from, poured out.

She cried for the long lost father and mother she had never known. She spoke of their tragedy, about how happy she was to have found his family. She promised to do her best to be the kind of a daughter that he may have hoped for. She talked a little of her troubled marriage, and her own lack of a child. About how her life had been difficult of late, and her hopes for a better future. She promised to pray for him and her mother in her own way when she returned home.

Her uncle gave her a warm embrace while he explained to the monk all that she had said. The two men seemed pleased with the words she used. The monk guided the two of them to a seating area and motioned for her to be seated. He began to talk to Lucy directly, Xin translating as rapidly as he could. For whatever reason, she found herself talking openly about all of the problems with her husband, what he had been through, the changes in him, even her affair with Sam Jones. She exposed her feelings of guilt in her love for Wang Jun, how that flame had never died. She told the monk of her American father, and all that was happening there. She left out certain things she assumed even Xin might want to keep secret. In the end she asked his advice about what she should do. She told him she had to go back to the U.S. but a big part of her wanted to stay, to find a life with her real family, and live where she was born.

When Lucy finally stopped, and Xin finished translating, she could see her uncle was pained by some of what he had heard. The monk, however, smiled and reached out. Taking both her hands in his he appeared to bless her. He reached behind his neck and slowly removed a necklace, a small jade Buddha on an old leather strap.

She listened to her uncle's translation. "This is for you, Miss Lucy. It has protected me for many years, and will protect you in the future. You are still young, you have much life ahead of you, and your heart will show you the way. Look into it and weigh carefully what it is you want. When you do, decide whom it will benefit, but also whom it will pain. Take time in choosing the way forward. The balance of life is not always in our own hands. When it is, we need to be careful which path we choose."

Lucy asked her uncle to tell the monk she hoped she would choose the right one, and the translation drew a smile from the man.

"Your uncle chose the path of light; he is a happier man for it. I hope you find the light you are looking for. The way of the Buddha is not easy. I know that better than anyone, but it has brought me such happiness I could never imagine life otherwise. If you are interested in our teachings, that would give both of us here great pleasure. It is a choice only you can make, but I wish you peace in this life, Miss Lucy, whatever you decide. I thank you for making your uncle a very happy man."

The monk told them he had to leave and gave both of them a final blessing, after which her uncle presented him with a small contribution for his main temple. The monk tried to refuse the gift, but Lucy's uncle made sure he accepted it.

As soon as the monk was gone he spoke to her. "That jade necklace has been his for decades, Lucy; it is a very special gift to you. He gave something of immense meaning and value to him tonight, but he asked nothing in return. I hope you recognize how significant a gesture that was on his part. And before you ask, he did not tell me he was going to do that, or request any money."

Lucy told him how much she appreciated meeting the monk, and that she understood the significance of his gift. She promised she would honor the gift and wear it faithfully every day forward. Her uncle seemed pleased and mentioned how happy he was with the way the whole evening had gone. He led her to another area, where Lucy was totally surprised by what she saw.

Chapter 20

"Where did you get these, Uncle?"

The wall in front of her was filled with photos. She gazed at them and understood instantly they'd been taken ever since she opened the flower shop.

She looked at her uncle, puzzled as she moved from one to another. "Who took them? I don't remember anyone with a camera?"

Xin smiled and held her hands in his. "Lucy, the monk led me some time ago to the realization that I needed to find you again, at least to know you were well, and safe. It was not difficult for me to find your father and discover where you lived, that you were married, and starting your own business. I arranged for someone to see you regularly and to send me these; that way I knew you were okay."

"But why didn't you just have someone tell me all this?" she asked.

"Because John Wainright, your father, was against it, Lucy. He felt it best that everything be left the way it was after your mother's death. He told my people you were settled and happy, that all of this would be too much for you."

Lucy grew angry to hear yet again how her father had blocked her from learning her true identity, where she came from, or that her real parents were dead. She asked Xin how he had found her. Who had taken the photos without her knowing?

"Lucy, you have a visitor every month. You know him as Don Roberts, don't you?"

"Don? He always told us he was buying flowers for his wife. He never had a camera with him, as I recall. We talk a lot whenever he comes in. I thought he was one of my best customers, but you're telling me he isn't. Who is he really?"

"He is Don Roberts, really. The flowers are for the wife he loves dearly; that part is all true. What you don't know is he was with your American police, the FBI you call them. He is based in Greensboro; that's also true, but he does undercover work on the side. We came to know him through a corruption investigation involving one of our sister companies over there."

"And his wife?"

"She is very ill, cancer. Whatever he earns from us for this small task helps with her medical care, nothing more." He raised his hand before she could speak, "And before you ask, the photos were taken with one of those small lapel cameras. You may have noticed he always wears a jacket in your shop, even on the hottest days. He did complain about that."

Lucy shook her head as she looked at the photos and thought about the lengths her uncle had gone to keep track of her, even as her father tried everything to keep him away.

"And those flower orders for the conventions in Greensboro? You were behind those too?"

"Only the first ones, until Don said you were doing fine and we did not need to do anything more. He was afraid you would get suspicious."

Lucy gave her uncle another embrace, and thanked him for all he had tried to do for her. Her uncle tried yet again to convince her to come to China, divorce her husband, and find true happiness. He promised her that her husband would never want for anything again if she agreed.

As much as Lucy wanted to start a new life, she could never bring herself to leave her adoptive father or tormented husband. She told him her first priority was to pull her father from the abyss he seemed to be sinking into, though no longer sure how she felt about him after what he had done.

"Lucy, do not let hatred into your heart. Your father was a good man in his own way. He did what he thought was right for you. Maybe he did not know what happened to Li Buyun. Be careful condemning him before you know for sure. I think your plan to get them together will help him."

"I'm not sure it'll work with Madame Li alone. It seems my father was desperate to locate his real daughter, just like you wanted to find me."

"We will redouble our efforts. You only have a few days left here . . . unless you stay longer."

"I'd love to stay, really I would, Uncle, but I can't. I have to go back as soon as I get my passport and book the flight."

—————

Lucy was led back to the main part of the house to await Wang Jun's arrival. Xin's wife told her he would be there shortly to pick her up. The process of saying farewell to everyone began; the gifts she had received were too numerous to take with her, though she wouldn't let the small parcel from the aunt out of her grasp. They promised to send everything over to her the next day, not to worry about any excess baggage charges; they would be taken care of.

The final embrace with her uncle brought the evening to its close; however, the happiness of the reunion was marked with sadness as she told them one last time about going back to America. She promised to visit them again in the future, as soon as she could afford it. The family all laughed together; Madame Xin assured her tickets could be sent to her whenever she wanted to come, that this home was hers now, as was the rest of the family.

—————

Wang Jun was led into the main courtyard where he found Lucy wiping her eyes, as were many of the relatives standing there to bid her farewell. As he walked toward her he smiled at Xin and his wife, noticing the looks of approval directed his way. He embraced Lucy somewhat formally, but she held on to him in a way that everyone could see the two were more than good friends. Xin jokingly told him they hadn't convinced their guest to stay in China, so it was up to him. Wang told everyone he would do his best, then led Lucy to the car. She was leaving with him, but he could sense in her the desire to stay. This time he drove, taking her to his private apartment where he planned to spend the last few nights with her, unless he could persuade her to stay longer.

~~~

When Lucy entered Wang Jun's apartment building she was surprised to be walked into a sparsely decorated apartment, guessing correctly it dated back to the sixties. Despite being in an old apartment block, the rooms themselves were immaculate, the furnishings luxurious nonetheless. There were only two bedrooms, a lounge area was right next to the small but well-appointed kitchen; inside it was like so many of the older apartment blocks being demolished or renovated. It had a small balcony enclosure where a washing machine and dryer sat under overhead rails for drying his clothes, so typical in Beijing. An antique desk in the spare bedroom was littered with paperwork; a computer and printer indicated Wang Jun worked there often.

"This is my special retreat, Lucy," Wang Jun said, as he held her close. "It was my mother's at one time. I kept it to get away from everything, and remember where our family came from. It keeps me grounded. I hope you can bear spending the next few days with me here . . . longer if you like."

"It's a surprise; that's for sure. I'm happy just to be here with you though. We've so little time left and I want to make the most of it. Don't waste anymore time trying to persuade me to stay. I have to leave, and that's the end of it. Promise me you won't bring it up again? I can hardly bear it as it is."

"I'll try, Lucy, I really will . . . but promise you? That I can't do."

She was led by Wang Jun to a wardrobe where all of her things were hanging up already, or neatly folded inside drawers. He suggested she check to make sure everything was there, but she said she didn't care. She backed herself to the bed and sat on the edge, pulling him towards her. He knelt in front of her and kissed her gently. She felt the warmth of his kiss, and reached down to caress him, letting him know that she wanted him and would wait no longer. It started tenderly in the way he undressed her, and how he held her to him on the bed. It was not tenderness she wanted; she needed him to release what her body was craving.

She moved gradually until she was on top of him and gazed into his eyes. She pulled a part of the bed sheet over his eyes, then stretched his arms out to support herself. She rose up on him and told him she wanted to make love to him in her own way, that he should say and do nothing.

She started slowly, intending to make love to him for as long as she could, but once their feelings intensified everything changed. Her self-control ended as he ripped the sheet from his eyes, holding her tighter than ever. She felt herself fighting him as he tried to turn her back onto the bed and under him. She could contain her own emotions no longer, and was lost in a world of pleasure she had never experienced so deeply. When their desires were met they lay together for what seemed like hours and said nothing; there was no need.

They slept the rest of the night, and at breakfast talked more about their situation. Lucy was disappointed to hear Wang Jun needed to go to the office for a few hours. He suggested she come with him and use one of their spare offices near Mei Rui. She could spend time looking through the documents they'd shown her the day before. She thought it was a good idea and would be able to talk to her uncle too, particularly about getting Li Buyun to change her mind about her daughter, at least to allow them to meet one another. Wang Jun still doubted Li would ever agree, but encouraged her to talk to her uncle about it.

Lucy dressed for the office while he sat at his desk checking e-mails. She felt at ease in his apartment. It was small yet comfortable, a different world from Mei's apartment or his other home. She thought about how happy she could be living with him in such simple surroundings.

They arrived late at the office; people were already waiting to meet with Wang Jun, so his assistant led Lucy to an office alongside Mei Rui's. All the files from their meeting in the boardroom were neatly laid out for her. Mei soon stopped by to welcome her, she said she'd missed Lucy's company at the apartment, but hoped her evening was enjoyable, especially the night with Wang Jun. Lucy told her it had been exceptional, blushing at Mei's knowing look.

"I thought so," said Mei. "Look how red your face is!"

They talked about the evening at the Xin home in particular, then Mei said she needed to get some things done and excused herself. Lucy busied herself going over the files, especially the photo album her uncle had given to her. She used the office phone to call Sarah and Sally. All was well there; Phil was due back at the weekend. Lucy said little about anything personal.

Sarah said Don Roberts hadn't stopped by that week for his wife's flowers. She hoped there was nothing wrong with him or his wife. Lucy told her she was sure he was okay, then thanked her for taking care of everything. She asked her to pass along to Phil that she hoped he would be home when she got back.

With Sally it was a far different call. She told her all that had transpired over that weekend, including the kind of intimate details they always shared since they were young girls. Sally told her again that she thought Lucy was insane not to take advantage of the new life she was being offered, adding how neither her father, nor Phil, deserved her. Lucy brushed off her comments and finally rang off, telling Sally she would check on her passport and let her know her flight schedule as soon as possible.

Lucy did not want to bother Wang Jun or Mei, as busy as they were, with the passport problem. She decided instead to call the American Embassy direct. It took time to get through to a human being, after running through various recorded options to choose from. She did not know her "party's extension" when asked; She needed someone to track down Michael Song who was in charge of her case.

Finally another American voice came on the line. "American Embassy, Julie Nelson. How may I help you?"

"My name is Lucy Summers. Thanks for taking my call. I'm trying to reach a Michael Song. I lost my passport and he's working on the replacement. I'd like to get an update so I can book my flight to head back home. Can you put me through to him please, Miss Nelson? I'm afraid I don't have his extension."

"Do call me Julie; everyone else does. Let me check for you. His extension's seventeen forty-three, should you need it next time. Hang on please; I'm going to put you on hold." Lucy waited patiently, listening to an audio yet again about the embassy's services.

"I'm afraid Michael is tied up right now, but I can check for you myself. Do you have your file number?"

"Sorry, I don't. A friend's company is helping me. I think they have the file number, but they're busy right now."

"Are you in a hurry?" Julie asked.

"I am, kind of. My husband is arriving back home this weekend and I 'd like to be there when he gets back. He wasn't too happy about my passport being stolen."

"I can imagine. He must be excited to get you back. Let me see if I can do it another way. Give me your address and social security number. I think I can trace where the file is from those." Lucy gave her the information and was put on hold again while the woman went off to check. She was on hold for another ten minutes.

"Sorry about that. It took a while but I found it. Can you also verify a few more things for me please?" Lucy gave her birth date when asked, and confirmed her mother's maiden name.

"Sorry about that, but we are being very careful with passports these days. Anyway, good news, you'll be able to get it back anytime you like. The passport's been waiting for you to pick it up."

"That's great . . . but waiting? Since when?"

"Three days ago. Let me see here . . . yes, there's the note, called through to a "Mei Rui" three days ago. Is that a problem?" she asked.

Lucy said nothing for a while. "Oh no, that's great. She's been traveling on business; maybe she was too busy to tell me. I'll arrange to come in for it. Thanks again for helping me."

"No problem. It's sitting here ready. Just make an appointment and come in during our open hours. Do you want to pick it up today?"

"I don't need it just yet. I still have a lot to see before the weekend, but thanks."

"My pleasure, enjoy the rest of your stay."

The phone clicked dead and Lucy sat back. They were obviously trying to keep her there as long as they could. She didn't know whether to be angry with them, or him. In any event she would make her flight reservations for the weekend. That would be the end of it; she would delay it no longer.

❦

She walked into Mei's office and asked if she could contact the airline to confirm a return flight to the U.S. for the coming Sunday. Mei suggested she ought to wait until they heard about the passport being ready.

Lucy glared at her. "Mei, make the goddamned reservation. I just called the embassy, and you've known it was ready for the last three days. I'm not angry with you, but I'll be really pissed if you don't get me on a flight this weekend."

"Okay, okay! We really hate to see you leave. Think about it, Lucy, you've found your family, and that man in the office over there is crazy about you. It doesn't hurt that everyone who cares about you is rich either."

"It's not that I don't want to stay, Mei; I just can't. If we can do something with my father and Madame Li, then I might think about it in the future. What do you think our chances are of getting her to travel with me?"

"Not good, I'm afraid. She won't get involved until the merger is settled."

"Can't I at least meet her?" Lucy asked.

"Chairman Xin 's working on that, and if anyone can get it done it's him. You might have to fly to Nanjing with me though to see her."

"I'd love to, but no more games, Mei. I'm leaving Sunday, whether I meet her or not."

Chapter 21

Lucy finally had a reservation booked by the office for a Monday flight. She accused Mei of trying to delay her return, even though it was only for one day. Mei said it was either coach class on the Sunday flight, or first class on Monday. Lucy agreed Monday would be better.

The last days were passing quickly. Wang Jun was spending as much time as he could with her, but the merger with Sunrise Chemicals and the discussions with Li Buyun were now in full swing. Their remaining evenings were spent alone, eating out in small restaurants, walking in parks, and simply enjoying each other's company.

She eventually confronted him with not telling her about the passport being ready, but only chastised him mildly, unaware of his involvement in its theft.

Her recent phone calls to Blowing Rock added to the regrets of leaving Wang Jun and the new family she had come to know. Her mind was filled with thoughts of the future, and if she was going to bring her father out of his malaise and improve her relationship with Phil. She made up her mind to give it one more try, but she would leave him if they couldn't make it work.

Saturday came quickly; they stayed in bed later than usual, and only ate lightly at breakfast. They spent most of the morning talking about their time together, Lucy revealing more about her husband than she had to anyone other than her friend Sally. The more she talked about her life with Phil and what happened to him overseas, Wang Jun grew more sympathetic, but adamant he could take better care of her and make sure Phil had a good life ahead of him.

"I just can't," she told him. "He may not be the man I married, but I promised myself to him . . . in sickness and in health. Those were my vows. I can't change them so please don't ask me to."

"You can't live like this forever, Lucy. If it gets worse you have to do something. I'm here . . . your new family is here. Just promise me you won't stay with him if it doesn't get better."

"I'll try. I promise," she said.

"Will you tell him everything when you get back? I mean about your new family of course, not us."

"I don't know yet. I think I have to though with my father's situation."

"He needs to know some of it; that's for sure."

The conversation brought Lucy more tears. There was so little time remaining, and farewell meetings with Mei Rui and her uncle would take up precious hours.

⁕

Lucy met Mei later as planned in one of the restaurants at the Solana outdoor shopping area, alongside the Chaoyang Park Lake. It was a glorious day in Beijing. The sun was shining, and any hint of pollution had been wafted away by the winds earlier that morning. Mei arrived with Han who was following her with three large boxes. She told Lucy Han was not joining them, but had something for her.

"My god, Mei! These are all for me? I'll never get them in my case."

"No problem, Lucy. Only one of these is for you to take back. We promised you something for Phil. I just need you to pick the size you think will fit him.

Han laid the three boxes on the table. Mei ushered the waiter away, until they were ready to order. Han opened the first box and held the contents in front of Lucy, turning the article around to show her what they had bought.

"That's perfect!" Lucy said as Han continued to show her a leather jacket emblazoned with local badges on the front and a unique Beijing Harley Davidson logo on the back.

"Pick one you think will fit and Han will take the others back. Wang Jun was going to order him a new bike, but I told him that might be a bit over the top."

"Oh my god. Thank goodness he didn't do anything so stupid. The jacket is perfect. Anything more and Phil would have definitely thought I was up to more than just finding a family here. Let me look at the others; this one is definitely too small."

"Maybe he was hoping he'd fall off it, the bike I mean."

"That's not funny, Mei."

Lucy settled on the one she thought would fit Phil well. She hugged Han before he left with the other jackets, thanking them both again for their thoughtful gift. She assured them Phil would be over the moon with it, and the envy of his buddies in Blowing Rock.

Mei called the waiter over to order wine while they studied the menu. After ordering, the two talked at length about her father's situation and Li Buyun's daughter.

"Do you think Madame Li will tell her daughter? Would she ever bring her daughter to my father?" Lucy asked.

"I doubt it. She's stubborn. I know your uncle's been talking to her, but so far she won't do anything until the merger is settled."

"Why not? I mean, you have a firm agreement, right?"

"We do, but this is China. She's not going to move until it's all spelled out on paper. She wants to see our company chops are on the documents. I know she's pushing for more for her daughter too."

Lucy asked about the daughter, Zhao Wen, and what she was like. Mei told her how different she was from her mother. She thought the daughter ought to be told about her past too. Eventually the conversation moved back to her relationship with Wang Jun, but Lucy cut Mei off before she could say anything on his behalf.

"Don't even ask! I can't stay, no matter how much I'd like to, or want to. You all make it harder for me by even talking about it. My minds made up. I may be making the biggest mistake of my life, but I have to help my father, no matter what he's done. And I need to help Phil get better."

"I won't push. I just want to tell you one more time that you and Wang Jun belong together. In some ways you and he are both so hard-headed! I can't get him to give up that bitch of his, but you could. For you, he'd leave her in a heartbeat. I like you, Lucy, I really do. I think we could work well together if you were here. If you ever felt like going back to real work I'm sure we could find something for you in the U.S." She smiled. "Then you'd have a good reason to come here for company meetings . . . or for us to visit you in the U.S."

"Tempting, but I've got the flower business and my family to worry about. Getting back into the corporate world might be too big a step these days. I won't say I wouldn't consider it, especially if things get worse with the store."

"Lucy, you can do whatever you like right now. You have two of the richest guys in China on your team. There's a great life ahead for you, if you want it."

"Money isn't everything, Mei. It's good, that's for sure, and I've had the best time of my life these last couple of weeks, but life is more than money to me. I'd still love my uncle and Wang Jun, whether they were wealthy or not."

"Not me," Mei joked.

The food arrived and they started to eat. The conversation turned to all that had happened on Lucy's trip, how it was marred by the break-in to Mei's apartment. By one thirty lunch was finished and they sat with coffee waiting for Wang Jun to arrive and take Lucy off to the Western Hills.

As soon as Mei saw him coming, she gathered her things and readied to leave. "I'll leave you to it then. Enjoy the rest of the day and I'll see you at the airport before you leave. Take good care of my boss, Lucy; he's very fragile right now. He needs you."

"I'm fragile too. It's harder for me than any of you think. Let's stay in touch. And thank you for everything, I can't thank you enough."

The two women hugged. Wang Jun invited Mei to stay when he got to the table, but she told him the last thing they needed was her hanging around. After she left, he embraced Lucy, then sat down to order a coffee. They talked about their days together when she had been an intern and he was the Global Industries chief rep, laughing at the precautions they'd both taken to avoid detection.

They drove back to his apartment; she looked forward to the night ahead, but knew Sunday night would be especially hard. She asked to stay in the apartment that last evening. She wanted to cook for him there and be alone. She told him she looked forward to the farewell lunch with her uncle, but regretted the loss of time on the last day before she left.

Chapter 22

Lucy arrived early to meet her uncle. The traffic had been lighter than Wang Jun had predicted. He insisted on driving her there to the restaurant her uncle selected, an elegant place near the Forbidden City. It featured fine vegetarian dishes in a peaceful, Buddhist atmosphere, ideal for her uncle, and a place he thought she would like too. She was surprised to be led into a private dining room and to find three place settings with her uncle already there to greet her. He was pleased to hear how her weekend had gone, but disappointed she was soon leaving.

"So, our friend hasn't convinced you to stay?" he asked.

"No, sorry, Uncle. I want to, but I have to go back. I hope you understand. Can you forgive me?"

"Of course I forgive you. You're a true Xin; you have principles you feel you must follow, just like my brother. I may not agree with them in your case, but I have to respect you for it; I know he would have."

"We can talk whenever we want, Uncle. It's easy using social media these days. We can see each other on our computers or phones anytime we like."

"Yes, a good idea. I can have my nephew set me up with it at the house, I guess."

"I'm sure Mei can do it anytime for you. She's good at that sort of thing. So who's joining us?" Lucy finally asked, pointing to the third place setting.

"An old friend who should have been here an hour ago."

"Someone I know?"

"Let me go outside and check."

Her uncle left the room, and the waiter brought her a glass of water while she waited. Lucy found the room peaceful. The decorations and simplicity of it all put her at ease. She began to think about her flight the next day, the harsh reality of going home to Phil, and the routine of her life in Blowing Rock. Would she miss all of this too much? Was her decision to go home a bad one, as everyone here and Sally at home had warned. She was shaken from those thoughts when her uncle walked back in, his guest following. Right away she knew who it was. The attractive but expressionless face told her the lady was none too happy to be there.

"I'm sure you've guessed who this is, Lucy. Let me introduce Madame Li Buyun to you at long last."

Lucy rose, walked over to the woman and held out her hand. "Madame Li, I'm Lucy Summers, John Wainright's daughter. I'm so pleased to finally meet you."

"I'm only here because of your uncle. It's not by choice, I can assure you."

The icy silence hanging over them showed no indication of thawing as she joined them. Lucy could feel the chill from her eyes as her uncle seated them facing each other.

"I appreciate you coming before I leave, Madame Li," Lucy said, twisting her napkin under the table to calm herself. "I'm grateful you're here, and I think I know why you feel the way you do. I just want to understand things better. I need to try to help the father I've known all my life somehow if I can. "

"I should not have agreed to come today, Mrs. Summers, but every time I refused your uncle, our merger terms improved. I'm not sure if I am being blackmailed to be here, or bribed, but it's clear he thinks a lot of you. I knew it was you when I walked into this room. I see your real father in you. He was a colleague and friend of mine too."

"And I see my adoptive father in your daughter's photos, Madame Li."

"We will not involve my daughter in this. Is that understood? I've made that quite clear to Xin here."

"So I hear," Lucy added quietly while nodding to the older woman.

Xin changed the subject by insisting they pause to order their food, something neither Lucy nor Madame Li seemed too interested in. He indicated they needed to eat, that if they didn't feel like it, then he certainly wanted to. The two women never bothered to pick up their menus. Xin was left to order, hoping that somehow the process of eating would ease the tension. He talked first about Lucy, how Madame Li and his brother had been close friends, to the point that she interrupted and told Lucy about how she had her own eye on the brother, until he met the American woman. It was around that time she became infatuated with John Wainright.

Xin watched Lucy let the older woman talk about those past times in her way, even though she had heard much of the story. She told Lucy how her political views had been shaped by the events of that time and her desire to see the country move forward. When the subject moved more to Wainright himself, the expression on Madame Li's face visibly hardened, the hatred clear to the two sitting at the table. Xin noticed, however, a slight softening in the way the woman began to speak to Lucy.

Xin interrupted. "Li, I know you don't believe this, but John Wainright never knew what happened to you when he left. We're convinced the document they showed you was a forgery. He never saw it. They used it to get you to talk."

Madame Li shook her head vigorously. She refused to believe him.

"Madame Li, from what I've been told you were incredibly brave in those days to protect your friends and colleagues." Lucy said. "The man who saved you and became your husband must have been a very special man. I'm truly sorry for your loss."

Li bowed her head slightly to Lucy, acknowledging her husband's passing, her pain clear to both of them.

Lucy continued. "That I was different from my parents bothered me my whole life, especially as I grew older. I was called many bad things, but my parents helped me through it. Still, they never told me who my true parents were. They lied to me. Your daughter is lucky; you are her real mother, but I suspect she too has wondered who her real father was. The photos of her tell it all. How can she not have yearned for the truth as I did?"

Li sighed. "She loved my husband. Her real father is of no interest, never has been. She is happy to remember a loving father and the life we shared with him; that's all there is to it, and will remain so."

"But what if that's not the case, Madame Li? What if she knew something of the past, how her biological father is still alive and sick, and that you could both help him recover? Shouldn't she at least learn the truth and be given the choice to help or not?"

"You remind me so much of your real father, Lucy, but he was far more persuasive than you will ever be, better than his brother here. I've agreed to terms with Xin that once the merger is signed I will make myself available to you, not before. One visit only. My daughter cannot, and will not, be dragged into this. Take it or leave it."

Xin leaned back in his chair, far enough that Madame Li couldn't see him smile, or mouth the word "Lucy." She understood exactly what he was emphasizing; Li had finally addressed her by her first name instead of Mrs. Summers. Lucy surprised him when she left her seat, and walked around the table toward Madame Li. She knelt in front of her, as tears streamed down her face.

"I beg you, Madame Li, in the name of the Xin family, please ask your own daughter, Zhao Wen, if she wants the truth about where she came from. If she says no, I'll accept her decision, I promise you. We're somehow sisters in this matter, not by blood, but we've traveled similar paths. I'd like to meet her someday as a friend. Whatever the father who raised me did or didn't do to you I want to have it cleared up. He may not be the man your husband was, but all of the hatred of the past years may have been misplaced. Shouldn't that be settled once and for all? What if you are wrong?"

Lucy stayed on her knees, refusing to get up without an answer. Her tears were genuine; she resisted any attempt by Li to get her to stand up.

Finally Madame Li looked at Xin, "For the sake of your gods Xin, get your niece up. I'll think about what she said, but that's all I promise."

Lucy stayed kneeling, her head bowed until Xin came and held her. "Lucy, get up now, please. Madame Li has promised to think about what you said. You cannot expect her to agree to a request like this after all those painful years so quickly. We must give her time. She is an honorable woman and will give this serious consideration, won't you, Li?"

"I made a promise didn't I? What more do you expect?"

Lucy finally rose with her uncle's help; she bowed slightly to Li and hurried out, wiping her eyes, then asked a waitress where the ladies room was.

———— ≈≈≈ ————

Once she was gone, Madame Li told Xin the girl reminded her so much of her real father that it was eerie. Xin asked only that she give her own daughter the opportunity to learn about her past. If she didn't want to have anything to do with it he would ensure she would never have to. Before Lucy returned, Madame Li obtained Xin's agreement to accompany her to the States to meet John Wainright, giving him little choice but to agree. She warned him that any more involvement than they agreed to already was going to cost him, one way or another. She laughed when he told her he never thought it was going to be any other way and gave no further promises.

When Lucy returned and heard that her uncle had agreed to accompany Madame Li to the States, she was overjoyed. "Relax, Lucy," Li told her. "We still have to agree on merger terms. Don't forget that. Now let's eat, I'm starving."

As the lunch wound down there was conversation about Lucy's upbringing, her mother's death from cancer, and when and how her parents had met. Lucy understood that Li was trying to line up those dates with everything that happened. She even listened with a softer attitude as Lucy described her father's illness. The idea that its onset had anything to do with the search for his biological daughter drew a curt dismissal by Madame Li. Lucy said it was too coincidental to be discarded. Her argument remained that knowing the truth surrounding what happened all those years ago and meeting Li and her daughter could bring him back— and bring peace to everyone involved.

———— ≈≈≈ ————

It was time for Lucy to leave with Wang Jun, he was waiting outside, deliberately avoiding any conflict with Madame Li. Lucy regretted leaving without an agreement involving Li's daughter. She desperately wanted to meet her. She felt a bond between them, a connection of sorts through the relationships of those involved all those years ago.

Lucy rose from the table after thanking Madame Li for coming. She kissed her uncle and told him she hoped to at least see him one more time before her flight. As she walked to the door she understood the two would be talking for a long time about her. She said a quiet prayer that her uncle could somehow convince Madame Li to speak to her daughter.

<hr />

During the drive back to Wang Jun's apartment Lucy told him about their discussions, adding her disappointment that she'd not succeeded in getting an agreement over the daughter.

"Lucy, you've got a lot to learn about your native home and its culture. I've listened to all you just told me, and if I read it correctly you made a lot of progress today. "

"I didn't make any progress, I'm afraid."

"You're letting your emotions cloud everything. You've forgotten what you went through in those meetings years ago. This is China, Lucy, not the U.S. We don't sit across a table, argue for a while, then reach across and shake hands on some kind of compromise deal. It doesn't happen that way here."

"This is not 'a deal', John, this is different."

"It *is* a deal, Lucy. It absolutely is. And from what you told me I think you're farther along than you think. Your uncle hasn't given up either. I guarantee you he's talking to her right now, pushing for everything you're after. He can be very persuasive."

"You mean offer more money on the deal? Is that it? I don't want that."

"I'm not talking money at all, but if it comes to that don't worry about it. Madame Li has no idea what value we can unlock from our merger, and once she finds out she's going to be kicking herself — more likely me. We have so much more to lay on the table if we have to, but that's not the point. Your uncle is going to do what's right . . . for you, and the business."

⌘

Their remaining hours were spent alone in the apartment. They promised each other it was not the end, but Lucy offered little prospect of any change in commitment to her husband, only that she would rethink everything if things worsened, or Phil became violent towards her. Wang Jun told her he was going to be there for her, and that he could wait for her. He reminded her of the patience of the Chinese, and how they could wait a long time to get what they wanted.

Their last night together wasn't hurried; their physical needs were taken care of, more tenderly than the hungered passion of their earlier evenings. Lucy struggled to control her tears at times, despite their agreement not to waste a second of their time in sorrow. When she cried, he cried, comforting each other in those moments, holding each other close. This was what she wanted, and where she needed to be. In the end she couldn't look beyond her father's illness, nor sorrow for the life her husband walked into the day he was captured. The words, in sickness and in health, ran like a broken record in her head, over and over. Would they ever go away?

Chapter 23

Lucy's departure from Beijing was as emotional as she had feared, especially with Wang Jun there. Mei Rui came to see her off, but didn't stay long. There were long hugs and promises they would be seeing each other in the future. Mei whispered in her ear again not to be foolish, to come back soon to where she belonged. Lucy thanked her for all she had done and promised her to stay in touch. Mei told her she might accompany Madame Li later. Lucy hoped she would, but she told her not to expect too much from Blowing Rock.

Her uncle arrived with one of his grand nieces by his side. The pretty young girl was clutching a beautiful red envelope that she seemed excited about giving her. Holding the envelope, Lucy thanked the girl warmly, then hugged her uncle. She knew exactly what the red envelope would contain, but she recalled how impolite it would be for her to open it right there.

"I can never thank you enough, Uncle. I'm blessed to be a part of your family. If my father was anything like you, then he was a wonderful human being," she said.

"I may not be that, Lucy, but my brother was. He loved your mother and would be proud to see how you have grown up. The envelope is to help you come back to see us soon. Anything you ever need, you call me. Understand? We are a close family, and you are part of it now. I hope to see you soon if we can get this merger done quickly enough; then maybe Wang Jun and Mei will come too."

"I'm looking forward to it. But don't rush the merger needlessly. It needs to be done right. How was the meeting with the Madame, after I left?"

"It was good, Lucy. You made an impression. I hope she will relent about her daughter, but it's still difficult for her. At least we are talking. The merger means she can't avoid contact with me again."

"And my sick father? Did she say anything more about him?"

"She still believes your father abandoned them, that he used her, then gave her up to the authorities to save his own skin. She'll see him for sure, but the daughter is not likely to."

"There's nothing more we can do?" Lucy asked.

"Mei and I aren't giving up. We're trying to track down people that were involved back then; some may still be alive, some not. I have friends who have promised to search through the files for me; perhaps there is something there we can use. As bad as they were, those interrogators kept meticulous notes of everything. We're hoping we find the right records to change her mind."

Lucy told her uncle again how much she appreciated what he was doing for her, and Wang Jun for allowing Mei Rui to continue to help. When it was time to go through immigration she hugged both of them. Her uncle left first to allow Wang Jun the few last minutes with Lucy alone.

Their farewell was tender, but they were careful of any public display of their emotions. There had been more than enough tears shed in his apartment. They promised to contact each other daily by e-mail, phone, or video call. Wang Jun held onto her hand as long as he could before she finally slid from his grasp. She looked back several times to see him still watching her walk toward the international departure area, onto the train toward customs and security. She spent the next hour in the first class lounge waiting to board her flight, suddenly physically and emotionally exhausted from all she'd been through.

———— ✺ ————

The plane was full and she was pleased to be flying first class; at least she would have a bed, better food, and not be bothered by other passengers. The initial acknowledgment from the woman in the next seat was the only words to pass between them until the plane landed. Unlike her early flying days, Lucy was asleep within an hour of dinner being served. She had only one glass of wine, but made sure she drank plenty of water before sleeping soundly for a good seven hours.

Once awake she went over in her mind what she would tell Phil; she had talked to Sally about her arrival time in Greensboro and learned he was back from his ride, happy, but worn out. He'd been relieved that Sally was going to pick Lucy up, and asked her to pass on that he was looking forward to seeing her at home. His not wanting to be in an airport didn't surprise Lucy; he hated being around planes and airports. She was glad Sally would be there to meet her first; she needed advice as to how much she would tell him about her trip.

Prior to landing Lucy remembered the red envelope and began to worry about getting through customs. Was it better to leave it unopened, or check what was in it? She decided to open it. Inside was a letter, indicating the gift was for her to set aside for tickets to China. She was shocked as she counted out twenty bank notes, each of them crisp thousand-dollar bills. She was really concerned. What if she was stopped?

As it turned out her passage through immigration, baggage, and customs went smoothly. Exiting the plane in New York, an airport representative with a sign bearing her name escorted her quickly through the entire process. She'd been nervous going through customs, especially with the two large suitcases on her cart, but the officers waved her through. They were focused on a couple with far more cases than anyone else in front, and the man accompanying her knew the officers well.

After he made sure her bags were checked through to the Greensboro flight, he asked if she needed any more assistance. Lucy told him she could handle everything from there on, that she really appreciated all his help. She tried to give him a large tip, but he waved it aside. He appreciated her gesture, but told her not to worry about it. "Mr. Wang Jun has covered everything . . . with extreme generosity. It was a pleasure."

Lucy was tired, but excited to see Sally after arriving on her connecting flight to Greensboro. The pair hugged as an exhausted Lucy told her how thankful she was for her being there to meet her. Sally told her she looked tired, but could see something new in Lucy's face, attributing it to "this Wang Jun of yours." Once the couple were out of the airport and into the car, Lucy called Phil to tell him they'd arrived and looked forward to seeing him in a couple of hours. That done, Sally suggested Lucy get some sleep while they drove home, but she had no desire to; she insisted on telling her about the rest of the visit. She told her everything that had happened over the last few days, and left nothing out. The more she talked about her uncle and Wang Jun, the more she realized what she had left behind, and that what she was coming home to was going to be a huge letdown.

Sally was nervous about agreeing to keep Lucy's uncle's gift in their safe, but Lucy pressed her to help. She did not want any bank records around that Phil might see and brushed off any concerns about it being stolen.

———— ❧ ————

Lucy was surprised to find herself nervous as Sally's car pulled into the alley beside the flower shop and parked by the stairs to the apartment. Sally helped her out with her cases, then got back in the car to wait until Phil could come down to greet Lucy and help with her bags. Within minutes the side door flung open, Phil came down to greet Lucy and waved to Sally. As the two embraced, Sally saw Lucy quickly draw away. She signaled to Sally it was okay, but Sally could see that Phil had been drinking. She held back a little longer until Lucy indicated she should leave.

As Lucy climbed the stairs, with Phil lugging the cases ahead of her, the contrast of life in Beijing with what she had come back to struck home. This was going to be far more difficult than she imagined.

———— ❧ ————

It was late and Lucy was exhausted. She had no desire to talk to Phil that night about her trip, only to get to bed right away. Phil seemed more anxious to tell her about his trip than to hear about hers. In some ways she had the feeling that she could have stayed longer, and he probably would have said nothing about it. She went to bed and lay there feeling alone, despite his presence by her side. He had reached out to her, but she feigned sleep; she could not get Wang Jun out of her mind. The last thing she wanted that night was to have Phil trying to satisfy her— in the only way he could.

Wang Jun was a noisy lover, but a quiet sleeper. Phil was the opposite, and the snoring she'd become used to ground on her senses now. She finally dragged herself out of the bed and headed to the guest room for solitude, struggling to clear her mind for sleep.

When Lucy came into the kitchen the next morning Phil had already made coffee and was eating a piece of toast. She began to tell him more about her trip, but there was much she couldn't bring herself to tell him. She said nothing about traveling first class, nor about the red envelope Sally was holding for her, or more importantly that she had discovered her real family.

She described Wang Jun to him simply as someone she worked with at Global who had done very well after the opening up of China. She described Chairman Xin only as her "adopted" uncle, a name given him from business all those years ago. She told him about being able to stay with a woman from the company, Mei Rui, who'd invited her to stay and save her the expense of a hotel. She told him in great detail about the whole business of the break-in and passport theft, and gave Phil only a hint about looking into something that might have affected her father's condition. She was thankful for his apparent lack of interest, determined to keep silent about the real story of her two fathers and Chinese family— at least until she was sure she could confront her father with Madame Li.

Phil occasionally interrupted her with some story from his road trip. Any other time it would have angered her, but this time she was thankful that he had few questions of her. His excitement grew, however, when she went to the bedroom, opened her suitcase, and brought out his special gift.

"What's this, Lucy? For me?" he asked, holding the package and squeezing it to guess what it may be. "What's really in here?"

"It's for you. Everyone was upset over the passport thing, and you having to wait another week for me. They bought it as a special gift since you couldn't fly over . . . remember?"

"Oh yeah . . . right . . . now I remember." He tore the wrapping off, understanding quickly it was a heavy leather jacket. As soon as he saw its emblems he leapt out of his seat to try it on. Lucy saw right away he was more excited to receive this than listen to anything about her trip.

"My god, Lucy, this is incredible. The guys will shit when they see this. Man, is this something! We have to thank them, really. Can you do it, for me?"

"Of course. They'll be pleased you like it." She smiled at the sight of him acting like a teenager, getting something he'd never dreamed he would own.

"Like it? I love it! I know my Harley stuff. This sucker's expensive. And feel it, feel that leather, Lucy. You don't get that here, not even in New York!" He took it off and showed her the emblems on the back, glowing with pride over it. "Now these ones here, they're real special. I can't wait for the guys to see them."

Lucy rolled her eyes when Phil turned around and was taking it off. She smiled at his reverence in the way he laid it over a chair back. "Okay, I'm going to unpack the rest of my things, then head down to the office," she said. "Are you taking the day off?"

"I don't go back till tomorrow. Are you going to be real busy in the shop?"

"I think so. In any case I'll be too tired to do much with the jet lag and everything. I've got something to take over to Sally later." She knew what she was about to be asked, and didn't really care.

"Do you mind then if I go off for an hour or so, show this to the guys? I need to break it in anyway. Is that okay?"

Lucy told him to head out whenever he was ready; she was going to be busy enough. She got up, gave him a reassuring hug and kiss on the forehead, then headed back to the bedroom. She closed the door behind her and leaned against it. Tears rolled down her face as she hit the doorjamb with her head several times. "What the hell have I done?" she asked herself over and over. She locked the door, slumped onto the bed, and buried her head in the pillow, muffling the sounds of her sobbing.

"Are you okay, honey?" The words brought her crying to a halt. She yelled out as best she could that she was fine. "Well, I'm off then. See you later. Love you." Lucy was relieved when he was gone.

It took her time to stop crying, wipe her eyes, and begin to empty the rest of her cases. She opened the first one and began putting everything away in the various cupboards and drawers. She threw anything she thought needed cleaning, or was heavily creased from the trip, onto the floor. The second case contained more clothes and a few gifts she'd bought for her father, Sally, Sarah, and even her former lover. She was surprised to find a package at the bottom of the suitcase, wrapped beautifully in red paper. She recognized right away what it was.

"Oh shit," she said, as the wrapping fell to the floor, revealing the chipao she had worn to the celebration for Xin. It was too beautiful, and valuable, to leave in the apartment. It meant everything about Wang Jun to her, but she wanted it to have nothing to do with Phil. She carefully rewrapped it, hoping Sally wouldn't mind keeping it in her safe along with the money. She had no idea when, or where, she could ever wear it in a place like Blowing Rock.

There was yet another red envelope in the bottom of the case. She was thankful that Phil had not been there to find it. She knew right away it was from Wang Jun. Somehow he must have slipped the dress and card into her suitcase before she left. The fact that he had cared enough to do it gave her a warm feeling, despite the trouble it could have caused with Phil. She opened the envelope carefully and sat on the bed to read it.

The letter was handwritten; he had obviously taken care in writing it. She read, absorbing every word and image that the paper yielded. He wrote of their time together, the joy she'd given him, his love for her, and the emptiness he would feel when she was gone. She quickly put aside any thought of destroying the letter, but knew she could not keep it in the apartment or the shop below.

Lucy read the letter several times, thankful that Phil had left without seeing it. She wondered for a moment if it might have been better if he had, bringing everything into the open. No, she told herself, she wasn't ready. What if Wang Jun did show up in Blowing Rock? Phil had already taken on three tough guys, requiring several of his friends to pull him off, just for a few lewd comments. The idea of an angry Phil meeting Wang Jun was something she dare not think about.

Chapter 24

L ucy came down to the flower shop around eleven in the morning to a warm welcome. Sarah told Lucy she had been busy, that the week ahead looked promising with a large number of orders to fill. She could barely contain herself talking about her recent sales, beaming as Lucy ran her eyes over the numbers and congratulated her. Lucy made a mental note to put something extra in her paycheck at the end of the month.

"That's really great, Sarah! I can't thank you enough for what you've done, but this is for you . . . a special thank-you." Lucy passed over the package to Sarah who oohed over the elaborate packaging, not wanting to damage it in any way by opening it.

"For god's sake open it, Sarah. You'll be here for hours trying to open it like that."

Sarah would have none of it; she spent the next fifteen minutes working at the package like a cosmetic surgeon on a delicate area of someone's face. When it was finally opened, she was delighted. There were several things inside: a beautiful cashmere scarf, an ornate table runner, and a wooden box containing four sets of gorgeous chopsticks with elaborate silver work. She tried on the scarf and flung her arms around Lucy, delighted with everything. Lucy could see Sarah was going to wear the scarf all day, as warm as it was, just to show it off.

"I'm glad you like them, Sarah. Are you okay if I disappear into the office for a while now?"

"Course not. You must be worn out after your trip. I'll get to work on to-day's flowers. Oh . . . and that Don Roberts was by for some flowers for his wife while you were gone. He's such a nice man. Anyway, he'll be back this week. She's going into hospital again and he wants something special. She'll be there quite a while, he says. Do you think it might be cancer?"

"I hope not. When he comes in let's do something special for her."

Lucy was surprised Don Roberts was still stopping in, especially since she knew everything about him now. Besides, she would be in touch with her uncle on a regular basis. She would talk to Don about it when he came in.

Lucy went into her office. It was too late to phone Wang Jun but he had told her to phone him at any hour, how he would be in his apartment waiting for her call the day after she arrived. They talked for a good hour that morning using her phone and the video chat program she downloaded in China. Using the shop's Wi-Fi would keep the cost of calls to almost nothing, and there would be no record of the calls for Phil to stumble upon. Not that he ever paid any atten-tion to the details of the various bills Lucy managed; he showed no interest in them at all. She spent another couple of hours helping Sarah, then called Sally Sweetland to see if she could come over to the grill to talk.

⸺⁂⸺

She arrived at the Supper Club Grill around two thirty. The lunch crowd was gone, and Sally and John were already cleaning up. Their other waitress had already left after clearing away the tables. Lucy was greeted with hugs from both Sally and John. Sally asked if she was hungry, or wanted to join her in a glass of wine.

"I'm not hungry right now, Sally, but a red wine sounds good. My body clock's all screwed up. I guess it thinks it's two thirty in the morning."

Sally poured two large glasses and suggested that her husband get back to the kitchen to do some food preparation for the evening. Lucy put down the back-pack she was carrying with her things inside, and the gifts for her closest friends.

"So how was it with Phil?" Sally asked.

Lucy looked at the ceiling and rolled her eyes. "Oh god, Sally. What a moron he's become. All I get to hear about is his frigging road trip, his buddies, and have him rave about the leather Harley jacket the Chinese bought for him."

"I'm not surprised. You know how I feel about him, don't you? Why you ever came back to this, I'll never know. Anyway, on the positive side you didn't want him asking too many questions, did you?"

"No, you're right. I have another favor to ask, by the way."

"What's that?"

" Can you keep something else for me in your safe? They were slipped into my case by Wang Jun before I left, without me knowing. Thank god Phil hasn't seen either of them, or the money."

"Course we can. There's not much in the safe. Should I ask what they are?"

"Sure, this is a dress Wang Jun bought me. I wore it at the celebration for my uncle. There's one other small thing, a personal letter from him. I can't throw it away . . . I probably should though. If Phil found it he'd probably kill me, or Wang Jun. Promise me you or John won't read it."

Sally laughed and joked how reading it would be the first thing she would do after Lucy left, swore on her mother's grave she wouldn't look, and promised to make sure John didn't either. "Now the dress, that's different; I want to see it! Let's go upstairs. At least show it to me before we put it away."

⸺◦⸙◦⸺

In Sally and John's bedroom Lucy carefully unpacked the red chipao. She held it in front of herself for Sally to see.

"Oh my god, Lucy!" Sally ran her fingers carefully over the designs in gold thread, then gently touched the areas highlighted in pearls.

"You like it?"

"Like it? Are you kidding? This is the most gorgeous dress I've ever seen. And those slits up the side. I bet it's sexy. Was your Wang Jun able to keep his hands off you?"

"Not for long." Lucy replied to Sally's knowing look.

"And these things here. Imagine if they were real pearls! It would cost a fortune."

Lucy blushed. "They are real. I think it is worth a lot. He told me if I ever needed money, or wanted nothing more to do with him, I could sell it back in China and live a good life on the proceeds . . . for a while at least."

"Oh, Lucy, do you think I could try it on just once . . . please? I promise not to do anything to it. We're about the same size. Can I? Can I? Oh please let me."

Lucy laughed at her acting like a young girl that has just seen a princess's dress and cannot wait to try it on. "OK. But be careful . . . here . . . let me help you."

Sally was in her underwear in no time. The dress was a bit snug on her, but was not overly so. Lucy led her over to the bedroom mirror, surprised to see that it looked great on Sally too. She grabbed a brush, a hair clip from the bathroom, and pushed Sally's hair up to highlight the dress's neckline even more.

Sally stood before the mirror, occasionally turning to let the side slits open in a sexy manner. "See, Lucy, the old pins still look pretty good, don't you think?" Lucy was surprised to see Sally's eyes suddenly well up and tears appear. "It's so beautiful, Lucy. I've never worn anything like this in my life. Would you mind if John saw it on me? This once, I mean. Then it can go away, we'll never touch it again, honestly."

"Of course he can. Just don't tell him the pearls are real. Let's keep that between us."

Lucy told her to wait while she fetched John from the kitchen. She asked him to come up and look at something in his wife's bedroom, but did not say what it was. She made sure his clothes and hands were clean before leading him up the stairs and asked him to wait while she knocked on the door. She called out to Sally that John was about to come in, then led him in after he'd promised to cover his eyes.

"Okay, John, take a look at your wife."

He took his hands away. "Holy mother of god! You look gorgeous. I don't know what to say. It's beautiful. Wow."

"Isn't it, John? It's Lucy's though. She's let me wear it this once for you; then it's off to the safe. Phil can't see it, or be told about it, okay?'

John couldn't resist kissing his wife right away, and running his hand up her thigh to where the slit ended. "Would you mind, Lucy, if I took a photo of her, for me I mean? Could I? I won't show it to Phil."

"Of course, John. Get your camera and then Sally can take it off afterwards. I've got something I want to give you both downstairs."

John came back with his camera; he was an accomplished photographer in his own right. Lucy sat on the bed, bemused by his excitement, watching him lovingly photograph Sally. When he was finished, both women looked at the screen on the camera back to see the photos he'd taken. Lucy thought they were exceptional. Sally hugged Lucy, thanked her for letting her try the dress on, and allowing John to take the photos. John went downstairs while Lucy helped Sally off with the dress, carefully folded it and wrapped it for storage in the safe. Sally was beaming as they came down to the restaurant area.

∞∞∞

After carefully placing the letter and the dress in the safe, Sally poured a second glass of wine for both of them. She continued to tell Lucy what an incredible dress it was until Lucy reached down to the bottom of her bag and brought out two more packages, one for each of them. "These are for you two, for being the best friends anyone could have."

Sally called John over and began to open hers, as careful with the packaging as Sarah had been. Sally took out two small ornate boxes and timidly opened each one, as if the enclosures themselves were somehow precious. Inside the first was a large, single-pearl necklace with a gold clasp. Sally gasped and threw her arms around Lucy. "Oh my god . . . it's beautiful . . . you shouldn't have." The other box contained a broach in the shape of a Chinese character. "What does it mean?"

"Fortune, to bring you luck. I hope you like them."

Sally put the pearl around her neck, and John commented on how well it suited her. Lucy suggested she get it appraised and insured, confessing that her new friend over there, Mei Rui, had bought it from her friend's store in the Silk Market of Beijing for her to give to Sally.

"The broach is from me, but Mei insisted on getting this for you. I tried to pay her for it, but she told me I couldn't afford it. Anyway, it's a gift from you know whom really, so she didn't pay for it herself." Lucy noticed her handling the pearl with a lot more care after hearing it could be expensive.

Sally put it away gently in its box, and then insisted Lucy pin the broach to her blouse right away. "You'll thank him for me, won't you? Tell him I really love it, and that I hope one day we'll meet."

"Of course. Now John, please open yours. I wasn't sure what to get you. The first one here's from my friend again, the second from me."

John opened the package to reveal an impressive leather wallet embossed with the Louis Vitton logo. Before he could say anything Lucy pointed at it and turned to Sally. "Oh, and it's genuine, not a fake."

John loved it, telling both of them he always wanted something special like it, how he usually shopped for wallets in the bargain section when he needed one. "They never last," he said. Grinning he opened the larger box with Lucy's gift, shocked to see a fine gold Rolex watch nestled in an elaborate case.

Before he'd finished whooping with excitement, Lucy gave him a dig. "That's from me John, and that one *is* a fake! Actually it's the best copy you can get your hands on over there, not cheap. My friend helped me make up the difference, so you have to thank him for that too. Only thing is, if you need it fixed you better be careful, but the seller says it will last you for years, no problem. Apparently Wang Jun's done business with him for years, bought real ones and copies from him, never had a problem. "

"I don't know what to say, Lucy, really I don't," John said. "They're both great gifts. You didn't need to buy these, especially not your friend, but we thank you both. We care about you, Lucy. We just hope one day you can be happy again."

There were hugs all around before she left the restaurant, asking the two to say nothing to anyone about the gifts, except that Sally could show off the broach as Lucy's gift from China. They promised to keep everything to themselves; John joked that his customers would accuse him of overcharging to pay for his new watch. He was still admiring it on his wrist as she walked out.

As the days and weeks went by Lucy settled into a routine. This "new normal," a phrase she was hearing more and more on the evening news, was far from it. She was living a lie. She knew it, but still could not bring herself to face the reality of what she wanted. Her calls to Wang Jun continued, as often as she could and when he was available. Her uncle called every couple of days, as did Mei Rui, about the merger. Mei also filled her in on how Wang Jun was doing, the discussions with Li Buyun, and her own situation. Mei never stopped trying to talk her into going back, or at least working for them in the U.S. The difficult conversations were whenever Mei wanted her to open up about Phil, obviously checking her out for Wang Jun and her uncle.

Lucy was frustrated; the merger discussions were dragging. When she told Mei she feared that Madame Li would back out, Mei told her she shouldn't worry. It was China after all, and these matters always took time. Mei said Lucy's uncle was spending more time than ever talking to Li Buyun, and she felt sure he was making progress with her.

Lucy had told Uncle on her own calls that her father was not improving. He had shown little reaction to her getting back from China. She'd steered clear of talking to her father about Xin or Li Buyun, but sensed relief more in what she hadn't told him. She was more convinced than ever that her plan was the best way to shake him out of his malaise.

⸺ ⚬⚬ ⸺

Every two weeks, on Friday evening, her regular customer Don Roberts came by to pick up flowers. The first time he showed up after her trip she took him into her office to talk in private. As soon as they sat down Lucy told him how pleased she was to see him.

"How's your wife doing now, Don?"

"Not well I'm afraid, Lucy. She's in the hospital again. I'm not sure she'll get out of there this time. The flowers are the one bright spot while she's suffering there."

"I'm so sorry. My uncle told me all about it. I was a bit surprised to see you back actually, now that I know about everything. I see you've stopped wearing a jacket. No more lapel cameras, I guess."

He laughed, reached in his pocket, and pulled his cell phone out. "Yeah, wearing the jacket on some of those hot days was a pain, now I can just use this." He took a few quick photos to her amusement, and then continued. "Actually, your uncle is more interested in you than ever. I'm to keep a closer eye on you and your husband. You might as well know that. I'm also going to give you a new number to call me on . . . this is it . . . use it twenty-four seven if you need my help . . . or anything at all."

"I'm sure I won't need it, but if it makes my uncle happy, that's fine with me."

"Your uncle's been very generous to my wife and I, Lucy. Way beyond any agreement we ever had. I think she'd be dead now without the care we've been able to afford, thanks to his generosity. The company health insurance we had wasn't worth a damn."

"He's a wonderful person. I only wish I'd known him all these past years."

"He's changed though, Lucy. I've known him a long time; he used to be ruthless in his business dealings. I hate to tell you that, but back then he could strike fear into the people he dealt with. Somehow he's changed over the last couple of years."

"I never saw him that way, even when we were negotiating years ago in Beijing. I did meet his Buddhist teacher on this visit; maybe he's helped him change."

The two talked about everything during their first meeting after her trip. From then on it became a biweekly ritual Lucy looked forward to; somehow she felt Don gave her another connection to her uncle. The flowers for the man's wife became more elaborate, always more blooms than she charged him for, and despite knowing her uncle was likely paying for them. But Lucy remained far more evasive with him when talking about Phil.

Things were not improving in that regard. She worried that her husband's mental stability was slipping worse than ever, but she said nothing about it to Roberts. Thankfully Phil was still not physically violent; in every other way he was, however, and difficult to live with. In times past she complained about his being out with friends all the time; she now encouraged it. Her main concern was the increasing use of alcohol her husband seemed to need to ease his pain.

The questions Don Roberts asked in subsequent meetings were becoming subtler about Phil, but posed in such a way that he seemed aware of that something was going on. Her uncle had told her the man was a good investigator. From his pointed questions now, Lucy could see just how right her uncle was. The lies became more difficult for her to tell, and she knew he didn't believe her. She wondered what he might be telling her uncle.

Chapter 25

It had been four months since her return from Beijing. That morning the phone rang in the flower shop. Sarah answered it and rushed to tell Lucy someone from China was calling. Lucy picked up the phone expecting it to be Wang Jun.

"Hello . . . John?"

"Sorry, it's Mei. Wang Jun's in meetings, but he wanted me to call right away. Great news! We initialed the papers today. The deal's done, Lucy."

"What?"

"Madame Li is waiting for confirmation of when you want her and Chairman Xin to come. She needs at least a couple of weeks notice though. How about that?"

Lucy was stunned for a few moments; she had waited so long for this to happen and now was tongue-tied. She had not told Phil anything about this yet.

"Lucy? Are you there? Are you okay?" Mei asked, concern in her voice.

"I'm sorry, Mei. It's just a bit of shock after all these weeks. And just like that! I can hardly believe it."

"Oh, you better believe it. Thanks to your uncle, of course, and Wang Jun. She's extracted one hell of an agreement though."

"That doesn't sound good."

"Don't worry. There will still be tremendous benefits all round; I'm sure of that. I need to get back into the meeting, but let us know when they can come. Allow us a couple of weeks to arrange everything."

Lucy thanked Mei, but told her she had to think things through. She still hadn't told her husband what was going on. Either way, she was anxious to get her planned confrontation with her father over with. She promised Mei a reply within the next day or two.

Lucy began to think about dates. She had given up on the daughter coming over and was now worried about Wang Jun showing up there, especially while Phil was in his current state. Would he figure out what was going on between them? Where they would stay was another worry. Blowing Rock had few decent places to stay. The local Holiday Inn Express was probably decent, but she figured her visitors would be unhappy there, the hotels they used were pretty fancy by comparison.

The nearest place with any high-end hotel was Greensboro, but that was going to mean a good two-hour drive each way to the hospital. She made several calls before she settled on recommending the downtown Hyatt Hotel. A quick call to Don Roberts about it, since he lived there, took away any concerns she had. He confirmed he would be taking care of them while there, and drive the pair to and from Blowing Rock. He told her not only was it his pleasure to do it, but he had already discussed it with her uncle the day before.

The decision on how and what to tell her husband took a couple of days. Finally she decided to simply tell him that while in China she had met two people who knew her father when he was with Goldman Sachs. They planned to be in the U.S. on business and had agreed to visit her father, as "old friends," nothing more than that. Wang Jun was on her mind constantly; any feelings of love for Phil were gone. All she had left was sympathy for what he had endured overseas.

She eventually stopped by Sam Jones' office to give his assistant two small gifts— a tablecloth and chopsticks. For Sam she had an attractive cardholder she thought he might like, which he did. He was pleased to see her again, but she steered clear of anything to give him hope she was there to rekindle their past relationship. She told him the same story she had given Phil about her trip, not knowing what he might let on to Phil during his therapy sessions. She was there primarily to understand if Phil was making any progress, telling Sam things seemed to be deteriorating with him. She confirmed her husband hadn't sunk to any kind of physical violence yet, but was more distant than ever and drinking heavily.

Sam was not surprised; he said Phil seemed introspective of late, angrier with himself, and more frustrated than before. As much as Sam probed the past with him, it was clear to Lucy that Phil hadn't revealed any details of his torture and what had been done to him.

He urged her to be careful and watchful of him, that if she was worried about anything to call right away. She left his office, promising to stay in touch. She knew he was disappointed that she showed none of her past feelings towards him. She wondered what he would have said to her if he knew the full story of her visit to China. She still cared for him, but in a different way, hoping they could still be good friends. She was going to need his insights into her husband's state of mind, especially if things got worse. She might also need his help one day. Don Roberts was a good two hours away if anything happened; she needed to keep Sam as a close friend, but not too close.

Chapter 26

Suicide is a terrible thing. Lucy Summer's loss of her husband left her devastated, mentally and physically. Her father's condition had been traumatic enough; now she couldn't see herself surviving both situations. Wang Jun, Mei Rui, and her uncle all told her they would come to her aid, but she was adamant she be left alone to grieve until the time was right for them to come. She broke down in front of her father when she gave him the news. He held her close, but his silence, even over her tragedy, led to angry words. She had slammed the door behind her on leaving, yelling to the nurse's surprise, "The asshole can go to hell as far as I'm concerned."

The whole town of Blowing Rock was talking about her. She knew small towns were like that; everyone knew each other's business, their personal affairs, and more. She was devastated. Feelings of guilt wouldn't leave her. She wondered if she had failed her husband. She chastised herself for losing it with her father, even questioned her love for Wan Jun. She began drinking at home again, not enough to worry about, but certainly more than she'd done in years.

What they were saying about her in the town, and its bars, became apparent one evening in Jake's bar. It was a small place with a jazz trio playing there most evenings, soulful music that appealed to her sense of loss.

She had decided to meet with Sam Jones there. She knew she needed Wang Jun more, but she wasn't ready for that yet. Arriving at the bar early, she hid herself in the corner near the small stage to avoid other people. She recognized three of her husband's friends sitting in the next booth; fearful they might see her meeting Sam she sat back from their view. As soon as she saw him appear she told herself to catch him at the entry, to go somewhere else. She could not help overhear the men talking.

"Damn shame, Joe," one of them said.

"You're right, and what a babe," Bill said. "I mean, she could have any man she wanted in this town, anywhere for that matter."

"I'm talking about Phil, you moron. How can you say something like that after what's happened?"

"Look, what Phil did, he did, and no one held a gun to his head or anything. He chose his own way out. I mean . . . he was happy enough on our road trip, right? Others have done it too you know; vets that is. Some of them who went through what he did have already beat him to it. Who's crying for them?"

"Jesus, Bill, he's not even buried yet!" Fred said.

"All I'm saying, guys, is she's a real honey. She shouldn't be alone. Suffering with that spaced out father of hers can't help either. She needs someone to help her with that too."

"You two are a couple of heartless bastards, Lucy's a real lady around here."

"Now calm down, Fred, he's not serious."

"None of you should be talking like that. I can't imagine what she's going through right now."

"I'm just saying what she is, Fred. Aren't I right, Joe?"

"Yeah, well Phil would beat the hell out of you if he could hear you talking like this. He'd want us to help her, not throw around stupid remarks like that."

Lucy could bear it no more. She started to rise out of her seat, upset at the way her husband's old buddies were talking. As Sam looked over to her and smiled, she quickly got up and walked by the three men, stopped herself from blurting out what she really wanted to say, sweeping Bill's beer into his lap, missing Joe's by an inch.

"Screw you, Bill. You too, Joe."

She rushed over to push Sam outside before the three men could see him, or try to offer apologies for any offences they may have given.

⋙

Fred chuckled, told Bill he was lucky it was only beer she spilled on him, that he didn't get the glass dropped on his head.

"Sorry, guys, I'll try to call her and apologize tomorrow. I had no idea she was sitting behind us. I mean she *is* a honey isn't she? Am I wrong, guys?"

Fred stood up, gave his best friends a last disgusted look before leaving the bar. "You just don't get it do you, Bill? Sometimes you really are an insensitive prick."

"What the hell did I say wrong, Joe? I gave the lady a compliment didn't I? Don't you think she's hot?"

Joe got up and left too, shaking his head. Bill just sat there, shouting after his friends, "What the hell's got into everybody tonight?"

⋙

"What's wrong, Lucy?" Sam asked as she dragged him outside the bar.

"Let's get out of here before I lose it. I can't stand these people sometimes. Just take me somewhere to cool off . . . anywhere."

"Are you hungry?" he asked.

"Not any more, but don't let that stop you from eating."

"Okay, how about the Supper Club? It's close by and quiet on Monday nights. We can talk in peace there if you like.

"Fine by me. Let's walk. I need some air."

By the time they reached Sally and John's bar and grill she had calmed down. The cold air of a March evening in that part of North Carolina had helped clear her head; perhaps she could eat something after all. She had arranged to meet Sam Jones earlier that night, specifically to talk about her father. Their past relationship had been complicated, hidden she hoped from prying eyes and gossipers; Blowing Rock was filled with them, people who had nothing better to do than spread whatever juicy scandal they could find, or make up. He had been her husband's caregiver right up to the tragedy, but fallen for Lucy, along with every other male in town. She had not turned him away like all the others, responding instead in a way that even surprised her. It was a serious breach of ethics for Sam, as the doctor overseeing Phil Summers' mental health. She knew the fact that he was divorced would matter little to any medical board of governors, even in light of her situation. That had been one of the many reasons she had ended the relationship, apart from other concerns about what Phil would do if he found out.

Sally Sweetland welcomed the couple into the restaurant, but Lucy could see the puzzled look on her face. Before Lucy could whisper anything to her, Sally led them in. "Come in, come in. It's good to see both of you. The place is quiet tonight. You know what Monday's are like around here, Sam. One of these days I'll get John back there to shut the place down, but he won't listen to me. I'm sick of hearing how his family has kept this place open on Monday nights for forty years."

"Well, I'm glad you're open, Sally. I need a drink," Lucy said.

"Me too," Sam added, giving Sally a reassuring pat on the arm.

"Let me take care of it right away. Ignore what I just said; I'm glad you two are here. Sit wherever you like. The usual?"

Sam said yes. He was about to get a stiff brandy Manhattan with just the right amount of special bitters that Sally kept behind the bar for him. Lucy surprised both of them by ordering a large vodka martini; she'd always been a wine drinker. The two picked the table by the log fire John Sweetland was stirring into life, giving a glow and warmth to take the evening chill off them.

Within no time Sally was back to their table with the two drinks. She offered to take their orders but both declined, and asked if they could be left to talk for a while. Sally said she wouldn't bother them until they needed another drink or were ready to order.

They sipped their drinks while Lucy filled Sam in on what just happened in Jake's with Phil's old buddies. Sam said he understood her frustration, but told her it wasn't worth getting heated up about. She cracked a half-smile when he added, "Lucy, you always were the hottest babe in town, for me too!"

The martini was starting to have its effect on her when Sam changed the subject. "I have to ask you something, Lucy, you can tell me if you want to, or not. I can find out from the cops if I want, but I'd rather hear it from you if it's not too painful."

"What do you want to know?"

"Well, they've already talked to me about Phil's mental state, for obvious reasons, but they declined to disclose how he did it. Can you tell me? Or am I out of line on that too?"

"No, Sam, I'll tell you. It's coming out soon anyway, now that the autopsy's finished. Wednesday, they warned me; that's the day the report will be made public. Officer Smith already called to tell me the chief wanted me to know first. They had to wait for a third-party investigation to confirm everything before releasing it."

"So what really happened, Lucy? I thought we were making progress with him. I was devastated when I heard about it. Phil let me believe things were going well, and I hadn't seen you for weeks. I want you to know I'm still here for you, professionally of course, but if possible I'd like it to be personally too."

Lucy thanked him, and told him gently that sometime in the future there might be a chance of rekindling their relationship, but it was way too soon to even think about anything like that. She warned him there were some tongues wagging in town about them, that her being out together that night would cause more rumors. He told her they could have met professionally in his office if she preferred, but she responded that was not what she needed just then; in the future she might. She said nothing to him about Wang Jun.

The first drinks gone, they ordered another, and put in their food orders. Sam excused himself to visit the men's room. Sally then leaned across and put an arm around Lucy's shoulder, whispering gently that she hoped she was feeling better, but what was she doing there with Sam. Lucy told her she was only there to talk, and would tell her later what just happened in Jake's. Sally told her she could take all the time she needed to talk, but cautioned her to make sure that was all it was.

———— ✺ ————

"You know the hills out back where we used to play as kids, then hike on up to the mountains above?" Lucy asked Sam when he sat down again.

"Of course I do. That's where I fell in love with you. I was only twelve."

"I know you did. Anyway, it was a special place for Phil too. That's where he proposed to me. We had many good times there hiking and camping. Phil's dad took him there from when he was only six to watch the sunrise and then fish together. Do you remember that area with the huge flat rocks? We used to call them Indian lookout mountains when we were kids."

"Sure do. One of my favorite spots for playing cowboys and Indians, as I recall, but I haven't been up there in years. I was never the outdoorsy type like Phil and the others; dad used to gripe at me for burying my head in all those medical books after school. Sorry, that's not what we're hear to talk about, go on."

"They found Phil up there . . . on the biggest boulder. You remember that flat one that sticks out the farthest? The one with the best view of the valley?"

"I think so, yes."

"Well, the autopsy report will say he died about thirty minutes after the sun rose, that he must have been sitting there just to watch it come up."

"I'm so sorry. Lucy. Which gun did he use?"

"There was no gun, Sam. They found him sitting in one of his hunting chairs with a case of beer by his side and an old fishing rod across his lap. I told the police it looked like the one he used with his father; it was missing from the garage wall where he kept it. He was sitting there, Sam, stone cold, looking straight ahead, hands draped over the armrests."

When she choked up he leaned over to comfort her, but she pushed his arm away telling him she needed to finish. "There was blood everywhere. He'd used his dad's hunting knife on both wrists. They told me he had a weird look of contentment on his face though, as if he was glad it was finally over."

"Was there any note left? Did he give any reason? Sorry to ask, but I've worried about that ever since I heard. Was it my fault, do you think? Did I let him down?" he asked.

"No, not you, but he left a note, said he'd had enough of hurting everyone . . . especially me. He regretted not being man enough to give me the child I wanted so badly. He'd always figured that could have helped our marriage. There was more, but that's the essence of it. He added a note at the end, scrawled in blood, his own blood!" She finally broke down. "He told me to forgive him, Sam, that he was at peace now, and he loved me." With that she left the table, her drink spilling as she headed past a concerned Sally to the restroom.

Sally walked over as soon as Lucy disappeared into the ladies room. "Is she okay, Sam? Should we bring the food now?"

"Yeah, please. Let's do that. She needs to talk though, Sally, she's bottling too much up."

"Well, take care of her, you hear."

"I will, if she'll let me."

"I'll say this once. Phil was an asshole to her, God rest his soul, but the son of a bitch should never have married her in the first place. He just wanted to own the best-looking girl in town. I tell you now, the only guy in this town she deserved to be married to would have been you. You've missed out for good now, but for god's sake take care of her, as a friend."

"What do you mean, I've missed out for good?" he asked.

"I can't say, Sam; leave it at that."

"I'll help her, Sally, don't you worry about that, but I haven't given up on her, especially now. Please be careful what you say around here about us, just yet anyhow."

"Don't worry. John and I are your friends, but you need to know those old hags out there have been talking for a long time about you and Lucy. Never mind what they've been saying about that crazy father of hers!"

"I thought as much. I guess that's one drawback of growing up in small town America, and staying here. Thanks anyway for tonight. By the way, I did see you turn your open sign to closed . . . does John know?"

"Heck no, he's still working in the kitchen where he belongs. He thinks it's just a quiet night."

"I can't thank you enough." Sam said.

"No need. That girl's been my best friend from middle school on. I love her like a sister. I never understood why she came back here, except of course for her father, and that thing with her mother. Don't let her down on this, Sam."

"It won't be for not trying, I assure you of that."

"Good. I'll tell John to get your food out. Stay all night if you like."

"I think it'll be a long one, thanks."

"Never thought we'd be providing facilities for psychiatric services by Sam Jones in the old Supper Club . . . Careful, she's coming."

<hr />

"What's up? Sorry about that."

"Nothing, honey. I just checked if Sam here was ready to eat. The poor man must be starving, and John's antsy to bring it out."

"Go ahead, Sally, I'm ready. I'm not finished talking though. Can we stay longer?"

"As long as you like. We'll clear away after you eat, if you don't mind. We'll leave you a nice bottle of wine, and head off to bed. You know where the lights are, right?"

"How can I forget."

"Just make sure you lock the door behind you properly, not like that damned prom night of ours. And before you say anything about tonight, our lips are sealed. I dread thinking about what those jerks out there say about John and me."

<hr />

In minutes the table was covered with more food than they ordered. John told them he had so much time while they were yakking that he was trying a few new dishes on them. He shook hands with Sam and kissed Lucy on the cheek. Lucy thanked him and whispered in his ear, "I love you both."

They were surprised to see it was ten o'clock when they began to eat. They talked about other things for a while, Sam's practice, where it was headed, and how well Lucy's flower business was doing. She almost told him the truth about her uncle, and Wang Jun, but decided the time wasn't right.

After the meal was over, Sam poured the wine Sally had brought out before clearing the last of their dishes.

"There's more about Phil I need to tell you," Lucy said. "He was never the same when he came back from Afghanistan, you know."

"Of course, not many were."

"I mean not being able to give me a child, Sam. That really got to him."

"But that's not such a big deal these days, with fertility treatments, adoption; there are many ways. He never said anything to me in our sessions about that, as I recall. I always assumed you two didn't want a family yet, what with your business and all."

"He never talked about it, Sam?"

"No."

"You didn't know he'd been tortured badly over there? That we couldn't have a normal sex life anymore?"

Sam suddenly put his wine down, almost breaking the glass. "You mean he was tortured like that over there? Oh my god! Sally, I could have done so much differently with him if I'd known. I thought I'd burrowed into his most innermost fears and memories of what he went through there. I believed I was bringing him out of it, but you're telling me I wasn't at all. Why didn't you tell me all this?"

"I promised him I wouldn't tell anyone. He was deathly afraid his buddies would find out he was impotent . . . worse, a eunuch, I guess. Not that any of those morons would know what the word means. In the end he just didn't love me after his last tour; that was plain from the abuse I took since."

"Well, on that score you're wrong, Lucy. The man loved you with a passion I've rarely seen. Every session was the same in that regard. To be honest I was jealous, and guilty about that when we were together. What you've told me sheds a whole new light on Phil; whatever he may have done to you, I can assure you he loved you. I see now why he was as abusive as he was; it's classic among vets, but with what they did to him over there, I'd say his problems were far worse than most."

"There's one more thing I have to tell you about a note in his lap," Lucy said.

"What's that?"

"Those last words in blood. He also wrote, 'See Sam. I want him to take care of you.' "

Sam was shaken. "Oh my god. Of course I will, if you'll let me. But I feel terrible knowing we were cheating on him."

"I'm sure he never knew. I've asked the chief to protect my privacy in not releasing all the contents of his suicide note, but I doubt they'll keep it quiet."

"I don't care, Lucy. We can get through this together."

"Don't think that changes anything between us. There's still more I have to tell you about where I go from here. I just can't tell you right now. I need you more than ever as a friend to help me."

"Of course, anything. I'm here for you any hour of the day. If you want to move into my house the door's wide open."

"That's not going to happen, Sam."

⸙

They talked until one o'clock in the morning. As they left she asked him again if he thought what she planned to do with her father was the right thing to do or not. He told her he would support her in any way she needed, that it was worth a try if she could pull it off and offered to help; she thanked him, but was sure it wouldn't be needed.

"Lucy, I'll be waiting until you're ready. I love you."

"Things have changed. Give me more time and I'll tell you everything, maybe then you'll understand. I just don't want our friendship to end."

"I'll always be your friend, no matter what."

She wondered if he really would, once he found out the truth about Wang Jun. She declined his offer to walk her home, as much as Sam worried for her safety, the shop was only a few blocks away and the street well lit, even that late at night.

Her husband's death had been the most prominent news story in years, and she knew rumors were rife in town about what may have happened. She didn't need another one surfacing about her and Sam, especially if someone saw him walking her home so late at night.

Chapter 27

The week following her husband's death passed in a blur for Lucy. It fell on Sally Sweetland to help her through those difficult days, along with Sarah in the flower shop. She was surprised and deeply moved by Phil's friends in their support of her after the Jake affair, Fred in particular. He had stepped in to organize the funeral for Phil once the body was released from the morgue, insisting she let him make all the arrangements when he saw how lost she was. She had resisted at first, in the belief it was her responsibility alone, but Sally persuaded her to let him take it over. Lucy was torn inside with Phil's death, her guilt over the relationship with Sam, and the affair with Wang Jun. Her only relief was the daily calls from Wang Jun, and sometimes her uncle. She continued to delay agreeing to their many requests to come over to help her.

The funeral itself, held within days of the body being released after the investigation, turned into a more moving event than Lucy had imagined. Phil had no other relatives that anyone knew of; his parents had passed away years earlier. Her own father was in no condition to attend, so she expected a few friends at most to be there. The sight awaiting her when she arrived at the small Episcopal church downtown was a shock. The pathway to the church was lined with military veterans and motorcycle riders to show their respect. Sally and John had to support her as she made her way into the church. Sarah had filled the altar with flowers and surrounded the area where the coffin would be positioned with red roses. There were people in the pews she had never met, but who somehow knew her husband.

It was Fred who eulogized her husband, something she could never have done herself. He spoke of growing up with Phil, his marriage to Lucy, the love of country that led him to defend it, along with a celebration of the times when the four close friends enjoyed the freedom of the open road together on their bikes. There was laughter and tears from many in the church at some of the stories. After Fred finished Lucy hugged and thanked him for his kind words. When she left the church, the hearse was trailed by a solemn formation of twenty bike riders, many with U.S. flags at half-mast on their bikes. It was a moving sight for a small place like Blowing Rock.

The move to the crematorium was a more private ceremony, except for four officers from the Marine Corps that Phil fought with in Afghanistan. They draped the coffin in their unit's flag before it was carried inside, then drove four of their badges, by hand, into the outside of Phil' coffin, and presented the folded flag to Lucy. One of them played a soulful trumpet, the last call, as the coffin moved out of sight towards its final moment. The Marine who presented the flag to Lucy had leaned forward, and told her how Phil saved their lives, even as he was captured. They were thankful Fred had contacted them, and presented her with official condolences from many others who could not be there. By the time the day was over Lucy was in a state of grief, anger, and guilt. Sally told her husband she was staying over with Lucy, who didn't object. She was thankful to not be left alone after such a heart-wrenching day.

—❦—

At eight o'clock that evening the apartment phone rang. After Phil's death, Lucy had arranged for all calls to be transferred after hours from the shop to the apartment. Sally had put Lucy to bed, along with a sleeping aid. She heard the answering machine kick in, knew right away who it might be, and rushed to pick it up.

"Is that Wong John?" she quickly asked.

"Er . . . close enough; it's Wang Jun. Is Lucy there?"

"I'm afraid she's sleeping. I'm Sally Sweetland."

"Ah yes, she's told me a lot about you. Is she okay?"

"She's sleeping now, but it's been a tough day for her. I know she would have liked you to be here, but it's difficult in a place like this," Sally said.

"We are all sorry here about her husband. I guess she told you about me?"

"Yes. Can I call you John, like she does?"

"Absolutely, I feel like I know you."

"Great . . . er . . . John, then. Listen, you need to get over here as soon as you can if you want her. To be honest with you she's feeling guilty. She shouldn't, but she's forgetting all the bad things about Phil, God rest his soul. I haven't met you yet, but I can tell she loves you. She should never have come back here all those years ago."

"Well, we're ready to come over, Sally, as soon as she tells us we can. Her uncle has been working hard on her father's situation, so I hate to see something happen there if we leave it too long."

"Let me work on her. Can I talk to you directly if I think I need to?" Sally asked.

"Of course. I'll send you all my information and private number. You'll be able to get me anytime. Just remember the time difference."

Sally gave him her e-mail address and phone number. Wang Jun gave his, promised to e-mail her for confirmation, and offered to pay for any calls she had to make. By the time she put down the phone she had a new determination to work on her friend, convinced more than ever this man was where Lucy's future lay. The day had been as moving for her as everyone else, but she knew more than anyone what Phil had put his wife through; it was too easy to lose sight of that. Lucy still had her whole life ahead of her, and Sally was determined to encourage her best friend not to waste it in mourning, especially over him.

It took two weeks for Lucy to come out of the apartment after the funeral, even to venture down to the flower shop. Sally came around as often as she could, and slept there for the first few days until Lucy assured her she was okay. Sarah came up from the shop frequently to check on her too, and reassure her that all was fine. She brought up more condolences and flowers from customers and friends that stopped by. Lucy refused to see anyone, except Don Roberts. Sarah brought him up to the apartment when he came. Lucy talked to him for a while, asking how his wife was and if he had talked to her uncle. She knew he was there to check on how she was really doing.

Sally's continual urging for Lucy to move on and have her uncle visit went nowhere; it was Don Roberts who finally convinced her and extracted the agreement for her uncle to bring Li Buyun over. She had called Wang Jun about it soon after Don left, but told him it was too early for him to come, that he needed to wait a little longer. Despite his pleas to the contrary she insisted he remain in Beijing; her grief was easing, but it was better for him to come once she was through the confrontation with her father.

<hr />

Sally picked up the phone in the Supper Club to an overseas call. She knew right away who it was.

"Sally Sweetland? Is that you? Wang Jun here."

"Yes it's me. What do you need?"

"I just heard from Lucy. She told me she's agreed to her uncle and another lady coming over in two weeks to visit her."

"That's great, Wang, er, John, I'll look forward to meeting you."

"Well, that's the problem. She doesn't want me to come yet. Can you change her mind? If you could I'll be forever thankful to you."

Sally promised to talk to her friend, but warned him Lucy could be very stubborn, as well he should know, and that she had to pick the right time to try. The call did not end quickly. She spent another ten minutes pushing him to ignore Lucy, to come anyway, whether Lucy could be persuaded or not. The two talked openly about his feelings, Sally grilling him at times as if making sure he was committed fully to her friend. Before they rang off she made certain he understood her.

"Look, John, this is my best friend we're talking about here. I've known her my entire life. She should never have made the mistake of hooking up with Phil. God rest his soul, but if you don't take care of her you'll have me to answer to. I promise to rip your heart out if you hurt her— with my bare hands if I have to."

Wang Jun assured her of his love for Lucy. He asked her not to say anything to Lucy until he told her himself, but he had begun the process after Phil's death of filing for divorce. He told her he was going to be somewhat poorer, but assured Sally he would have more than enough of a fortune that Lucy would live well for the rest of her life.

"I don't think it has anything to do with money, John. She loves you. I know she'll follow you over there even if you have nothing. I'm glad to hear you're serious. Don't let her slip through your fingers, okay?"

The call with China ended, Sally returned to the kitchen to fill her husband in on the call. John Sweetland liked what he heard about the man, and the discussion she intended to have with Lucy.

"Sometimes you just have to do what you think's right," John said. "She'll come around; I'm sure if it." Sally kissed him on the cheek, then told him it was time to get back to preparing the evening's menu. She picked up the phone and called her friend right away, said nothing of Wang Jun's call, and arranged to see her first thing in the morning at the flower shop.

Lucy was already worrying about the visit of her uncle and Madame Li's visit when Sally arrived. Things seemed to be moving faster than she expected. Don Roberts was on the phone discussing plans for the visitors' arrival in Greensboro, and coordinating the planned visit to the hospital outside Blowing Rock. She told Sally, after the call, that Sam had recommended arranging the meeting at the hospital, concerned how her father would handle the shock she planned for him. There would be adequate emergency care on hand, and her accompanying him there for a checkup would not be cause for alarm.

She filled Sally in on the visit details, mentioning her concerns, but also her relief that Don Roberts was going to organize everything on his end in Greensboro. She told Sally her uncle had said not to worry about anything, laughing at her concerns about the suitability of the accommodations, and what Madame Li might think about her small business.

"You worry too much, Lucy. It's going to be fine. Whether it works with your father or not, you need to start thinking about moving on," Sally said.

"Oh god, I hope it works. I can't move on with anything until he's settled."

"Shit, Lucy, you've got your whole life in front of you. His is behind him. I hate to be so blunt, but what's he ever done for you? Your mother dies and he goes off looking for his mistress? And lies about his past to you? No more, that's what I say."

"I hear you, Sally, but that's not me. I can't."

"So, do I finally get to meet this Wang fellow then? Is he coming too?" Sally asked.

"It's way to early. What would the hags say? My husband just in his grave and a lover shows up, Chinese at that! He's still married, and as much as I think he loves me it's going to take time."

"You don't have time, Lucy. Get off that high horse you keep riding. Screw the old hags around here. Do yourself a favor and get the hell out."

Sally was dying to tell her what Wang Jun said that morning about beginning divorce proceedings, but she'd promised not to. The two eventually moved out of Lucy's office, left Sarah in the shop and headed up to the apartment. Sally opened a bottle of wine to have with lunch. She hoped to use a little alcohol to convince Lucy of the need to invite Wang Jun over with her uncle, but she made little progress.

Sally stayed all afternoon, Don Roberts calling numerous times to firm up various arrangements. Lucy called the nursing home to talk to her father's care-givers, and she phoned the doctors at the hospital. One of the resident psychiatrists that afternoon expressed concerns about confronting John Wainright in the way she planned. It took calling Sam, and then his direct call to the doctor to clear the meeting date and time.

Sally emptied the bottle's last drops of wine into Sally's glass, "As much as you need Wang Jun in your life, Lucy, Sam's still a good man. Don't lead him too far, he needs to know sooner, rather than later, what's going on."

The talk of telling Sam about Wang Jun was going nowhere, nor inviting Wang Jun with the uncle. Sally decided it was time to get back and help her husband, promising to keep quiet about the visit of Lucy's Chinese friends. She left Lucy stretched out on the sofa, tired from so many sleepless nights.

———⊗⊗⊗———

Within minutes of arriving at the restaurant, Sally was on the phone with Wang Jun. They spoke for some time before he had to end the call and give her the cell phone number of Mei Rui, just in case anything happened and she couldn't get hold of him. Sally recalled what Lucy had said about Mei and was glad to have her number.

———⊗⊗⊗———

Lucy's uncle in Beijing used his connections to obtain U.S. visas for himself and Madame Li; he had been in regular contact with her since the merger of the companies was announced. Madame Li had insisted on Mei Rui being involved in the merger discussions, despite Wang Jun's original plans for someone else to lead them. Mei was surprised at the warming relations with Madame Li, in particular the growing closeness between the older woman and Chairman Xin. Wang Jun had not fared so well; he was frustrated by the contempt the older lady seemed to have for him. Xin put it down to her negotiating style, and used it to his advantage, allowing Wang Jun to be the heavy-handed negotiator, leaving him in the role of peacemaker. Mei led the team that put the flesh on the bones of the agreement, work that led to her negotiating the detailed language of the terms directly with Madame's daughter, Zhao Wen.

The two were ferocious enemies in negotiating the agreement terms, but in the evenings put aside their differences and shared more intimate details of their lives than they should have. It was classic Mei, plying her opponent with drink, far more than most would have survived; in the end they had to declare themselves equals, in that area at least. Mei reported everything back to Xin and Wang Jun as requested.

Zhao Wen's mother kept her abreast of some other developments, but only to a point. Madame Li had informed her daughter of a visit to the U.S. to meet with certain of the merged companies' investments, but said nothing of the real purpose of the trip. Wang Jun, on the other hand, pushed the chairman to use his influence on Madame Li to tell her daughter everything. Xin repeatedly told him not to push too hard, to focus on the agreements, and leave Madame to him. He reminded Wang Jun often that to move the mountain sometimes took one rock at a time, but his protégé replied that would take too long. They'd all be long dead by then.

The days passed and Wang Jun's calls to Lucy grew lengthier. Her concerns about her uncle, and especially Madame Li, seemed to worsen as the day of their arrival neared. She resisted his pleas to agree to him coming as well, always telling him the time was not right. He still said nothing about initiating divorce proceedings. His lawyers had warned him that his wife was taking a hard line, and advised him against involvement with another woman until everything was settled. He shared this with Mei and Sally. Mei recommended he follow his lawyers' advice; Sally, his heart.

On Chairman Xin and Madame Li's arrival in the U.S., there were several company executives waiting to greet them, as well as Don Roberts. He was to be on hand, ready to take the two to Greensboro and on to the hospital where Madame Li would confront Lucy's father. When they arrived at the Waldorf Hotel in New York other representatives were there to welcome them, they were booked there for only two nights, but had a full schedule ahead of them.

The following day they held a number of internal meetings on the merger itself. Next there were discussions with leading investment companies who were recommending them to list the new company on the U.S. stock exchange. Don Roberts stayed in the background, until called on to assist in their transfer to La Guardia Airport for the flight to Greensboro.

Xin took Don to one side while Madame Li was checking out. "Is everything arranged?"

"Of course, Mr. Chairman, everything."

As Xin walked back to make sure Madame Li was taken care of, Don Roberts breathed a sigh of relief, thumbing the shirt and necktie he was wearing as if it were too tight. He wondered if he should tell Xin or not. He looked at his watch, made a quick call, and then found Madame Li irritated at being kept waiting.

"Is there a problem, Don?" Xin asked on her behalf.

"Not at all. Just had to call my wife; she's not been well again lately."

"Sorry to hear that. I hope she gets better soon."

Xin spoke to Madame Li in Chinese, then Don noticed a visible change in her attitude.

"So sad. Forgive me, I hope she gets better soon," Madame Li said, touching his arm gently.

"Me too." Don said before thanking her for her kind words. He went back to organizing the bags out to the limousine.

He hoped none of this was going to change his relationship with the chairman. He had come to admire him over the years, and was grateful for all the help the man had given him for his wife. Her condition was deteriorating, but thanks to Xin the inevitable had been delayed for a few years. That some may have viewed his work for Xin negatively was of little concern to him; without it his wife would never have survived so long. He said nothing about the seriousness of her current situation, as he knew Xin would have insisted on him staying at the hospital with her. Don viewed Xin as his to protect while in the States, and he was determined to provide any and all assistance he could to somehow repay his generosity.

Chapter 28

Lucy Summers had slept poorly since Phil's suicide; plus she was apprehensive about her uncle and Madame Li's visit. She dined at Sally's restaurant the night before she was to travel to the hospital, not wanting to be alone. Nevertheless, she refused to stay at the restaurant that evening, or for Sally to sleep at her apartment.

Sally's husband made sure she ate well at the restaurant, despite her feigning little appetite. The cocktails they made for her were strong enough to ease some of her anxiety. Any doubts about the next day were fading in a fog of alcohol, and while she wasn't drunk, John Sweetland told her she was not walking home alone.

Sally had taken her arm for the short walk to the flower shop, the two talking about Lucy's plans for the morning, and the hopes riding on the father's reaction.

"What if all this doesn't work, Sally?" Lucy asked, suddenly turning gloomy at the thought of how embarrassing it might be if it didn't, for Madame Li in particular.

Sally held on to her shoulders and shook them, as if to waken her from some sad slumber. "Don't worry about it, Lucy! If it doesn't work, you've at least tried everything you could."

"I don't know. I'm having second thoughts."

"If it's the way he wants it to be then let it go . . . you've tried. Your uncle sounds like the kind of man who'll understand if it fails. Just be glad to see him again. As for the madame, so what? She's getting well taken care of for her trouble by your uncle's company."

"I hope you're right," Lucy said.

"I am, and you need to get on with your life. As far as I can see that means your Mr. Wang Jun. Get the hell out of Blowing Rock . . . while you can. Now, off to bed. You've got a big day tomorrow."

They arrived at the shop and climbed the outer stairs to the apartment; Lucy turned the key in the door and muttered to her best friend how much she wanted everything to be right. She gave Sally a half-hearted smile, turning one last time to thank her again before closing the door. She heard Sally yell for her to be sure to call as soon as she was back from visiting her father.

Lucy woke later than expected. She had assumed the night would be restless as so many nights before, thinking and planning what she would say to her father. She was relieved that, for once, she had slept well, ahead of what would be one of the most important days in her life. As soon as she was ready to leave the shop, Sarah arrived early to see her off. She had prepared a beautiful bouquet for welcoming Madame Li, as well as an extra one for Don Robert's wife.

Before getting into her car Lucy phoned Sally one last time, thanking her for her help the night before. She was dressed in an elegant suit she had purchased for the occasion, as much to create a good impression on Madame Li as anything else. Sarah complimented her on how well she looked. The showdown was now only a few hours away. Her nerves began to show as she put her car into reverse instead of drive and almost crashed into the rear storage area of the garage.

"Shit, shit, shit!" Lucy paused and breathed in deeply to try to calm down. This was not the way to start the day. She sat back, stared at the wheel of the car for a few moments, then cleared her thoughts and put the car in gear. She drove carefully out and into the main street of Blowing Rock, heading toward the nursing home. She would pick her father up to drive him over to the hospital for what he thought was a periodic checkup.

The phone rang while she was driving, and she pulled over to the side of the road to take the call. It was Don Roberts, calling to confirm all was well, that Madame Li seemed uptight but was not obnoxious in any way, despite the warnings. He also said Chairman Xin was in good spirits, and seemed anxious to see his niece, more than her father. He noted how Chairman Xin and Madame Li had a closer bond these days. Based on what he had seen, he told her everything would be okay with the visit.

One last call came in before she arrived at the nursing home from Wang Jun. He wished her well and assured her it would work out. Mei jumped in on the call at the end, telling Lucy she missed her, that all was well with the merger discussions but her boss still pined for "his Lucy."

<hr />

Lucy walked into the nursing home to find her father dressed in the waiting room. Her earlier requests of his caregivers to make sure he was presentable to meet old friends had been listened to. He was sitting in the wheelchair, still frail as ever, but wearing new clothes she had bought for him a long time ago. The staff had promised not to mention the special meeting, but she could see a hint of puzzlement on her father's face when she walked in dressed up. The nurses all commented on how elegant she looked that day.

She greeted her father, knelt in front of him, and kissed his forehead. "Time to go, Father. We don't want to be late for your checkup. How are you feeling today?" She neither expected nor received any response. The staff helped her father into her car, then loaded the folded wheelchair in the back seat. The drive seemed to take forever for Lucy as she began to anticipate what lay ahead. She babbled on the way she usually did for the journey to the hospital, her father acting as he always did on the trip, head slumped forward, staring at the dashboard. He said nothing, and only occasionally raised his head with little control when she braked sharply, something she did consciously from time to time to get some kind of reaction. She decided to set the stage by talking about her visit to China again, saying nothing about her uncle or the madame. She noticed something inside the stoic look he maintained as she talked, wondered if something was registering in him, then decided she was imagining it.

∞∞∞

The noise of the wheels over the tiled floor quieted as Lucy pushed her father down the hallway; then wheeled him onto the carpeted floor of a large consulting room. Dr. Weinstein was sitting in one of the easy chairs waiting for them to arrive.

"You're here already, Doctor?" She said.

"Don't worry. I'm not staying, Lucy. I still think I should, just in case, but I've agreed not to, as you requested. I'm not sure I agree with Sam Jones on this, but I appreciate his input. You're taking full responsibility if anything happens . . . right?"

"Yes, I understand your position fully, but thanks for agreeing."

"I'll be close by in my office should you need me."

"I appreciate it, Doctor, I really do. I'll call right away if we need you."

"I'll look in from time to time. Good luck to you both," he said, and walked out.

Lucy came around to look in her father's eyes, kneeling beside him. She spoke slowly and deliberately. "Father, there's someone I want you to meet."

Interrupted by the sound of a door opening she turned around, enough to see a young nurse peering in, her father still motionless even when she told him someone was coming to meet him. She looked intently into his eyes, frustrated by the lack of any curiosity or flicker in his eyes to show something awakening in him.

"Mrs. Summers?"

"Yes?"

"Are you both ready?"

"Yes," Lucy said.

"Well, I'll fetch them. They're here."

"Thank you, Nurse."

She rose shakily from her knees, now filled with trepidation about what was to happen next. "Oh god!" she said. "What have I done?"

She burst into tears as the door opened wider and the footsteps drew closer, still outside of her father's range of vision, his head lowered to the floor as usual. Lucy could bear it no more as Madame Li and Uncle Xin walked towards them. She held her father, pulling his head to the back of the chair.

"For fuck's sake, look at them!" she screamed in his ear, holding on to him as Madame Li advanced slowly, seemingly hardened by the sight of a man she had hated for so many years.

———— ∞∞∞ ————

At long last she felt her father stiffen. From behind the wheelchair she gave her uncle and Madame Li a look to convey her desperation. Madame Li stopped walking once she was close enough, and there was no doubt that she was in his field of vision.

At that point her uncle moved alongside the woman, and spoke directly to the man before him. "John Wainright, you may not remember me, but my name is Xin, the brother of your friend killed along with your colleague, Christine Meyer. I have to thank you for saving his daughter, my niece. She now knows everything and who her family was."

Lucy felt her father tremble slightly, but she tightened her grip, even as he fought to lower his head. Something was definitely happening to him.

"But, more importantly, the lady here suffered more than you can imagine in those days after you were in Beijing with my brother. She has something to tell you."

Before Madame Li started to speak, Lucy could see her father's hands grip the arms of the chair tightly and his knuckles whiten.

"How can you sit there like this, John?" she said to him. "What has happened to the man I once loved, who gave me my only child, and then left? A man who took in such a filial daughter as is standing behind you now, one who never gave up on you, even though she is not of your blood. Unlike what you did to your true blood daughter, and me. You had the gall to contact me, only when your wife died, to ask to meet her. After all you did to us, how could you imagine I would agree?"

Lucy could feel the shaking in her father, as if he was trying to respond to her, but nothing was coming out.

"My husband saved me from the hell we endured after you left. I would not be here today if it was not for your Lucy and her uncle, I can assure you of that. I need to hear everything from your own lips as to why you left us. You owe me that much, at least."

Lucy could hold back no more. She let her father's head slump to his chest, rounded the chair on him, and did something she had never done in her life before. She struck him in the face. Her uncle stopped her from striking him again

"No, no, Lucy! That is not the way of a Xin, and you are a Xin, believe me you are."

Madame Li moved to comfort her. Don Roberts thought he should leave the room, but was motioned to stay. Xin spoke directly to her father.

"John Wainright, you can be at peace, believe me. Madame Li is here because of your daughter's efforts to bring you back, but more importantly because my family has uncovered evidence that the charges against Madame Li were false. They were contrived by the guards to make her plead guilty. Those charges led to her and the baby being sent to a labor camp. For all those years, she assumed you had used her, then turned her in to save your own skin. Were you really that cowardly, John? I think not."

Lucy was being comforted in the arms of Madame Li when the first words she had heard from her father in months broke the silence. It was a whisper at best, but they all heard it. "Our daughter?" was all he uttered, as if he was learning to speak for the first time.

"Our daughter, John? Your daughter? Oh no, never! My daughter. Mine. If you think you'll ever see her again, then you really are as mad as you seem to want to be. Maybe Xin is right. Maybe it wasn't you, but you never attempted to find us . . . not once . . . only when your wife died did you try; before that, never."

A door opened again, breaking the deafening silence that hung in the air after Madame Li had finished. The doctor, who had been listening outside, motioned Lucy to the door. "Lucy, you may be going too far with this. I think he needs a break."

"No, Doctor, he needs to hear all of this, and more. If we need you we'll call right away."

The doctor left the room, not happy with being asked to leave, but understanding how determined Lucy was to go on. She returned to find her father looking straight at Madame Li; she was explaining everything that had happened to her. Lucy was relieved to see him finally reacting in a way she had not seen for a long time. He kept his silence still, but his face displayed a torment she could see straining to break free.

Lucy noticed Don Roberts step over to the window and try to call someone on his cell phone. He went over to the same door they had all walked through earlier, and was outside for a few moments before returning. Lucy recognized right away who was walking back in with him— Madame Li's daughter, Zhao Wen!

"Father?" she called out in a strong voice as she walked in. Zhao Wen's mother quickly stepped in front of her, as if to shield her from any view of John Wainright.

The torrent of Chinese echoing throughout the room told everyone that Madame Li had no idea her daughter was going to be there, nor wanted her to be. Lucy guessed Madame Li was demanding her daughter leave right away, but Zhao Wen was holding her ground. From the corner of her eye, Lucy could see Don Roberts was worried; he had obviously been involved in arranging for her to be there. Both he and Lucy soon received reassuring looks from Xin that told them to let mother and daughter work this out.

The two women stood toe to toe in the middle of the room for what seemed like an eternity, the mother pushing her daughter back toward the door, the daughter refusing to move, trying to get around her to see the man she only recently learned was her real father.

Lucy felt the chair shake a little. She could see her father stirring, trying to move his arms. Neither of the arguing women noticed the slight movement, but Xin and Don Roberts could see that something was happening. The two men came to the side of her father and helped give his wasted limbs the support needed to raise him to his feet.

"Don't. Please don't." Her father's whispered words grew louder as he repeatedly tried to call out to the two women, but his voice was weak and failed him. Lucy noticed tears forming on his face, showing anguish at the argument raging between the two women in a language she realized he understood well enough.

"Please, no, no, not this way, I beg you, no. I'm sorry, so sorry, please stop." Her father tried to shake Don and Xin off as he moved toward the women, his voice barely discernible. The two men released their support momentarily, but that was all it took for John Wainright to collapse forward. He glanced against Madame Li legs as he fell to the floor and rolled onto his back, staring directly up at the two women. Before anyone could say anything the doctor who was standing by rushed to his aid.

"That's it, he's had enough!" the doctor shouted, then called for the two nurses outside. They were crouching by the doctor's side in seconds to work to revive John Wainright.

Lucy was terrified, crying and trembling in her uncle's arms. Madame Li and her daughter stopped fighting and stood in silence. One of them looked down as if at a long lost love. The other appeared curious about the man whose looks had caused her so much derision in the early years of school.

"Who did this Xin?" Madame Li shouted in English. "I agreed to come only on the understanding she was not to be told. I swear by my ancestors I'll kill whoever allowed this."

"Calm down," Xin said. "We'll find that out as soon as we can. No matter how it happened, she must be here because she wants to. I'm sure nobody forced her to come."

"I don't believe it."

"Lucy fought to know where she really came from," Xin said. "No doubt Zhao Wen wants that too. She's not a child, Li; you don't need to protect her from everything. Thanks to you she's a strong and intelligent young woman. At least give her the choice to know."

"He's right, mother," Zhao Wen said, "I want to know. But not this way. No more fights. Let these people do their work. We can argue later."

John Wainright was placed on a gurney, breathing easier with the help of an oxygen mask. An emergency injection brought his failing heart under control. He was soon on the way to intensive care, with Lucy following. The others were told to wait for further news, to calm their rhetoric while the hospital did its work, or leave.

Chapter 29

Within minutes of the doctor and patient leaving, the group divided to opposite corners of the room. This time no voices were raised, and the uneasy silence was broken only by hushed conversations on both sides. Xin noticed the two women holding hands, obviously the mother trying to explain everything to her daughter as calmly as she could. Madame Li was crying; her head was bowed as she spoke, Zhao Wen listening intently, occasionally stroking her mother's shoulder and saying it was going to be all right.

The two seemed closer than any time Xin had seen during the merger negotiations. He stood up thinking he should go over and add his comfort to Madame Li, but Zhao Wen looked at him and shook her head. She half-smiled before refocusing on what she was hearing, telling him with her eyes all was well.

Xin turned to Don Roberts, giving him a suspicious look. "So, Don, who arranged this trip with Zhao Wen? Obviously not you, but you knew about it, right?" Don shifted uneasily, then leaned over and whispered what he knew in Xin's ear..

"I might have guessed," Xin said. "Say nothing to Madame Li unless Zhao Wen does. Meanwhile see what's going on with Lucy and her father, would you?"

"I'll try, Xin, but I doubt they'll tell me. Only family members get to hear that kind of information here in the U.S. We'll likely have to wait until the doc, or Lucy, can tell us."

Don Roberts was out of the room for a good fifteen minutes, returning with the news that Lucy was still with her father. A nurse assured him the patient was stabilizing, the worst over, but that it could have easily gone the other way. Xin strode over to the two women and broke the news. Both seemed relieved, Zhao Wen more, asking if he thought it was likely she could talk to him that day. She looked disappointed when he told her it was unlikely, but they would wait to see what developed. With that Madame Li waved Xin away so she could continue talking. Zhao Wen assured him everything was fine between them.

Xin talked again to Don Roberts about the situation. Then told him to make the arrangements that were needed. He was to do nothing this time without keeping Xin informed.

Two hours later Lucy walked in with the doctor to announce her father was stable and expected to make a full recovery. It was going to take weeks for him to gain his strength back, however, and a peaceful recovery process was paramount.

"Can I see him?" Zhao Wen asked right away, surprising Lucy.

"He does want to see you, Zhao Wen," Lucy replied, "but he wants to talk to your mother first . . . and alone."

"I've given him something to calm him," the doctor said. "I really don't think he can see anyone for at least two more hours. You can wait here, or come back later. It's up to you all."

"We'll wait, thank you. If that's all right with Mrs. Lucy?" Zhao Wen asked, looking at her mother for agreement.

"If you like, or perhaps we should come back tomorrow," Madame Li said.

"Today, please, Mother. Let's not wait . . . anyway, I want to talk to Lucy if I can."

Xin smiled as the mother shrugged at him, as if there was no way to refuse her daughter anything.

"I would really like to talk to Zhao Wen and get to know her too," Lucy said. "We can all go to the hospital café if you like and talk there, together or separately. A change of rooms would probably do us all good, maybe a walk outside for some air?"

"Yes, a walk would be nice." With that Zhao Wen jumped up and grabbed Lucy's hand, pulling her toward the door before her mother had time to react and join them.

"Alone, Mother! Talk to your old friend, Chairman Xin. I'm sure you two can discuss the merger, if you can't think of anything to talk about."

The two left the room visibly warming to each other.

"I understand you were in Beijing recently, Mrs. Lucy, and years ago too," Zhao Wen said.

"Just call me Lucy, Zhao Wen. Can I guess who told you about me? My uncle?"

"No, not him. He would never go against Mother. It was your friend Mei Rui; she's far less principled, but I like her all the same."

"When did she tell you? Why?" Lucy asked.

"I don't think she meant to. We'd been negotiating the merger all day and into the evening. I'm afraid we ended up drinking way too much at dinner. We'd been talking about Wang Jun actually. I was interested in him myself, but Mei put me straight in that department."

Lucy was puzzled. "But that doesn't seem much of an introduction into getting you involved in this?"

"She told me all about the situation with your uncle and how happy you were to have found your real family. I guess when I told her I was in a similar situation, desperate to find my own father too, it was all the opening she needed."

"So it wasn't an accident that it came out?"

"Lucy, I'm not that naïve. No, she planned all along to find a way to involve me. I'm not angry with her; in fact I'm thankful. Not knowing has been eating at me for years. My mother is another story. We better keep Mei out of this if we can. Mother can be very vindictive. I won't tell her, but your uncle may."

"I'll talk to him about it, but meanwhile let's talk about my father, or is he your father? And what are we now? Sisters? Half sisters? What do you want to know about him?" Lucy smiled. "This could get confusing."

Zhao Wen grasped her arm as they walked. "Let's just be like real sisters; that's all, Lucy. I'd like that."

They talked for over an hour in the gardens, Lucy telling Zhao Wen everything she knew about her father and, carefully, what she didn't understand about him. She also told her the story of how she came to know Wang Jun in the first place, and most recently what led to her discovery of her real parents. Zhao Wen said it all seemed to be in line with what she'd heard from her mother.

That they had been so closely linked through their parents all those years ago, and were now reconnected, was a miracle of fate as far as both were concerned. There were still questions, however, that both of them had about John Wainright, which they hoped would be answered. Lucy wanted to know why her father had used the name Richard Towers when working for Goldman Sachs, and the secret world he seemed to have lived in. Zhao Wen needed to hear directly why he deserted them and had never sought her out.

Don Roberts called the two women in from the gardens; the doctor was looking for Lucy. They hurried back to the consultation room, where the doctor was talking to Madame Li and Lucy's uncle.

"How is father?" they said in unison, glancing at each other with a look of surprise, a warmth between them that the others could see. Zhao Wen's mother was clearly displeased at her daughter using the word "father."

"He's stable, thankfully, and doing well," the doctor said. "I don't want him taxed too much, but he's sitting up and ready to talk. He sounds weak but his voice is improving. I can only give him an hour today, but by morning he'll be able to talk to more of you."

Lucy began to walk toward the door when the doctor signaled her to wait. "I'm afraid he's insisting on talking to Madame Li first . . . alone. Apparently he doesn't want to talk to anyone else until he's seen her, but thanks you all for being here. He wants to talk to each of you in turn, but I've told him he can see only one person today. He told me to tell you that, Lucy, and hopes you'll understand."

"Perhaps it's best, Lucy," Madame Li told her. "Take care of my daughter here and I promise not to hide anything from either of you when we are finished. Is that okay?"

Lucy was visibly hurt, but her uncle came to her side and gave her a reassuring hug. "It's okay," he said. "Really, I expect it's something that has needed to be said between them for many, many years. There will be time for you and the rest of us tomorrow."

⸻ ◦◦◦ ⸻

The doctor led Madame Li to the intensive care room. Before letting her in he alerted her to a red alarm button by the bed if anything happened, something he told her seemed highly unlikely now. She walked into the room and somewhat reluctantly approached the foot of the bed where John Wainright was struggling to raise himself. He pointed to one of the chairs by the bed, motioning her to sit closer, so he would not have to raise his weakened voice. She moved around the bed, the man before her looking nothing like the strong character she fell in love with all those years ago. She wasn't sure whether to be angry with him for leaving her, or to pity the broken individual that lay before her.

Finally he spoke to her, shifting wires and drip feeds that were connected to him. "Thank you, Thuzi, for coming. I want you to know right away that I never, ever knew what they did to you. You have to believe that, whatever you think of me, you have to."

"Thuzi?" she repeated, "That's a name no one has ever called me, other than you, a rabbit on our Chinese zodiac. And you, May born, the boar. What happened to all that hair you had back then? I called you hairy boar, mao mao Zhun. So many years wasted, and what for? A revolution that never happened until later!"

"They told me I couldn't go back, they said you'd been arrested. They said if I did the Chinese would torture me and use the information to kill you, that your people knew what I'd done with Lucy. They threatened to send her back, or worse if I tried to contact you."

"They? Your CIA friends? Is that who they were? Is that what we were really all about? For you to penetrate every part of me, and take what information you wanted? Was that it?"

"It wasn't like that, not at all."

"We thought we were making a difference, Xin's brother and I. We had access; we had political secrets, and willingly gave them at great risk to families and ourselves. And what protection did we get from you, or anybody? None!"

"I tried. I wanted to protect you."

"Tried? That was all you could do? I was saved by one of my own, a man who was more than you could ever be. You are not the father of my daughter, John Wainright, and you never will be, no matter what she wants, or thinks."

"I did come back," he responded. "Once I finally heard you'd been arrested, and about the baby. I tried as John Wainright so many times, but the State Department blocked it every time. When I tried on my own your embassy denied me; they warned there would be trouble for me in Beijing."

"A likely story."

"Why do you think I became Richard Towers of Goldman Sachs? I know Lucy is wondering. You may not believe me, but it was the only way to try to find you."

"I don't think so." Li scowled. "You could have found me if you wanted to, with all your experience and connections. You or your government could have done that if you really tried."

"I did everything I could think of. I quit the service. I used old contacts to get me into Goldman as an employee. I searched around Beijing for you whenever I could. I never dreamed of looking in Nanjing . . . that's the truth."

"So much concern that you married someone else? That was how much you cared for us? I don't think so, John Wainright."

"They told me you were dead, for Christ's sake, Li. I believed them for a long time. I can take you to the man who told me you were alive and where you were. He can vouch for everything I'm saying if you want. He's still alive. Talk to him at least."

"For what? Even if what you say is true, it means nothing to me. You mean nothing to me. Thanks to you I got to meet the most wonderful man I could ever have known. Where? In a godforsaken labor camp, but together we made a life for ourselves few could dream of, and he loved Zhao Wen as his own. What about the life of your Lucy? What did you do for her? Nothing as far as I can see! So what can you do for my daughter? Ruin the glorious memories she has?"

"I can't change any of this, Li. I know it's too late. That was never the point. I just wanted you to know the truth, and to see my daughter while I could. Like you with your daughter, I tried to keep the truth from Lucy. I thought it would be bad for her to find out what we'd told her all these years was a lie, that I was a lie, but I know now I was wrong. I lost a good partner too, Li, maybe not some-one that I loved or cared for as much as you, but she accepted me even when she was told everything about us. She made me promise to get in touch with you and your daughter if anything happened to her. I was crushed by her death; then you refused to see me, and when I saw the things you wrote back I just wanted to join her, to tell her I'd tried. If your daughter doesn't want to meet me I have to accept it, but I beg you, give her the choice I never gave Lucy."

"I'm sorry, I cannot forgive you for what you put us through, never. Can we talk more about it when you are really well? Not as far as I'm concerned. As regards Zhao Wen, I know she wants to meet you. I'll allow it once, but Lucy is your daughter, no matter what you may think. Zhao Wen is of your seed, that is true, but she is not yours and never will be. Start to worry about Lucy, John Wainright, before you lose her too."

With that Madame Li turned and walked out, listening to her former lover pleading for her not to leave. She did not look back, nor say good-bye as she slammed the door behind her.

When Madame Li returned both young women stood together asking the same questions: had everything gone all right? Was Lucy's father okay? Madame Li turned to Uncle Xin and Don Roberts, ignoring their questions. "I am finished here!" she said as she grabbed her things. "There is nothing more for me to say or do. I have honored my commitment to come here. Now I am leaving, with or without you Xin. As regards Zhao Wen, she has my permission to talk to this man tomorrow. What she chooses beyond that is up to her. If she wishes to remain in the Zhao family and our business she needs to get this over with and return to Beijing. Forget this excuse for a man, Zhao Wen. If you do not, then you are no longer a daughter of mine."

Zhao Wen tried to object, but her mother stormed out of the room, ordering Don Roberts to open the car so she could wait there. Lucy tried to comfort Zhao Wen, who was clearly upset, and Uncle Xin was quick to console her in Chinese. Lucy understood from the facial exchange her uncle was assuring her the anger would pass, that her mother simply needed time. Finally he switched to English so Lucy could understand.

"Your mother has every right to feel the way she does, Zhao Wen. But some day we have to learn to forgive and leave this world in peace. Your mother will understand that soon enough, as I have learned in these last few years. I believe from everything we know now, John Wainright was also a victim of our years of struggle; he deserves forgiveness at least. But you, Zhao Wen, need to understand that Zhao Chungang was your real father and your mother's husband. The man in that bed loved your mother a very long time ago. By all means respect him and learn what you need to know, welcome Lucy as a new sister into your world, but leave it at that. Your mother loves you more than anyone ever has or will. She deserves your love and support."

"I know, Chairman Xin," Zhao Wen said, " I have no desire to change what my mother and I have been through together, or shame the love that my father Zhao gave me. I simply want to know my real father's story, where I came from, what their lost love was like, and then I will be at peace. I have wondered about this quietly for so many years. Mother would never answer any of my questions. I knew I was different, just like Lucy here. All I want is to know."

Lucy told everyone they should leave, that she would stay to make sure her father was comfortable through the night. She checked with the doctor, who said her father would be able to talk again in the morning, after ten o'clock. She told Zhao Wen that she could see him first, if she wanted to. They agreed they would leave Madame Li at the hotel for the morning, if she hadn't left already on her own. Xin and Zhao Wen would come back to visit Lucy's father. Xin still had questions about his own brother.

Chapter 30

Lucy's father had a peaceful night thanks to sleeping aids his doctor prescribed. By morning she was advised he would be comfortable receiving visitors. Lucy had slept poorly with so much flooding her mind. She was more confused than ever about her father, whether she still felt the same about him or had lost whatever love for him remained.

She tried to call Wang Jun during the night to talk, but he didn't answer. His office line recording told her he was in meetings. She did get in touch with Mei Rui, who assured her again things would work out, that Madame Li would come around.

Lucy spent the time before her visitors arrived talking by phone to Sally, filling her in on all the developments. She laughed when Sally pointed out how incredible her story was, the stuff of movies, especially compared to her own life running the restaurant and her uneventful marriage. Lucy told her she wasn't sure all this was what she had in mind when she decided to break into her father's private office; Sally pointed out she would have had to do it one day, like it or not. At least now she was learning something she always wondered about and gaining a family in the process.

Lucy ended the call as soon as she heard Don Roberts arriving with the Chinese. She promised to call again as soon as she was back home. Sally told her they would take care of her that evening and feed her a good meal.

———⊗———

There were embraces all round as Xin and Zhao Wen came into the room. Don Roberts gave Lucy a reassuring smile, sitting off to the side when the doctor strode in, patient files under his arm. The doctor welcomed everyone, only to be told Madame Li would not be visiting again.

"That's probably a good thing. I hear things didn't go well yesterday. At any rate I'm here to tell you all, especially Lucy, he's doing well today. His vital signs are good; his voice is becoming stronger by the hour. One of our nurses can attest to that, he chewed her out this morning for not waking him early. I think he's all set, but let me know if he has any problems. We have him monitored, but whoever is in the room make sure you know where the call button is . . . okay?"

"How long do we have, Doctor?" Lucy asked.

"Oh, I'd say the morning at least, based on what I've seen so far. We'll bring some lunch in around eleven for him, and I'll look in from time to time. Just leave one of the blinds up for me to see how he is between patient rounds. I'm sure everything will be fine. Lucy, would you like to go in?"

"No, I think it's better for him to see Zhao Wen here first, then my uncle. I can see him anytime, maybe even this afternoon."

"As you wish. Follow me, Miss Zhao, or is it Mrs.?"

"It's still Miss, Doctor, for now at least. Lead the way."

Zhao Wen thanked Lucy for letting her go in first, and promised not to take all his time. Lucy told her to take all the time she needed.

———⊗———

Zhao Wen walked through the door of the new room the patient had been moved to. She stood in the open doorway while the doctor announced her arrival. The man sat upright in bed; he looked different from the beaten down person Lucy Summers wheeled in the first day of their meeting. Zhao Wen was nervous after her mother's visit, but relieved to see warmth in John Wainright's eyes. He was alert, looking straight at her with a welcoming smile. Before she could say anything, he waved her over to the chair by his bed.

"Zhao Wen, thanks so much for coming. Please sit down . . . here . . . by me. I'm sure you have more questions than I do." She walked over to the bed, shook his hand, sat down, breathing a sigh of relief as quietly as she could.

"How's your mother? I'm sorry things didn't go well between us yesterday. I'd really like to talk to her again. I feel much better today and my voice is stronger."

"How should I address you?" Zhao Wen asked politely.

"Oh, that. Just call me John for now. We'll see where that goes later."

"Okay, John then. I'm afraid mother has left, and I don't think she's coming back. Can you understand that? I do."

"I do too, Zhao Wen. Is there something else I should call you? What name do you prefer I use?"

"Wendy is the English name I used at university. It's funny; once I graduated it was back to Zhao Wen. Whichever you'd like to use."

"Then Wendy it is. I suppose you have some questions of me, right? You can ask whatever you'd like, but I want to say some things, if that's okay?"

"Of course, maybe you'll answer some of my own questions."

"First of all, Wendy, you need to know that I never knew what was done to you and your mother until some time later. Your mother doesn't believe me; I know she probably never will. I also know enough about what went on in China in those days to understand what she and you were put through, whether she believes me or not. Over on the table there's the name and phone number of someone I want you to call, your mother never will, please call him. He'll vouch for everything I tell you."

"How do I know he isn't telling me what you've asked him to?" she asked.

"You'll have to decide for yourself. I can't force you to believe me, or him."

Zhao Wen listened intently as John Wainright began the story of how he came to meet her mother. He described how he graduated from university with no idea what he would do, until approached by the government because of the language he had chosen to pursue. He told her Chinese history fascinated him growing up, and how he had been drawn to learning the language by a desire to visit the places he read about. His professor and mentor at the university counseled him on what he saw as an emerging power, telling him the country would one day offer opportunities if he mastered the language. It was through the same professor that a recruiter from the State Department contacted him about working for them in China.

"So did you go from there to the CIA?"

"I was never officially CIA, not then. I was always working with State after Nixon's visit there, but I can't deny we overlapped. They did want me to go over to them, but I refused."

"Why?"

He explained his interest was politics, nothing more. The State Department's activities at the time were heavily monitored and infiltrated, so people could have easily thought he was one of them.

"How did you meet my mother?" she asked.

"I was part of a team visiting Beijing, assigned to a Boeing trade group. They were one of the first commercial companies in there after Nixon's visit. My job was to assess the political direction the new government was taking, how its relations with Russia were evolving, and what if anything the military was up to. I thought my main purpose was to report as much on what Boeing was revealing in their meeting as what the Chinese were up to.

Your mother was involved in all the reviews and negotiations, thanks to her English skills, but I could tell the others in her group were jealous of her abilities. They were uncomfortable that someone so young held sway with their own leaders. That's what got us, and your mother in trouble."

"How so?" Zhao Wen asked.

"They were watching her and her young colleague Xin. The pair was being monitored far more than we realized at the time. The meetings were endless back in those days, and tough. No one wanted to appear to give anything away on either side. Many of them were against any American company getting involved in China. They made that pretty clear to all of us there. Your mother and Xin were different. They wanted to know as much as they could about America, what was really going on in the outside world."

"Was that how your relationships started?"

"I guess so. We would end up doing a lot of report writing, composing memoranda about he topics discussed in the meetings, that kind of stuff. None of the senior negotiators or technical staff wanted to stick around late at night. They were happier to join banquets and drink too much. We were left to do the homework every night. It was perfect for me. Your mother and Xin thirsted for knowledge about us, and I probed for the information I was looking for. The more we talked, the more information we exchanged."

"So my mother was a spy, a traitor to our country? Is that what you're saying?"

"Not at all, Wendy, no way. The two of them wanted positive change, for China to open up to the West, move away from the Soviet sphere . . . raise more people from poverty, that kind of thing. I'm sure the authorities would have seen her as a traitor. That's why our discussions became more secretive. We took great care, the four of us, about where we met. They were both very brave. To be honest, Wendy, I fell in love with your mother the first time I saw her at the airport when she was welcoming our contingent. It took time for her though."

"How did it happen?"

"I remember it like it was yesterday. We were working late one night in the Beijing Hotel near the Forbidden City. I guess I found a way to get your mother to come to my room to work on something for the next day. It all happened quickly. We were soon madly in love, and from then on saw as much of each other as we could, as did Xin and Christine Meyer, Lucy's mother. They had their own thing going. I expect you know now they were Lucy's parents."

"Yes, but if you knew you were being watched, why did you expose the woman you say you loved to so much risk? Look at what goes on today over state secrets, let alone what you were doing back then." Zhao Wen waited for an answer.

"You're young, Wendy. Did you never feel invincible? That you were smart-er than everyone else out there? We took as many precautions as we could, some of them a bit ridiculous frankly, but when you're in love you do foolish things sometime."

"Like two huge mistakes . . . Lucy and me?" She said.

"That's an embarrassing question, Wendy."

"I'm a big girl. I have sex. I've never gotten myself pregnant, but you four managed to do the most dangerous thing at that time you could."

"Ours was an accident, pure and simple. And don't tell me accidents like that don't happen anymore, because they do. As for Christine, she *was* with the CIA. She told me she got pregnant on purpose, had this crazy idea she could convince her people to get him out with her. They loved each other a great deal too. The Chinese claimed it was an accident when they were both killed, but I've always believed otherwise. Her grandparents kept the baby, at great risk to themselves."

"How was she able to hide that she was having a baby, along with my own mother?"

"Christine was small; you can see that in Lucy. She managed to hide it somehow. If she'd shown more she would have been pulled out of the country right away. She did start to wear a lot of loose clothes, and for the last few weeks it was hairy, to say the least."

"And my mother?"

"She got pregnant shortly before the accident. I'd promised to get Christine's baby out if anything happened, and I assured your mother I'd take care of her too."

"But that didn't happen, did it?"

"It didn't, Wendy, and for that I've never forgiven myself. We got Lucy out overland. It was risky but we did it. Whatever Christine had in motion caused them to at least agree to getting that part done. How we did it is a long story. Your concern is more about yourself. I understand that."

"When and why did you leave us then?" she asked.

"I didn't want to leave. There was so much business to develop I could have been in meetings for years and still had reason to be there. But things happened so fast after we got Lucy out. I knew your mother was pregnant, and I was trying to figure out a way to get her out of China, but I never got the chance. Security people arrested me and later took me to the airport. They told me they knew everything I'd been up to. I was not welcome in China, and it had only been thanks to the intervention of one of the leaders I was only being deported. Relationships like ours were off limits. I was ordered to leave right away, or I and the person I'd associated with would be in serious trouble."

"So you left? Just like that?"

"No, not just like that at all. They arrested me, Wendy. Put me in a cell for days, wouldn't let me communicate with anyone, and questioned me about what I had been up to. I was beaten regularly. They asked me all the time about your mother and Xin, but I never told them anything. They knew though . . . I could tell that. I thought I was dead or would never see the light of day again, but somehow my people got me out through diplomatic channels. I was never able to communicate with anyone over there again. The official word was I resigned for personal reasons and had gone back to the U.S."

"But you knew my mother was pregnant. Weren't you worried about her?"

"Of course I was. When I got back I was told your mother had been arrested. I about went crazy, like now. When I tried to find out where she was, I was told she'd been reassigned to another department, that if I wanted to protect her I needed to break off all contact."

"Which you did."

"What else could I do? From that day on no one could tell me anything, but I always wondered what happened to her, if she'd had the baby or not. I guess it was guilt over you that I determined to formally adopt Lucy, to be sure she was at least safe. That was the least I could do. I married a very special lady to do it, not unlike your mother, to be sure Lucy had good parents, something I couldn't do for you. I grew to love my wife very much, Wendy, but the love for your mother has never left me, whether you believe that or not."

So why the effort to finally find me now?"

"I told my wife everything from day one. She knew she wasn't my first choice, but accepted me all the same, even when I worked with Goldman Sachs and was involved in China again."

"Using a false name, I hear."

"Yes. My name came up at State again in the nineties. Business was booming, and people like Goldman were looking for China specialists. It was the CIA who got me involved. They knew all about my deportation, but I'd been badgering everyone to go back. I told them it would be easy under a different name. I'd throw on some glasses, change my hair, that kind of thing."

"Sounds dangerous."

"Not really. At least I didn't think so. In the eighties all of the visa procedures and immigration were manual. Files on me were there, but all Americans looked the same to them. I might have been spotted if I'd gone over using my real name, so I convinced everyone to name me Richard Towers. They forced Goldman to take me on."

"So you were CIA after all?"

"From that point on, yes. I tried to find your mother, but never could. How we missed locating her is something I can't explain, but we did. We never picked up on her being married to your father. Finally though, the man on that piece of paper over there called me. He was retiring and wanted me to know the truth. Told me the higher ups had known all along where she was."

"Seems a little too tidy," Zhao Wen said.

"Just call him, Wendy. At least do that. Anyway, all along my wife told me, especially when she was dying of cancer, that before I left this world I needed to find you, if you existed. Once I had the information I tried to contact your mother, but I was falling apart. My wife and partner had died, I was rejected by the one person I had loved more than anything, and I was told I would never see my daughter for what I'd done. She believed nothing of what I'm telling you, wouldn't even talk to me."

"I'm not sure I blame her. What is it you really want?" she asked.

"To be forgiven, to be friends with both of you, to know my daughter and how she is doing, from there . . . whatever's right."

"And Lucy?"

"I'll tell her everything, but I expect she knows a lot already. She's as smart as her real mother was, and her father of course."

"That she is, but you are in danger of losing her too, if you don't do something about it soon."

"I know, and I will do something about it. I'm afraid I've messed that up too."

For the next hour Zhao Wen asked more questions, the conversation shifting to questions about her life, what she remembered from the labor camps they were in, and about her father. There were many questions about her mother, which told her John Wainright really had loved her, and likely still did. He was interested in how she had grown up, studied, and ended up working alongside her mother. She found herself telling him more about herself than she had imagined she would. She could see that he genuinely cared too. He was not her father by any means, but she missed that relationship so much that the man holding her hand made her comfortable again, talking openly about everything.

The doctor came by to check on his patient, found him in good spirits, and reminded him there were others waiting to talk to him. It seemed a good time to finish and Zhao Wen rose to her feet. "I think that covers what I wanted to know about you and mother," she said as she picked up the paper with the name and phone number on it.

"Please call him, Wendy. At least do that for me, and your mother."

"Let's see how everything goes. What do you want of me going forward?"

"To stay in touch, maybe to be friends one day. It's up to you, of course. I'd like that with your mother, but I suspect that can never be."

"No, I don't think so either. Let's see what happens. I'll give Lucy all my details and you can contact me again when you are out of here. Get well and we'll see where it goes after that."

"Thank you so much for coming, Wendy. Now I can be more at peace than before. Tell your mother I was very impressed with you. You're a beautiful young woman like your mother, and a tribute to both your parents. I'm so sorry for her loss. I understand he was a very special man. Please wish her well for me."

With that Zhao Wen headed back to the consultation room. As she walked down the hallway she stopped and leaned against the wall, tears welling up in her eyes as she went over all Wainright told her.

Chapter 31

Lucy could see when Zhao Wen came in that she was unusually emotional. She went over and hugged her. "How is he? How'd it go?"

Zhao Wen asked to sit down, and went over everything. Lucy's uncle sat with them, nodding from time to time when there was something he already knew. Lucy thanked her for telling much of what she had wanted to know about her father, John Wainright, and was never told.

"Can I have a copy of the phone number he gave you? I'd like to call too." Lucy said.

"Of course, here it is."

"I want to hear directly from that man what happened. Do you believe what my father told you?"

"I'm not sure yet. It was a lot to take in. But if your father is not lying my mother is going to claim he was," Zhao Wen said.

As soon as the doctor cleared Lucy's father for another visitor, her uncle left the two talking, happy to see them growing closer by the hour. Walking into the recovery room he was pleased to see how well Wainright was looking compared to the last couple of days. He went straight over to the bedside, shook his hand, and smiled broadly.

"So, John Wainright, finally we meet and are able to talk. I'm glad you feel a little better. May I sit?"

"Of course. I definitely can see your brother in you, Mr. Xin. Have you talked to Zhao Wen yet?"

"I just listened to her speaking to your daughter . . . my niece. And please, no Mister, just Xin will do. Usually it's Chairman Xin these days, though I hope to retire soon. Once my successor is ready, then no more 'Mr. Chairman.' I'm looking forward to that."

"Hang on as long as you can, Xin. Retirement isn't all it's cracked up to be."

"You are probably right about that. Now I must tell you what I wanted to meet you for. I wanted to thank you."

"Thank me? For what?"

"For saving my niece, of course! She has another family to support her now, and we all love her dearly. She's a tribute to how you and your wife raised her, and the good seeds that brought her into this world."

"Your brother was a fine man, Xin. He wanted nothing for his country but the best. Christine loved him very much, and I know he loved her too. She was a good woman. What happened to them both was a tragedy."

"We know."

"I never understood why they went out so late that night; I've always believed the authorities were waiting for them. Something made them go down that particular street, Xin, but we never found out what it was. They were murdered, I'm afraid. I'm sure of it. The man whose name I gave to Zhao Wen assured me they were."

"That has been on our minds for years, John, if I may call you that. It's been confirmed by our research into your situation with Madame Li."

"How did you find out?"

Xin laughed. "The Party was always good at keeping detailed files on their activities in those years. You would be surprised how accessible they are, if you have the right connections."

"And money?" John asked.

"Let me say that can help; it always has."

"And does Li know this?"

"Not only that, but we showed her the documents. They indicate the interrogators used fake confessions signed by you to get her to admit what she was doing. That she was pregnant came out when they started to beat her and she begged them to stop. She wanted desperately to protect the child in her, but they threatened her with a forced abortion. Somehow she traded that too for information. For whatever reason she wanted to keep the child."

"I can see why she hates me so much," John said.

"Yes, and I don't think that will ever change. It may soften, and she may allow you to know her daughter better, but anything more is unlikely. I've tried, believe me, for Lucy's sake; but I cannot get her to change how she feels. Even if we can get her to see the truth, it's gone too far and for too long. Maybe as we work together on our companies' merger, and Zhao Wen takes over, these things will improve. I really don't know."

Xin asked Wainright more questions about his brother's relationship with Christine. He wanted to know what went on during those months the group was together, in particular what exactly his brother passed on to the Americans, not what the authorities claimed he did. He shook his head when Wainright told him much of it was political insight that is public information today, like Party organization charts available on the internet. The economic data they passed along was the kind of information most countries published regularly, except his brother was passing along data on what was really going on with the economy, not what the government was lying about to their people.

"To have been murdered for all that? Today I can pull up that information in seconds. How things have changed. My brother was no traitor. He wanted more for our country, and we have that today, but he never got to see it."

"Xin, the two of them loved each other deeply, as I did Li. He wanted a better life. We never found out who put the finger on them but we knew it was one of the leaders. How high it went we never found out."

"Well, you can be sure I found who it was. It wasn't easy, but it's over anyway now, he's dead —"

"Dead? Who was it? How?"

"I can't tell you that, John. Let's just say he died in a tragic road accident. Appropriate, don't you think?" Xin smiled with a satisfied grin.

The two talked for more than an hour, going over much of the same ground,; however Xin did tell him how the family recovered their fortunes, as did the Li side, both families taking advantage of the changes in China. That everything had come full circle was something both men would have said could never happen, but it had. Wainright thanked Xin for all he had done for him, and especially for Lucy. He told him bringing Madame Li and her daughter along had saved him, though it had not gone as well as he would have liked.

Xin rose from his chair, but before leaving had one more thing he wanted to say. "Don't thank me, John; it was all Lucy. She is the one you need to thank. She is quite a young lady; she has a bright future ahead of her, which she must tell you about . . . not I. You made her life difficult; the tragedy of losing a husband on top of that could have crushed her, but she is strong, a true Xin. Holding her back now is something you must never do."

"Hold her back? From what?"

"Maybe she doesn't fully know herself yet; I'll leave it at that. Madame Li is leaving and I need to accompany her back. We have much work to do on our merger. I hope in the future we can have some kind of relationship. Lucy has been a special gift to our family, and we do not intend to lose her again. If you need any help in the future you may contact me through Lucy. Until we meet again, get well as quickly as you can."

"Thanks again for everything. Your brother was a fine man, Xin. He would have made a difference in this world if he'd lived, I'm sure of that."

Lucy and Zhao Wen were still talking when Xin returned. He spoke briefly about his conversation with her father before advising they needed to get back to the hotel and pick up Madame Li. The plane was waiting to take them all to another shareholder meeting later that evening. Don Roberts was anxious to get moving too; Li was calling frequently and not happy they were still there. "She'll get over it," Zhao Wen told them. Lucy said it was probably a good time to leave; according to the doctor her father was too tired to see anyone else, and should be left to sleep for a while.

The farewell between them was emotional; assurances they would all be in touch in the future were made, phone and contact details exchanged. There was an especially warm parting between Lucy and her uncle. He assured her all would be well, that he felt for the loss of her husband, but happy John Wainright at least was recovering.

"Don't forget, Lucy," he said to her as they left, "Your future is with us now, not here. Don will watch over you until that time. Call me if you need anything, anything at all."

"I will, Uncle. I can't say what my future is right now. Everything's happened so fast. I'm still a bit confused, but we'll talk soon."

Lucy gave Zhao Wen one last hug, promising to stay in touch as she walked everyone to the car. She stood waiving them off until they disappeared from view.

———ⲟⲝⲝⲟ———

Dr. Weinstein was waiting to see Lucy, pleased to hear the visitors had finally left and that things could settle down. He said her father was doing well, despite being exhausted from the last couple of day's events. He told her he planned to get him out of bed and into a wheelchair soon, and that some fresh air would do him good. He was confident that a little rehab work could have him out of his wheelchair and starting to walk in short order. Lucy thanked him for everything; she would stay and make some phone calls until her father was ready to see her.

She called her best friend with an update. Sally was pleased to hear the progress with her father, but wanted more detail, especially about what transpired in China all those years ago.

"Can you come over tonight?" Sally asked. "Mondays are always quiet. We can talk while hubby cooks for us. I'm sure you need a break and a good drink . . . I know I need one."

"Okay, I'll try," Lucy said.

"Not try, Lucy . . . for sure! I want John to cook something special for us. Say seven, no earlier though. How's that sound?" Lucy thought for a moment before replying. She felt worn out physically and emotionally; going out was the last thing she needed, then again Sally was her best friend.

"I should say no. I'm really tired, but maybe you're right; some good food and a stiff drink might help."

"So that's a yes?"

Lucy told her she would be there on the dot at seven.

She was surprised at how well her father looked sitting in the wheelchair by the window. He beamed as she approached. "Lucy, can you forgive me? I'm so sorry for everything I've done, and haven't done for you. And the loss of your husband . . . how could I have been so selfish in my own grief? I've never comforted you or helped with yours. I'm so, so sorry. How can I make it right?"

Lucy pulled one of the chairs alongside her father, purposely silent, leaving him to wonder what she was going to say. "All these years you knew who my real father was, who my real mother was, and you said nothing. You told me so many lies about where I came from. I've had a family all along, when I thought I had none. How do you think it feels to find out the truth from someone else, and not from you?"

"I'm so sorry, Lucy. I do understand why you feel hurt."

"Only hurt? How do you live with yourself?"

"I can't expect your forgiveness, Lucy, but we honestly thought we were doing the right thing. I never did what Li thinks I did. I assume they've told you everything?"

"They've told me. To be honest, I wasn't inclined to believe you, and frankly right now I trust Uncle Xin more than you. At least he seems to support what you've told Madame Li and Zhao Wen, but I want to hear it from you again for myself."

Her father went over much the same story she had heard from the others, but this time she asked more questions about her birth mother and father, trying to understand who they really were. That she had been conceived in love, not some random affair, was at least reassuring. And the fact that he adopted Lucy to ensure she would have a good home in America was something she admitted being grateful for.

"You could've been so much more of a father to me if you'd talked to me about this a long time ago. Don't you see that?" she asked.

"Of course I see that today, but believe me, back then we thought it was best for you. One thing I can promise is to be more of a father to you now, if you'll let me."

"It's not that easy. I haven't told you everything about me of late. There was far more to my trip to Beijing than I ever told you."

"I had that impression from Xin. Do you want to tell me about it?"

"I do. I've met someone again, a man I met on that trip with Global Industries years ago. I don't know what's going to happen yet, but it's serious. The other thing is that uncle Xin wants me to come to China, make a new life there, especially now that Phil's gone."

"You'd seriously consider going over there? Leaving the place you were raised in . . . your friends . . . me?

"Actually I've considered it carefully already. I haven't made up my mind yet, but if I'm going to do something like that I don't want to leave it too long."

She stopped, watching her father's expression change; she sensed hopelessness in him, a look that seemed to say "You'd leave me like this?" She waited for him to say something, but he only shook his head briefly, muttering under his breath about deserving everything coming to him.

"I don't want us to grow apart, Lucy," he said. "Your mother would never forgive me for that. I don't want you to leave, never would, but you need to do something for yourself while you can. If you must go, I'd rather you went with my blessing and we made things better between us. I can take care of myself, so don't worry any about me. What about your business? Have you thought about that?"

"That's the least of my concerns, I've got some ideas about it, and so has Uncle Xin. Nothing's decided yet. I just want you to know things will be different for me here on out."

They talked for the rest of the afternoon. She shared all that happened during her visit to Beijing, how everything had been set in motion when she broke into his office and computer. She was surprised he was not angry about it, but told her he was impressed with her resourcefulness in the way she sought to uncover the truth. He told her there was maybe, after all, some Wainright in her. She told him about more about the Xin family, and eventually Wang Jun, how without their help the connection to Madame Li wouldn't have been uncovered. He expressed concerns hearing Wang Jun was a married man, but Lucy told him not to worry; she was a big girl now. More importantly, she was not about to do anything foolish.

He told Lucy things about his past he had not told the others. She was surprised by his nonchalant description of events in his life that were clearly dangerous, and could have landed him in prison . . . or worse. That he loved Madame Li was beyond doubt as she listened to him. He never wavered in his remorse for what happened to the woman and the daughter he had fathered. When he described his efforts to find the child, a daughter he had never known, Lucy began to feel she was unduly critical of him, that maybe he was more hero than villain after all. The final judgment would take time.

The doctor, looking in on his patient, brought their discussions to an end. He said it was time for her father to get some rest. It had been a long day; there would be plenty of time for them to talk in the days ahead. Lucy thanked the doctor for everything and he wished her well.

"Will you come back tomorrow, Lucy?" her father asked.

"Of course; maybe later though. I'm seeing Sally and John tonight for dinner, and drinks. You know what Sally's like; anyway I think I need one myself. I don't really want to go, but she's insisted . . . John's cooking something special for us."

"You should go, it'll do you good after all this."

"I guess I will, but I think I'll sleep in late tomorrow. Everyone else has left and Don Roberts is already driving them back to Greensboro. They've a private plane or something waiting to take them back for meetings in New York. At least that's where they said they were headed. They're all very wealthy, you know, Dad."

Her father smiled. "You called me 'Dad', Lucy, not 'father.' That's nice. I appreciate it. And yes, I do know all about the Xins' affairs, as well as Li's husband's business interests. I was checking them out before all this spun out. "

"You weren't worried about that when I was in Beijing? About me finding out, I mean."

"I wasn't in a shape to think too much about anything. Losing your mother was difficult enough. But being rejected and sworn at by someone I'd loved just made something snap in me. I know it's you I have to thank for bringing me back, and for that I'm grateful. You've earned whatever it is you want to do. I just want to be a part of it, until I'm gone too."

With that Lucy gave him a hug and a kiss, assured him that he wasn't going anywhere soon, and that things would work out for the best.

Chapter 32

The apartment had seemed eerily quiet after two days at the hospital. The first thing she did was turn on music to break the dreary silence. She dropped her bag in the corner of the living room, cast off the clothes she was wearing by the bathroom, and headed into the shower. She let the blast of hot water run over her for some time as her mind cleared, thinking about her father and what he had told her.

Those thoughts soon moved to calling Wang Jun as promised. She told herself she would do it once she got back from Sally's, or maybe while she was there. She toweled off after showering and dried her hair thoroughly, finishing off with the remains of some hairspray, tossing the empty bottle in the bin. She dressed quickly in a plain shirt and jeans, applied a little makeup as neatly as she could, then grabbed her bag and headed down through the shop to the front door. A quick look around told her all was well in that department; thanks to Sarah everything looked neat and tidy. A note was lying on Lucy's desk; it showed the last couple of day's sales. She was impressed with the numbers and grinned at the smiley face drawn next to the totals. "Atta girl, Sarah!" she said out loud, opened the door, and walked briskly over to see Sally.

———

It was a short walk, but she was suddenly struck with feelings of guilt. It dawned on her that for two days Phil had been out of her mind, barely talked about by anyone. She knew her father never approved of her marriage, but even he had not mentioned Phil much in all the hours they had talked. She asked herself if there was something wrong with her; was she being callous in some way over the whole situation? Was she glad he'd killed himself so that she was free? She tried to push it from her mind as she approached the Supper Club Grill, but knew it would likely never leave her.

"Uh-Oh!" Lucy thought. The restaurant was darkened. The main curtains were drawn, but she noticed the one side move, as if someone had been looking out for her. The sign on the door said "Closed." She pushed it, but it was locked. She could see a couple of figures through the dim light over at the bar. She rattled the door a few times, knocking to tell John and Sally she was there. The door opened, with John Sweetland standing there, apron on, clearly in the middle of cooking. He took her in his arms, welcomed her back, and asked if she was okay.

"I'm fine," Lucy replied. "You're closed? Where's Sally? Is she okay?"

"She's fine. Go on through; she's waiting for you. Watch out though, she's already had a few. I think she's ready for a good night!" He closed the door behind him. Lucy walked past the host desk and into the restaurant, turning back to see him closing the curtain and locking the door again.

As she approached the door she heard laughter and the clinking of glasses, the backs of two women looming large before either one of them turned to greet her. She was shocked when they did.

"Oh my god! Mei! What the hell are you doing here?"

The two women burst out laughing, and rushed to meet her. There were hugs and kisses all round. Lucy could see Sally and Mei had been drinking all afternoon. "When did you get here?" she asked.

"Two days ago. And by the way, I'm a good communist. There is no god; you need some other good phrase," Mei joked.

"Like . . . fuck?" Sally suggested.

"How could you come here and not say anything? Why didn't you come to the hospital? None of them said you were here. Zhao Wen said nothing about it."

"That's because they didn't know. I came separately. I'll explain that later. Meantime you need a drink. We all need a drink, don't we, Sally?"

"Oh yes, we do, but Lucy more than us."

"I do?" Lucy asked.

"Oh yes!" Sally said, "because *he's* here."

"Oh my god! Wang Jun's here? I mean, look at me? Where is he? Sally, Christ almighty, I need to change. Can I borrow something?"

"Of course, but you've got only thirty minutes to get upstairs and fix yourself. Your chipao is on the bed in the spare room. You have a half hour; no more!"

Lucy was in a panic. She gulped down the drink Sally handed her, and, Mei commented that maybe she would be good at drinking baijiu after all. They refused to tell Lucy where Wang Jun was, but to get moving and be back down in thirty minutes.

As soon as Lucy went upstairs, the two women set about getting the tables ready for all of them. John Sweetland was soon out of the kitchen, complaining about how long they were taking.

"Look, Sally, and you too, Mei. I can't keep delaying these dishes. If it's more than forty-five minutes they'll be ruined. Where is he anyway? Does this Wang fellow even exist?" he asked.

"He'll be here by seven thirty, guaranteed," Mei said. "He's arrived from New York on the company plane already, and Don Roberts is driving him here while Xin and Li head back to New York. They'll be surprised. We never told them he was coming, or borrowing their plane for a day. Now let's get this table set, Sally. I need another drink as soon as we're done. And, John, make sure there's plenty of champagne on ice, will you?"

"I've no idea where you put all that stuff you've been drinking this afternoon. You better slow down a bit."

"Don't worry, John. Mei Rui is a professional in that area. I've yet to have any man drink me under the table in China . . . you're more than welcome to try."

"Don't even think about it, husband," Sally said. "You always were an amateur in that department. Let's get on with it. I just called Sarah; she'll be here any minute. We need to get the tables done."

The laughter continued in the restaurant as Sally and Mei set out the two tables, stopping occasionally to drink and toast each other. John kept calling out for them to get a move on, quit laughing, and stop behaving like a couple of teenagers. Sarah soon arrived with a delivery van full of flowers. She left the giggling women to finish up the tables, while she sped around the room, setting out the floral arrangements.

Before Sarah left, Mei thanked her profusely and gave her a red envelope in appreciation. Sarah set it on the bar, politely telling Mei she was happy to do it for her friend Lucy. Then she told Sally to take photos of the evening.

At 7:45 there was a loud knock at the door. Mei told Sally to go upstairs and warn Lucy, but she refused, determined to first meet the man she had talked to and heard so much about. The two were at the front door as Sally unlocked it. Don Roberts walked in first, ahead of Wang Jun, who immediately embraced Mei Rui.

He asked if everything was under control, then turned to Sally. "You must be the famous Sally. It's a pleasure to finally meet you. I've heard a lot of good things about you from Lucy, and Mei this afternoon."

"It's so good to finally meet you too. We're not finished yet though. My husband's in the kitchen cooking; Lucy is upstairs still. I need to tell her you're here. What should we call you tonight, by the way? Wang? John? Wang Jun?

"Just call me John; that's what Lucy used to call me. Or Wang Jun will do. My Chinese first name is Jun, of course."

"I better call you Wang Jun then. Don't want to confuse you with my own John. I need to get up there to Lucy. She's a bag of nerves."

As soon as Sally disappeared, Mei led Wang Jun and Don over to the bar. John came out of the kitchen briefly, enthusiastically greeting his new guests.

He told Mei to get everyone drinks; he was sorry but he needed to get back to work. She looked at him quizzically.

"Now come along, Mei," he joked. "You've been here all afternoon. You know this bar from end to end. Give your friends whatever they want."

Everyone laughed; Mei shrugged and skipped behind the bar to mix three drinks for them. Don only wanted a small beer; he was driving later that night. Meanwhile Wang Jun and Mei sat at the bar together going over what she had heard happened at the hospital.

"How was the meeting at the airport? Were they surprised to see you?" Mei asked.

"It was fine. Xin was glad I'd come, but Li was cold as always. Just doesn't like me, I guess."

"She'll come around. What about Zhao Wen?"

"She was fine, better than her mother. I think she's going to do great when the merger's done . . . and Li's finally out of it."

"Better than me?" Mei asked.

"No one's better, Mei, except Lucy perhaps."

Mei gave him a playful jab, then warned him the other two would be down soon. It was already past eight and Sally's husband was groaning yet again about the dinner getting ruined. Wang Jun told him he would have to figure out how to hold the food back a little longer; he needed a good fifteen minutes alone with Lucy before everyone joined them. John headed back to the kitchen looking frustrated; Mei and Don were left talking together at the bar. Wang Jun headed to the table set for Lucy and him, chose the seat facing out on the restaurant, and sat nursing his drink, anxiously waiting for Lucy to come down.

Upstairs Lucy was being zipped into her chipao dress. Sally marveled yet again at how beautiful it looked. "Come on, Lucy. He's downstairs waiting. You can't take too long, you know. You look great already. John's tearing his hair out over the food; he's never cooked Chinese before, but it looks good. He's fixed some other dishes too in case we don't like the Chinese."

Lucy told Sally not to worry about the food; she was sure Wang Jun would enjoy the meal if John were cooking it. "I'm almost done. How do I look?"

"Unbelievable!"

"And Wang Jun, what do you think of him?"

"The man's good-looking. I'm impressed. And that Mei Rui . . . she's a doll. What a riot, and boy, can she put it away! You better watch out for that one."

"He's already tried that. They're just great friends and colleagues now. She loves him still, I know that, but you're right, she's great. Okay . . . I'm ready. You go, give me two minutes to calm down."

"Christ Lucy, this not a bloody wedding we're putting on; it's a friggin' dinner."

Lucy smiled. "We'll see."

⸺⸙⸺

When Sally told everyone Lucy would be a couple of minutes, Wang Jun rose and waited by the table. Meanwhile, the other four gathered around the bar to watch her come down. John was still grumbling, and Sally told him to quit whining. As Lucy walked down, John clapped and Don whistled. Mei pointed Lucy in the direction of Wang Jun.

The flowers all around took Lucy back; none of them were there earlier when she went upstairs. Wang Jun stood with his arms open as she ran to him. Their embrace lasted a considerable time, until Sally yelled they could get to that later. Wang Jun asked for a few moments in private, so John headed back to the kitchen, warning Sally one last time the dinner was sure to be a disaster.

⸺⸙⸺

After he told Lucy how lovely she looked, Wang Jun pulled one of the white flowers from the floral decorations and placed it in her hair. "There!" he said. "Perfect. I have something to tell you, Lucy; that's why I'm here. I think you know what I'm going to ask you."

"I've no idea."

" I understand there's a formal way to do this here."

He got up, knelt in front of her, and held her hand. "Lucy Summers, will you be my wife?" he asked.

"No."

"No?"

"I can't. You're married."

"Technically yes, Lucy, but the divorce is underway. She's agreed, and is about to become a very rich lady."

"So you're poor now; that's even better. Of course I'll marry you. I never wanted you for your money in the first place."

"Well, I'm sorry to disappoint you but I'll still be wealthy."

Watching them embrace over in the far corner, the others figured out what was going on. They all cheered and Sally swiftly popped a bottle of champagne, Mei brought glasses over for a toast.

"Now, for Christ's sake sit down. Dinner's served," Sally said.

With that John emerged from the kitchen with a tray of food to begin with, announcing that he and Sally would join them shortly, once the main course was served. Don was reluctant to join the group, but everyone insisted and the evening was underway. It turned out to be an incredible night that was as much of an engagement party as anything else. Lucy was the happiest anyone had ever seen her; happiness seemed to finally be coming her way.

There were serious moments when the events of the last few days were talked about, lighthearted times when each of them talked about their involvement in bringing it together. They thanked Don Roberts in particular for working with Mei Rui on the arrangements, at some potential risk by keeping Xin in the dark about it.

Sally told Wang Jun that since he was being so formal, then strictly speaking he should follow protocol and ask her father's permission for Lucy's hand in marriage.

Her remarks drew sharp looks from Lucy. "Sally, that's not a good idea; not at all. Anyway I don't need his permission for anything."

"No, no, " Wang Jun interrupted." I'd be honored to do that. But I want to do it alone. Would you take me there tomorrow?"

Over Lucy's objections Don agreed, finally giving in to Wang Jun, but only on the basis that Lucy would be there too, outside the room in case of any problems.

"What time shall I pick you two up?" Don asked.

Lucy looked at Wang Jun and read the mischievous look his face, "Eleven o'clock, please. We'll be waiting at the side door of the shop."

Sally told Mei and Don it was not a night for driving to Greensboro. They had two rooms upstairs and the pair had better stay the night. John agreed with his wife, told them he preferred they all stayed, if not to help clear up, then to help him drink too. It turned into a raucous evening; by two in the morning everyone was feeling the effects of the drinking, except perhaps Mei, who was as stalwart as ever in that department. It was Lucy who finally declared that she didn't care what anyone else did, but she was taking Wang Jun home to bed.

They were called party poopers and wimps by the others, but warmly sent on their way. Meanwhile Sally decided to take Mei Rui on. As far as she was concerned this was now a competition and the pair were drinking for their countries; she would not be beat. John and Don decided to sneak away, and leave them to it.

The next day John would be visited by the local police chief regarding reports of after-hour drinking at his establishment, along with a number of noise complaints from neighbors. Sally and he would sit in the kitchen eating together after the chief left, laughing at the old hags of Blowing Rock, and agreeing Lucy was better off getting away from it .

There was not much sleep for Lucy and Wang Jun that night. The air outside did little to sober them on their walk back to her apartment and shop. Neither had it eased their hunger for each other, but Lucy made sure they walked along the streets as inconspicuously as possible. When they were home Lucy was cautious in removing the chipao not to damage it, but that was the only piece of clothing either of them were careful with.

They made love several times, for him, and for her; sometimes for both. In between neither could sleep. There was talk about all Lucy had heard, some of it new to Wang Jun, but not much. At breakfast they talked more about the timing of his divorce and their marriage. Lucy was in no hurry. She told him that a wedding soon after Phil's death, would have more tongues wagging. Wang Jun could not understand her concern, especially with moving to China, something she'd readily agreed to do.

"That's all well for us, but my father will still be living here; he doesn't need all that gossip."

"I don't agree, Lucy. They'll talk no matter what you do. They will in China too. Look, I think my divorce will take six months, maybe more. I don't want to wait that long for you."

"Well, you have to. I need to get my father settled and decide what to do about my business. Sarah will be devastated with the shop closing. I can't do that to her without figuring something out."

"I have an idea for that. Don's checked it out already for me, and my proposal is that I'm going to buy you out. I'll give you the best price for the property, and an amount for the business development you've done— goodwill you call it. You can put that in an account and use it for yourself, or for your father. It's a very generous offer. Don says you'll be crazy to refuse."

"And what about Sarah? I have to take care of her. She needs the income for her family, and she's worked hard, especially of late."

"How about when the business is mine I lease it to her for nothing, and give her some working capital of her own?"

"Okay, okay, the business and Sarah is no problem. We can straighten that out, one way or another . . . but what about my best friends, Sally and John?"

"You sound like Madame Li. This is a marriage discussion, Lucy, not a merger," Wang Jun said.

"It's not?"

"Okay, an annual visit for them to Beijing, our expense. You can travel back to see them, and your father, anytime you like. Deal, Mrs. Lucy Summers?"

"Deal, Mr. Wang Jun!"

"Oh, and I want to find you some work alongside Mei. I can't have you lounging around by the pool all day, okay?"

"Yes, now we better clear our heads and get cleaned up. I need to press your clothes. I can't have you meeting my father looking like a homeless person."

Chapter 33

Lucy needed reassuring several times by Don Roberts that the amount of time Wang Jun was meeting with her father wasn't any cause for concern. While she said the night before that she could do whatever she wanted, something inside her still wanted the blessing of the man who had smuggled her out of China and raised her.

She was in a panic when Wang Jun came into the consulting room looking grim. "It didn't go well?'

He shrugged his shoulders, indicated it had not. Don said he was sorry to hear it until Wang Jun gave Lucy a hug. He said he was just kidding. It had gone fine and she could go in and see him.

Lucy kicked him harder than she had planned. "Ouch! That hurt. Maybe I need to reconsider. You saw that, Don, already she's beating me."

"Big baby, you earned it. Wait for me for a while. I'll be back." She left the two laughing and went to see her father.

———

Lucy found her father standing by the window, somewhat shaky, but out of the wheelchair.

"I didn't want him meeting me in that thing," he said, pointing to the wheel-chair and opening his arms for her. She went straight to him, feeling a renewed bond between them. It was different, somehow stronger, even though she now knew the truth behind the lies he had told.

"What do you think of him, Dad? Did he tell you about himself? Do you approve?"

"Lucy, don't look so worried. You don't need my blessing. We're beyond that now, but I give it gladly. I think he's a fine man . . . really. He's told me everything about himself, including his marriage and divorce plans. Actually he was impressed with my Chinese, and how much I still know about his business world over there."

"What else did he say?"

"He's invited me to visit anytime, and to be at your wedding; here or over there. He's a very generous man, Lucy. I can see a tough businessman in him, but not like some I used to deal with."

"I'm so glad you like him. He's promised we'll take good care of you too."

"I can take care of myself, Lucy. I'll miss you when you're gone, but I'll manage. It's you I worry about. Remember, this is China we're talking about . . . living there . . . not just visiting. Things can change there, you know. Maybe the times I lived through won't come back, but you never know. He's promised me he'll make sure you're never at risk, and I think I believe him."

"China's changed so much, Dad. I'm sure there'll be things I'll miss— you, Sally, and John— but I'll have a whole family there, maybe even work to do. Phil's gone, and I do feel guilty about what I'm doing, you know, so soon after, but it feels right."

"Look, Lucy, I can't say your mother and I were happy when you married Phil. Mother always blamed herself for that, pulling you away from your career and all, but she'd be as happy for you now as I am. And if I never say it again, I can't thank you enough for dragging me back from the edge, not giving up on me. I still can't believe how losing your mother and the Li thing hit me, or how I've treated you."

Lucy asked if she could bring Wang Jun back in. She wanted him to see them together now since he would be flying to New York to join shareholder meetings with the others. When the two came back in holding hands, her father was still standing, despite being told he ought to sit down.

"Now you're here together," he said, "let me give you my best wishes for the future, and for my wife who can't be here to see this, or your real mother. Take care of our daughter, Wang Jun. Tell Xin I send her back to her birth family, to take care of and cherish. Her real father was a fine young man, as was her birth mother. All of this is something of a miracle really. My only regret, after all these years, is Li and I can't be friends again, but I understand the way she feels about me. Please tell her for me."

Wang Jun assured Lucy's father he would, that he and Xin planned to work on it; he was sure Zhao Wen would be in touch with him and come around too. The merger of the businesses was going to bring them closer together in the months ahead.

"These things take time, John, you of all people know us Chinese. We don't think only of today, tomorrow, this year or next year; we can wait for what we want. You need to do the same. I'm sure the time will come when you will be meeting Madame Li again, as friends."

"I hope so. I really do."

It was time for the couple to take their leave. Her father finally sat in the wheelchair and asked to be pushed with them to the exit to say good-bye. Don Roberts joined them at the exit; he already had the car doors opened for them. Everyone said their farewells, with Lucy promising to visit the next day. She declined Wang Jun's suggestion to come to New York with him, but her father urged her to see him off in Greensboro.

After they returned to Blowing Rock, Don dropped Lucy off at her apartment. Lucy thanked him for everything, and said she hoped he would still stop by for his wife's flowers, whatever happened. He assured her he would, that until she married and moved to China her uncle wanted him to look in on her; after that he was supposed to check on her father regularly.

"He's quite a man, my uncle Xin."

"Oh yes . . .that he is," Don replied.

Wang Jun had arrived earlier that evening in New York with Mei Rui and they all dined together with Madame Li, Zhao Wen, and one of their company presidents. They discussed the merger and future listing of their stock on the exchange; afterwards he and the chairman sat alone in Xin's suite. The conversation soon turned to Lucy, and Xin laid out the plans for her future that he expected him to follow. Wang Jun assured him he would honor all of his instructions, that he was pleased to care for and protect his niece in every way he could.

That night, sitting alone in his suite. Xin poured himself a last drink before going to bed. He was scheduled on a flight to Beijing the next day. He planned to leave the others in New York but would phone Lucy in the morning to congratulate her on her plans to marry. He would tell her that he was going to make arrangements, through Don Roberts, for her father to be very comfortable in the coming years.

He reached into his briefcase and pulled a sheaf of papers out and looked at them again. He knew he should have destroyed them earlier, but for reasons even he couldn't understand had not. He made out a check, a large check by any standards, and placed it in the envelope to go to Don Roberts. He looked over the invoice and added a few lines of gratitude for all Don Roberts had done, reminding him never to do anything again like he did for Mei, or anyone else, without telling him. He placed it in the envelope along with the check and sealed it. The other pages he looked at one last time, wondering what his

Buddhist teacher would think of him. He looked around for something to burn them in, but the room was non-smoking. He decided to rip them up first, and then dispose of them carefully.

The pages covered an FBI report provided to him by Don Roberts, and an "associate" covering the suicide of Phil Summers. The official report highlighted the toxicology analysis, confirming there was nothing in the man's system, other than painkillers, that could have caused death under suspicious circumstances of any kinds. That the deceased had been able to cut both his own wrists was evidenced by the fingerprints on the hunting knife and further analysis of the blood splatter around the victim. Reference was made to the extreme sharpness of the blade, the skills that the deceased had been trained for in the military, all borne out by the medals of valor he had earned.

The location of the body on the large flat rock, and traffic pattern had revealed a number of footprints. Some of them were disturbed by the intervention of poorly trained local police. The prints were deemed irrelevant after careful review, adding nothing that would indicate foul play. The third-party report concluded, for the police in Blowing Rock and state troopers in Greensboro, that this was indeed the suicide of a troubled veteran. The report noted the regrettable tragedy for his wife, Lucy Summers, and stated the deceased's state of mind, based on discussions with his psychiatrist, clearly provided support for the suicide verdict.

It was signed, Don Roberts, Special Investigator – Federal Bureau of Investigation, Greensboro, North Carolina.

Xin tore the report into as many pieces as he could, then knelt to pray.

"Forgive me, Brother, for bringing your child back to China in this way. I swore on your tomb I would find her, and I have. She will return home where she belongs as I promised you and our ancestors."

THE AUTHOR

Stuart Cotterill continues to draw from his experience living in China, and from his love for its culture and people. He visits Beijing annually, gathering material for his stories. Cotterill's travels and corporate work took him around the globe before he finally settled in Asheville, situated in the scenic Blue Ridge Mountains of western North Carolina.

Following two recent mysteries, *The Legacy of Ma Jun* and *Ma Jun's Lost Treasure*, this latest book takes readers outside the themes of the earlier "Dragon Script" series. The story, set in the U.S. and China, unravels the secrets of a father's past life, a daughter's secret love affair, a troubled marriage, and a death with mysterious undertones.

www.ingramcontent.com/pod-product-compliance
Lightning Source LLC
Chambersburg PA
CBHW061949170626
46813CB00006B/2589